THE FINAL RESTRAINT

'Suck it,' he ordered. Rick obeyed: he knelt in the water and took Adrian's cock in his hand, before guiding it into his mouth. He was rough; Adrian gasped with a mixture of pleasure and pain as Rick's teeth scratched at his shaft and helmet, while his hand squeezed Adrian's balls. In return, Adrian sought out Rick's tit rings, pulling them until the young man gasped. But he didn't stop sucking Adrian – if anything, he attacked Adrian's prick even more energetically. Rick's other hand climbed up Adrian's leg, stroking his thigh, his arse cheek, until it found what it wanted. Adrian's arse.

THE FINAL RESTRAINT

Paul C. Alexander

First published in Great Britain in 1999 by
Idol
an imprint of Virgin Publishing Ltd
Thames Wharf Studios,
Rainville Road, London W6 9HT

ISBN 0 352 33303 0

Cover photograph by Colin Clarke Photography

Typeset by SetSystems Ltd, Saffron Walden, Essex
Printed and bound in Great Britain by
Mackays of Chatham PLC

SAFER SEX GUIDELINES

These books are sexual fantasies – in real life, everyone needs to think about safe sex.

While there have been major advances in the drug treatments for people with HIV and AIDS, there is still no cure for AIDS or a vaccine against HIV. Safe sex is still the only way of being sure of avoiding HIV sexually.

HIV can only be transmitted through blood, come and vaginal fluids (but no other body fluids) passing from one person (with HIV) into another person's bloodstream. It cannot get through healthy, undamaged skin. The only real risk of HIV is through anal sex without a condom – this accounts for almost all HIV transmissions between men.

Being safe
Even if you don't come inside someone, there is still a risk to both partners from blood (tiny cuts in the arse) and pre-come. Using strong condoms and water-based lubricant greatly reduces the risk of HIV. However, condoms can break or slip off, so:
* Make sure that condoms are stored away from hot or damp places.
* Check the expiry date – condoms have a limited life.
* Gently squeeze the air out of the tip.
* Check the condom is put on the right way up and unroll it down the erect cock.
* Use plenty of water-based lubricant (lube), up the arse and on the condom.
* While fucking, check occasionally to see the condom is still in one piece (you could also add more lube).
* When you withdraw, hold the condom tight to your cock as you pull out.

* Never re-use a condom or use the same condom with more than one person.
* If you're not used to condoms you might practise putting them on.
* Sex toys like dildos and plugs are safe. But if you're sharing them use a new condom each time or wash the toys well.

For the safest sex, make sure you use the strongest condoms, such as Durex Ultra Strong, Mates Super Strong, HT Specials and Rubberstuffers packs. Condoms are free in many STD (Sexually Transmitted Disease) clinics (sometimes called GUM clinics) and from many gay bars. It's also essential to use lots of water-based lube such as KY, Wet Stuff, Slik or Liquid Silk. Never use come as a lubricant.

Oral sex
Compared with fucking, sucking someone's cock is far safer. Swallowing come does not necessarily mean that HIV gets absorbed into the bloodstream. While a tiny fraction of cases of HIV infection have been linked to sucking, we know the risk is minimal. But certain factors increase the risk:
* Letting someone come in your mouth
* Throat infections such as gonorrhoea
* If you have cuts, sores or infections in your mouth and throat

So what is safe?
There are so many things you can do which are absolutely safe: wanking each other; rubbing your cocks against one another; kissing, sucking and licking all over the body; rimming – to name but a few.

If you're finding safe sex difficult, call a helpline or speak to someone you feel you can trust for support. The Terrence Higgins Trust Helpline, which is open from noon to 10pm every day, can be reached on 0171 242 1010.

Or, if you're in the United States, you can ring the Center for Disease Control toll free on 1 800 458 5231.

Prologue

'Ah, yes, that's perfect.' Adrian Delancey leant back against the black marble sides of the Jacuzzi and gasped as the young bodybuilder's lips slid up and down the thick shaft of his cock, his fit, tanned body clearly visible beneath the bubbling waters, his head between Adrian's thighs. 'Amazing breath control, don't you think?' he sighed, as his hands massaged the young man's solid shoulders. This one had definitely been worth bringing along.

Adrian allowed the bodybuilder to continue pleasuring him while he surveyed his new apartment, hoping – insisting – that his guests showed the same degree of enthusiasm. But he knew they would: in Adrian's opinion, they simply had no alternative.

Look at James, faithful James Simonson, for example. Whatever his master wanted, whatever his master ordered, James had no choice but to agree. Adrian Delancey owned James, body and soul. Just the way that James liked it. Which was a good job, really, because he didn't really have any choice in the matter. The thickset, tattooed thug had followed him around the world like an obedient puppy, doing everything that he was told. *Good dog*. Of all his hired hands, James was Adrian's favourite.

'This place is amazing, Adrian,' said Ian Burke, Adrian's

financial controller, as a young skinhead, tattooed and pierced – just as Ian liked them – gently wanked him below the waterline. Ian was a good-looking clone in his late twenties, a city high-flier who had initially attracted the attention of the Elective . . . and then Adrian himself. But their relationship had been very one-sided: Ian enjoyed the sex and the collateral benefits – such as his little skinhead admirer – while Adrian enjoyed the freedom of the Elective's deepest financial secrets.

So, of course Ian would say the right thing about Adrian's apartment. Not least of all because, with one word from Adrian, Ian would find himself in prison for the rest of his life on charges ranging from fraud to murder, depending on how Adrian felt. Adrian laughed to himself as Ian groaned with pleasure.

'And it's not just the company, Adrian.' Ian nodded towards the huge archway that led into one of the many courtyards surrounding Adrian's villa: this one was covered in black and white slabs of smooth marble, making it resemble a chessboard for the gods. At least, that was how Adrian liked to think of it. 'This place is stunning.'

'Of course. No half-measures with the Syndicate, Ian. And what do *you* think of my little pied-à-terre, Mr Burroughs?'

But Andy Burroughs said nothing. He couldn't: the leather gag around his mouth made that rather difficult. Nor could he signal his feelings: the manacles that held his muscular, athletic body securely to the marble walls of the Jacuzzi room saw to that. Andy Burroughs had been a naughty boy, and Adrian always punished naughty boys. Perhaps, when Andy saw the error of his ways, Adrian would find a place for him in the Syndicate.

Perhaps.

'I do have you to thank for it, though, Ian,' said Adrian, lying. 'I was only able to build this place because of the financial success of the Syndicate – and you have to take some of the credit for that.'

Ian shrugged. 'It was nothing,' he said with enough false modesty to make Adrian want to puke.

Of *course* it was nothing, Adrian thought: all you did was make use of the information that I gave you like any half-good accountant. I need what's in your head – the last remaining secrets of the Elective.

Over the last three months, the Syndicate – Adrian's world-wide organisation dedicated to the pursuit of pleasure and profit – had made inroads into the Elective beyond anything than even Adrian could have imagined. The Elective – old, decadent, complacent – just hadn't been prepared for an all-out attack by something like the Syndicate: an organisation designed to take advantage of the economy and markets of the late twentieth century.

But Adrian himself couldn't afford to be complacent: despite all that he knew about the Elective, and all of the preparations he had put into creating the Syndicate, his rivals had been playing this game for a lot longer than he had. There were still a couple of things that needed to happen before the fall of the Elective was guaranteed: some internal, some external. But until Adrian was satisfied that everything was in place, he would wait until he set the final wheels in motion.

His bodybuilder surfaced from the Jacuzzi, a grin plastered over his square-jawed face. 'Was that OK?' he asked in a thick Mancunian accent.

Adrian nodded. 'Excellent. But that's enough for now, Mark. You can go and rest in the lounge.' He looked around the Jacuzzi. 'Ian, you and James as well, please. Apart from Rick, though. I'd like to get to know *you* a bit better,' he said pointedly. Rick had been brought over especially for Ian, but Adrian had already decided that he wanted him. And, if that pissed Ian off, then so much the better. He might be his financial controller, but he still needed to be shown his place.

Everyone did.

Ignoring the disappointed look from James – his good little puppy would have to wait – Adrian waited for the three of them to leave. He glanced at Andy, hanging from the wall, and smiled. Andy's eyes widened, but whether it was in anger or anticipation, Adrian neither knew nor cared.

3

'It's your lucky night, Andy – I've laid on some entertainment.' With that, he turned to look more closely at his little friend.

Rick had been recruited from a gay bar in the East End of London. Belligerent, violent, but quite a looker. And prepared to do anything – for a price.

And money was one thing that Adrian Delancey no longer had to worry about.

'Stand up – I want to take a look at you,' he ordered, and Rick complied. He was twenty, and had been a labourer before Adrian had offered him alternative employment. That showed: his body was muscular, but with the build that came from years of manual work, not the odd evening down at the gym. Tattoos – some professional, some done by himself when he was younger – covered his arms up to his shoulders. Both his nipples were pierced – like Adrian's – and between them a small bush of dark hair was beginning to grow, trailing down to his flat stomach and the thick bush between his legs. About six inches of thick, fat cock hung there, semi-hard. His whole body glistened with droplets of water from the Jacuzzi.

Adrian grinned, and received an arrogant smile in return. Rick had a short fringe of dark hair, now plastered to his forehead, and long sideburns. There was something insolent, angry about him – and that turned Adrian on. He imagined Rick with his mates back in the East End, sitting in some dirty flat, passing around the joints, getting stoned. Then one of them would put a porn film on the video, and they would sit there in silence, getting hornier and hornier. Eventually, one of them would take out his cock and start wanking, encouraging the others to do the same. They would sit there, slowly wanking themselves, until one of them decided to help out his mates. He would lean over and grab the nearest cock, wanking it while he wanked himself. Before long, he would take the cock in his mouth and start sucking it, tasting his mate's hot meat.

Then they would all start, sucking one another, fingering one another's arse until one of them had the idea of fucking. He would shove his mate over the nearest chair, and then force his cock into his mate's hungry, waiting hole, sliding it into the warmth, loving every second of it.

The image of Rick and his mates – and Adrian had seen some of his mates, *had* some of his mates – wanking and sucking and screwing each other, had gone straight to his cock. Eight inches of solid dick, desperate to be sucked, desperate to force its way into this East End rough's unwilling arse. Rick saw what was happening beneath the water and broke into a grin.

'Looks good,' he said. 'Wouldn't mind a bit of that.'

Adrian stood up, feeling the warm water drip from his body. His big balls were feeling heavy, desperate to be relieved, and Rick was just the person to do it.

'Suck it,' he ordered. Rick obeyed: he knelt in the water and took Adrian's cock in his hand, before guiding it into his mouth. He was rough: Adrian gasped with a mixture of pleasure and pain as Rick's teeth scratched at his shaft and helmet, while his hand squeezed Adrian's balls. In return, Adrian sought out Rick's tit rings, pulling them until the young man gasped. But he didn't stop sucking Adrian – if anything, he attacked Adrian's prick even more energetically. Rick's other hand climbed up Adrian's leg, stroking his thigh, his arse cheek, until it found what it wanted. Adrian's arse.

Adrian felt the finger probing at his ring, seeking entry. Normally, Adrian would have objected to such forwardness – James would never dare to do anything like that without asking – but he didn't care. He was in the mood to celebrate. This was his housewarming party, and, if a rough thug from the East End wanted to finger him, to suck him, wanted to *fuck* him, even, then Adrian wanted that as well.

And Adrian Delancey got whatever he wanted.

Rick's finger drove further and further into Adrian's arse, seeking and finding the tight bud of his prostate. Adrian groaned as Rick's finger stroked and flicked it, bringing him closer and closer. He could feel his balls churning with overwhelming pleasure as Rick's mouth played with his cock and his finger played with his arse, but this wasn't the way he wanted to come. No, Adrian knew exactly what he wanted.

'Fuck me,' he growled. 'I want that cock of yours inside me.'

Rick wasted no time in obeying. He got out of the Jacuzzi and virtually dragged Adrian over to one of the sun loungers.

'Lie there!' he ordered, and Adrian, feeling strangely subservient, did just that, pushing his arse upward to allow Rick entry. He heard Rick ripping open a condom packet, and fully expected to feel the wetness of lubricant – but Rick was having none of that. Adrian looked to his side, and could see everything in one of the mirrors that were hung on the walls of the Jacuzzi room.

Adrian watched as Rick climbed on top of him, his solid, straight body pinning Adrian to the wooden lounger. And then he guided the tip of his cock with one hand, so that it was waiting at the entrance to his arse.

Then he entered him. Adrian gritted his teeth with the pain as the thick cock forced its way inside him without lubricant, brutally sliding inside him, ignoring any resistance as the whole shaft went in.

'You like that?' hissed Rick, his mouth at Adrian's ear. 'You like me taking you like this?'

Adrian nodded, the pain too much for him to even speak. But then Rick withdrew slightly. Before Adrian could register the relief, Rick slammed his cock back in, and then out, and then in, building up a harsh, unforgiving rhythm that slowly made the pain subside into that indefinable pleasure that Adrian loved so much. As Rick continued fucking him, his right hand slipped under the lounger, and grasped Adrian's cock through the slats. Each time he slammed his cock into Adrian's arse he wanked him, pulling and fucking until the pleasure became indescribable. Adrian started groaning, aware that Rick, forcing his rough fat cock inside him, was grunting with a mixture of exertion and excitement.

'I'm gonna come inside you,' Rick said breathlessly. 'Is that what you want, eh? Is it?'

Adrian couldn't even nod. The feeling of this paid thug's cock ramming into him, his rough hand squeezing and wanking his cock, was just too much. His whole body convulsed as he came, wave after wave of release as his come splattered over the marble floor. As Adrian shot his last load, Rick let out a deep cry and came inside him, his fat cock pumping and pumping until he too was drained. With a satisfied sigh, he slumped on to Adrian's back and hugged him.

They lay like that for a few minutes before Adrian gestured for him to get off. Still a little unsteady, Adrian gave Rick a satisfied smile.

'Was that OK, boss?' he asked in his thick East End accent.

Adrian nodded. 'Expect a healthy bonus. Anyway, I need to see the others.' He pointed at Andy, who must have watched the whole thing. 'Take him to his room. And if he gives you any trouble . . .'

Rick shook his head. 'Don't worry, boss. He won't,' he said ominously.

'That's what I like to hear.' Grabbing a towel, Adrian wrapped it around himself before setting off for the lounge.

It was obvious that he hadn't been the only one taking advantage of the hired hands. Ian was looking rather flushed, his hairy chest matted with more than just sweat. James was sitting in the corner – he knew that it was more than his life was worth to do anything like that. On the other hand, Mark, the bodybuilder, was sitting in the armchair opposite, looking rather shamefaced.

And so you should – so you *both* should, thought Adrian. The moment I don't need you – any of you – you'll be sorry.

Before he could say anything, he was aware that someone was standing next to him. It was his butler, Mason, incongruously dressed in a tailcoat, holding a silver tray. Adrian took the piece of paper from the tray and read it. As the words sunk in, he smiled. No, he grinned. This was exactly what he wanted to hear.

'Mason – a magnum of Krug and ten glasses. And summon the others – I want them to hear this.' He glanced at Ian. 'And clean yourself up before the others get here.'

★

Five minutes later, they were all assembled in the lounge. All of his house guests were there: the members of the board that nominally ran the Syndicate – although Adrian knew exactly where the real power lay.

With him.

As soon as they had taken their glasses, he addressed the assembly. 'Gentlemen. Although this started as a housewarming party, I am delighted to be able to tell you that it has become a celebration of much, much more. I have just received word that the moment we have been waiting for has arrived. The five key share prices which dictate the finances of the Elective have sunk below their critical levels on the London, New York and Tokyo Stock Exchanges and on NASDAQ.

'We can now make our move. The time has come for us to preside over the final, utter defeat of the Elective. From this point on we will show them no quarter, no mercy.' He raised his champagne flute, but he was already intoxicated with the imminence of power. Within weeks, the Elective would be nothing, and the Syndicate would be triumphant. *He* would be triumphant.

'Cry havoc – and let slip the dogs of war.'

One

───────

Nathan took a deep swig of his Foster's and let out a heartfelt sigh. Other people had birthdays; why was he treating his like a wake? Why was he hiding away in the dark shadows of the Crossed Swords, rather than partying with his closest friends?

Which was how it *should* have been.

That was what Nathan had intended – once. Unfortunately, destiny had intervened, twist after twist of cruel fate that had led to his current predicament.

Three months ago, he had been planning a lavish party, hiring out the whole of his old stomping ground, the Brave Trader, inviting all of his friends to celebrate his thirty-fourth birthday. It was going to be a spectacular affair, with drag queens, singers, a disco, a lavish buffet provided by one of the premiere chefs in London – the climax of a successful year of his life. Indeed, the most successful year of his life. Nathan Dexter's triumph.

But not any more. No birthday party. No successful year. No triumph. Quite the opposite, in fact. The last six months had seen nothing but loss: career, friends, relationship, the Brave Trader . . .

He felt the all-too-familiar pang of loss as he thought of the Brave Trader, its comforts and charms now denied him. Then he took another, deeper swig of his pint and resigned himself to the serious business of being a miserable old bastard. So: who else could he share his misery with tonight? There was already a fair smattering of customers, a mixture of regulars and the passing business traffic that stopped off in the Crossed Swords after work. Nathan knew quite of few of them, but even the ones that he had once considered to be friends were doing their utmost to ignore him. Nathan wasn't that concerned, though: he could do without their false sympathy and their empty concerns. Misery is its own company, he decided.

Bitter, aren't we Nate? commented a little voice inside. *Getting a bit pissed, are we?* OK, so he was knocking the pints back, but what did that matter? It was his birthday – and it wasn't as if he had anything else to do, was it? Thirty-four years old, with no job, no friends, and virtually no money. Welcome to my life, he thought self-indulgently.

As he sipped his beer, he looked around the Crossed Swords, wondering – hoping – if any of his friends would remember that it was his birthday. But who was he kidding? Most people hadn't remembered, and those who had wouldn't have turned up anyway.

It hadn't taken long for Nathan Dexter to face the truth: on London's gay scene, he was about as welcome as an outbreak of crabs. Nothing had been said, that was true; but there were the looks, the whispers, the rumours. Enough to prove to Nathan that his credit rating on the scene was in the gutter. Thanks to the Elective, and the machinations of Adrian Delancey, his archenemy, Nathan was *persona non grata*.

Nathan's personal year had ended virtually without friends, without money, without a job. And, as far as the gay scene was concerned, as a nonperson.

As he drained his pint, his friend Sion – known as Mother to his charges in the Crossed Swords – nodded at the empty glass.

'Another?' Sion was the only person to have made the effort to be here – mainly because the machinations of the Elective were beneath him. Sion was virtually fireproof as far as the Elective was concerned: he knew where the bodies were buried.

If only you had met him earlier, said that annoying inner voice. *Perhaps you wouldn't be in this mess now.* But now wasn't the time for regrets: it was the time to party. Birthday party!

Yeah. Right.

Nathan shrugged. 'Why not?' It wasn't as if he had anywhere else to go, was it?

Sion pursed his lips. 'Not the attitude for my birthday boy,' he said pointedly, before striding off towards the bar.

As Sion entered the throng, Nathan looked around the darkened interior of The Crossed Swords, hoping to see someone he knew, somebody who might be bothered about seeing him.

The Crossed Swords on Charing Cross Road was large and cruisy, its main bar always about three deep with customers. The lighting was dim at this time of night, allowing people to sink into the shadows, to watch and to wait. Or to hide, Nathan decided.

Or to hide. Exactly.

Nathan was standing in the small raised area towards the back of the bar, next to the Round Table. It actually was just that: a round table. But to the regulars, it was *the* Round Table: the focal point for gossip and social interaction, where decisions were made and opinions were formed. The Round Table was the Crossed Swords' equivalent of the Royal Enclosure in the Brave Trader, the power behind the throne.

Since Nathan's fall from grace, the members of the Round Table had been his friends, his support network. They had kept him going while everything else had been falling apart.

But not tonight. When he had set off from his house in Docklands, Nathan had half hoped to see the Round Table surrounded by the regulars: people such as Uncle, Freddie, Ottavio, Alan – old friends, come to wish him a happy birthday. Come to show that they cared.

Instead, there had only been Sion. Not that there was anything *only* about Sion: he was at the heart of all of the gossip and goings-on throughout the entirety of the scene. Indeed, Sion had been there for Nathan on more than one occasion, warning him of places that would no longer welcome him, thanks to the Elective.

But what of the others? What of Marco, of Leigh, of Scott, his closest friends? Would they turn up? But Nathan knew that thinking that way was pointless: everyone that he knew, with the exception of Sion, and his old friends Paul and Neil, now steadfastly ignored him. Even Mike Bury had to work this evening. Still, there was always the possibility of a one-night stand, an empty gesture that would still help him to forget. Catching sight of his reflection in one of the mirrors on the wall, he knew that he was still quite a catch: stocky, with short hair, a goatee beard . . . And no one had ever complained after going home with him, he thought with a trace of conceit. Besides, if he couldn't be conceited on his birthday, when *could* he be conceited? He knew he needed the ego boost – even a one-night stand would do it.

At first all he saw was a row of dark faces, all blending into one sea of instantly available sex. It seemed so simple and easy . . . but was it what he was after that night? It was his special night: was he prepared to throw it away on some stranger whom he night never see again?

Well, yes. Six months ago, Nathan had been standing in exactly the same point in the bar, and had caught the attention of a young bit of rough standing by the stairs.

That person had been Scott James, a young student. And the one-night stand that had followed had developed into the most satisfying relationship of his life, fulfilling needs that he had never even realised he had – a relationship that Nathan had believed was invulnerable, everlasting.

He had been wrong.

And now? A life in ruins and a relationship in tatters. All because Nathan had miscalculated, underestimated the evil machinations of Adrian Delancey.

So why shouldn't he spend his birthday shagging some anonymous stranger? Well, not just any stranger. One particular person, whose face now stood out from the crowd, as if a spotlight had picked him out from the masses.

Fair enough, he might not be husband material, but there was something about him that drew Nathan's attention, enough to make him decide to take a closer look. He took a couple of steps forward so that he was able to get a clearer look at the guy.

It was as if the man had taken a mask off. From an object of desire, he became something quite different as Nathan got closer. Sense came back to Nathan as if someone had thrown a bucket of water over him. The guy was a *slug*, with thinning, greasy hair, a pointless, threadbare moustache, and far, far too much weight.

'I'm obviously losing my sense of taste,' he muttered, shaking his head, as Sion returned from the bar with a pint of Foster's and his own signature drink – the quad vod.

'So what have you got planned for the rest of this evening?' asked Sion as he settled the drinks on the Round Table. Sion was in his late forties, with well-coiffured greying hair and a lugubrious, lived-in face. 'I mean, it's only nine o'clock. The night is young. What about your mother?' Sion gave a wry grin. 'Your other mother, I mean.'

'I'm seeing my mum at the weekend. At least she'll be pleased to see me,' he said bitterly. What do I have planned, thought Nathan. How can I plan anything, when there's no one to do anything with?

'And I'm not pleased to see you?' said Sion, a hurt tone in his voice.

'That's not what I meant,' Nathan said defensively. 'It's just that . . .' He held his arms open to indicate the singular lack of friends surrounding them. 'What the about the others? It's funny how the whole of the Round Table found themselves with previous engagements this evening, isn't it?'

Sion placed a friendly hand on Nathan's shoulder. 'Nathan, I realise that this is hard for you, and it's not like me to lecture you on your birthday, of all days . . . but you have to pull yourself together. This wallowing just isn't the Nathan Dexter I know.'

PAUL C. ALEXANDER

'I know. But what can I do? I've lost Scott, my friends – most of my friends – have deserted me, I can't get a job for the life of me . . .' He banged the Round Table. 'It just seems so pointless. What's the future going to hold for me, eh?'

Sion smiled. 'Funny you should ask that question. Close your eyes.'

Puzzled, Nathan did what Sion asked.

'You can open them now.' Nathan opened his eyes and looked down. A large, triangular package and a smaller square one were resting next to Nathan's pint.

'Happy birthday, Nathan,' said Sion, and gave him a friendly kiss on the lips. 'Perhaps this will answer your question.'

Nathan unwrapped the blue foil paper and stared at the contents with a look of wonder on his face. It was a crystal pyramid, its geometric surfaces reflecting the lights and colours of the Crossed Swords in chaotic patterns. A bit like his life.

'Sion, I . . .' Nathan was lost for words. Mainly because he had absolutely no idea what it was.

'Open the other package,' Sion ordered, indicating the square one next to the pyramid. 'Then I'll explain.'

Discarding the wrapping, Nathan raised an eyebrow when he saw what it was. A pack of cards. Tarot cards, wrapped in black silk.

'Before you go to bed, you shuffle the Tarot pack, while concentrating on the question that you want answered. The pyramid is supposed to bring the card that tells you the answer to the top of the pack, which you then interpret.'

Nathan raised an eyebrow. He was predominantly a realist, and hadn't held much truck with superstition and magic. That was until he had been commissioned to write a feature for one of the Sunday broadsheets, exposing faith healers and fortune tellers as the fakes they were.

Except that he hadn't been able to. While visiting a fortune teller, all of his scepticism had immediately evaporated as he listened to the woman's words. There had been no way that she could have known so much, and no way that what she had

14

predicted could have come true. But she has been right. Her insights into his past had been one thing. But only in hindsight could Nathan see that she had told him all about his friend Paolo's death, Nathan's battle with the mysterious Elective, even his final fall from grace at the hands of Adrian Delancey.

'You might want to give it a go this evening,' Sion continued. 'It is your birthday – that should be significant.' Then his eyes followed where Nathan was looking and he broke into a broad grin. 'That's assuming you get home before midnight, of course.'

Nathan's attention had been drawn to a young, unshaven man standing at the bar – virtually the same position Scott had been in six months previously. Perhaps history could repeat itself. Who am I kidding? he thought. He didn't want a re-creation of Scott: he wanted Scott himself. But the young man by the bar was definitely Nathan Dexter material.

'Nathan's on the hunt, I see.'

Nathan shrugged. 'Why not? It's not like I have anything better to do, is it?'

Sion waved a warning finger. 'Not exactly an attitude conducive to a successful pick-up.'

'OK, OK!' Forcing a smile that he most certainly didn't feel, Nathan picked up his pint and nonchalantly sauntered over to his intended prey. Perhaps he could find a present for himself after all.

'For God's sake, Marco, snap out of it!' Leigh Robertson's patience was rapidly exhausting. His boyfriend, usually irritatingly cheerful, was currently about as much fun as an open grave. Marco was sitting on the sofa opposite Leigh, dressed casually in a pair of shorts and a singlet, showing off his solid, muscular arms and legs, his whole body covered with thick black hair. His square face was set in a frown, his mouth downturned. He was playing with his moustache: a clear sign that something was bothering him. And Leigh knew exactly what it was.

'Have you forgotten what day it is?' Marco muttered, his Australian accent colouring his words. After ten years in Britain,

Marco's accent was fairly muted, unless he was excited or depressed. And today he was definitely the latter.

Leigh sank down in the armchair. The two of them were sitting in the living room of Marco's flat in St John's Wood. Normally, Leigh felt relaxed, at home; why shouldn't he? He had moved in with Marco a few weeks after they had started seeing each other, back in January, and the place *was* his home. Wasn't it?

But, on nights like tonight, Leigh felt like an intruder, forcing his way into Marco's own world where he clearly wasn't wanted.

'Of course I haven't forgotten. May the seventh. It's Nathan's birthday.'

'Nathan's fucking birthday!' snapped Marco. 'Exactly!'

Leigh sighed. He knew the way this argument was going to go, whatever the reason for it. The same way it always went. And he knew how it would end: with one or the other of them storming out and spending the rest of the evening down at the pub.

But not tonight. This had been going on for months – and it would stop. Now. Because the way Leigh felt, if he stormed out he would never come back.

He adopted his most conciliatory tone. 'Marco: you know where he is. Why don't you go and see him? Try to bury the hatchet?'

'How can I,' said Marco softly, 'after what he's done to the Elective?' His voice may have been soft, but the anger at his betrayal was clear. As was the hidden message: after what he's done to *me*.

Ah yes, thought Leigh. The Elective. How could he ever forget the one thing in Marco's life that was more important than Leigh himself was?

Marco Capiello had been many things in his life: accountant, DJ, club manager . . . but his current 'job', if it could be called that, was far more mysterious. He was Comptroller of the UK branch of the secretive organisation known only as the Elective.

The Elective had been founded at the turn of the century by a group of philanthropic gay millionaires who had decided to help the gay cause in a time when homosexuality was hidden deep below ground, away from the prying eyes of 'normal' society. Using their financial knowledge, they had constructed a network of holding companies, which provided the cash necessary to fund the Elective – an unimaginably powerful body which now had influence in every country, in every section of industry, in virtually every government. The Elective existed to provide social and financial support to its members, a framework in which gay people could operate without fear of prejudice.

At least, that had been the original intention.

About five years ago, an ambitious accountant, one of the City's hotshots by the name of Adrian Delancey, had risen to the rank of UK Comptroller. Delancey had his own agenda for the Elective, and his exulted position gave him the freedom to carry that out.

However, Marco's first experience of Delancey had occurred when he and his ex-boyfriend Lawrence had started a club in South London that had proved incredibly popular. Its popularity had brought it to the attention of the Elective, which showed an interest in 'helping' Lawrence and Marco out.

Before Delancey, this would have been a more than acceptable offer: with the backing of the Elective, Lawrence and Marco could have gone far, both with the club and in the Elective itself. But, under Delancey, it wasn't an offer.

It was a vicious threat.

Lawrence's continued refusal to accept Delancey's terms had ended with a finality that Leigh knew still hurt Marco deeply. One night, while closing up the club, Lawrence had been jumped by two unknown assailants, and had been brutally beaten.

The result? Lawrence had ended up in a wheelchair, and Marco had been forced to agree to Delancey's terms. But at a cost. Marco had insisted that he become part of the Elective. But he too now had an agenda: by becoming part of the Elective, he could fight its shadowy power from within, and avenge Lawrence's injuries. He had eventually become Deputy Comptroller, hoping to stop whatever Delancey was up to, but there had been another cost: Lawrence, unable to understand why Marco was dealing with the people who had consigned him to a wheelchair, had ended their relationship, and Marco's reaction had been to bury himself even deeper in the Elective's work.

Which was the point at which Nathan Dexter had entered his life.

Adrian Delancey's plans had been reaching fruition: he had single-handedly built a slave ring, operating out of London's leather scene, drugging and kidnapping bears, clones and leathermen and shipping them out across the world. Having lost one of his closest friends – Leigh – Nathan had started to investigate the Elective, which had brought him head to head against Delancey . . . and into an alliance with Marco, who was almost ready to deal with the Comptroller's schemes.

Together, Marco and Nathan had defeated Delancey, and were subsequently asked by the absolute head of the Elective, the Director, to remove the last traces of corruption from the organisation.

Which was when the trouble had started. Both Nathan and Marco had taken to their new responsibilities enthusiastically, jetting across the world, righting wrongs and rooting out Delancey's influence.

Unfortunately, they had become so wrapped up in what they were doing, in the luxury lifestyle that it involved, that both Marco and Nathan had started to neglect their respective boyfriends. Leigh had given Marco an ultimatum: choose between him and the Elective – and it had worked. Partially. Until Nathan Dexter had stitched up the Elective, delivering a killing blow that threatened to destroy everything that Marco had worked for. Worse than that, it would probably mean the ultimate triumph of Adrian Delancey, which was something that Marco would never be able to face. Because of that, Marco had thrown himself into his work in a desperate attempt to thwart Delancey and save the Elective.

Leigh hardly ever saw him nowadays. And, when he did, he

was either too tired to do anything, or moping around like a bear with a sore head. Or, like tonight, both.

'Please, Marco, make an effort.'

'An effort?' Marco shook his head. 'No, Leigh, how can I? I trusted Nathan. The Director trusted him. We gave him the Director's Codes, because he reckoned he could finish off Delancey once and all. And what does he do? Gives the Codes to Delancey!' Marco's voice was ragged, angry. 'Thanks to Nathan, the Elective is on the point of complete financial collapse. The only organisation that could stand a chance of defeating Delancey and his Syndicate, dead in the water!'

Leigh went over and placed a comforting arm around him. 'Marco, I know Nathan. I know how much he cares about you, and how much he cared about the Elective. There has to be more to it than simple betrayal. Nathan just wouldn't do that.'

Marco sighed. 'I know. That's what makes it so difficult to understand. What did Delancey say to him? How did Delancey manage to persuade him?'

'Ask him. Meet on neutral ground, away from the Crossed Swords or the Brave Trader. Find out what really happened.'

Marco stared deep into Leigh's eyes, and a brief spark of the old Marco momentarily burnt brightly. 'OK, OK. I'll phone him tomorrow. One way or another, we'll get to the bottom of this.'

Leigh smiled. It wasn't much, but it was a start. Perhaps things would be back to normal before long.

He stood up. 'I fancy a drink. Coming?'

Marco shook his head. 'Got some Elective stuff to finish.'

Leigh sighed. Back to normal? he thought. Who am I kidding?

'No luck?' said Sion. Only minutes after Nathan had wandered over to the young man at the bar, he was back at the Round Table.

The expression on Nathan's face was one of unrestrained fury. 'I don't know why I fucking bother!' he growled, slamming the half-drunk pint on the table and making his pyramid shudder. 'I can't fart in this city any more without someone knowing about it.' He took a deep breath, trying to calm down. As he did so, he saw the young guy downing his drink and leaving the Crossed Swords. 'I'd been talking to him for about a minute. He seemed quite keen – then one of his friends called him over.'

'Let me guess: he made his apologies and left.'

Nathan nodded. 'Another of those friendly warnings. "Don't go near Nathan Dexter. He's trouble." ' It wasn't the first time it had happened, and it wouldn't be the last, that was for sure. Even in his last refuge, Nathan still wasn't safe. The Elective wanted revenge, but it wouldn't act openly. Instead, it had systematically destroyed his reputation, both personally and professionally. Every pub in London in which the Elective had influence had ensured that Nathan wasn't welcome, and even those in which the Elective had no say were soon seeded with people who were able to say, 'Don't go near Nathan Dexter. He's trouble.'

Not being able to get a drink – or a shag – was one thing; unfortunately for Nathan, the Elective's influence – even now – was far wider. Six months ago, Nathan Christopher Dexter had been one of the best-regarded investigative journalists in Britain. A byline from Nathan Dexter guaranteed a good story, one that would inevitably blow open some case of malpractice or corruption. There had been industry awards, glowing reviews, an endless series of freelance commissions . . .

Not any more. None of the newspapers, none of the publishing houses, would touch him with a bargepole. Nathan painfully remembered the exact moment when it had finally come home to him that he was unemployable.

He'd been standing there, in Marcus Moore's office, unable to believe what he had just been told. The *Investigator*, Marcus's magazine, had always been one place where Nathan had been able to place a story. The landlord scandal, the beer-pricing controversy, the gay serial killer . . . they had all been stories that Marcus had accepted without argument. Nathan had a reputation, and his copy sold issues.

Until now. Marcus mopped the ever-present sweat from his

forehead with a stained handkerchief and gave Nathan an embarrassed, apologetic look. 'I'm sorry, Nate, it's just . . .' He stared down at his desk, unable to keep Nathan's gaze a second longer.

'Let me guess. You've been got at.' Nathan's voice was cold. Part of him wanted to lose his temper, to slam his fists on the desk and demand that Marcus tell him who was behind this decision. But Nathan knew that it was no use. And, besides, Nathan knew exactly who was behind the decision. The one force he could no longer fight. The Elective. His best option was to swallow his pride and leave.

'I'm sorry, Nate,' Marcus repeated. 'I wish there was something I could do, but . . .' He held out his hands in a gesture of impotence. Six months before, Marcus had been asking for proof of the Elective; now he was in its pocket. How things change.

Nathan paid no further attention to the stream of platitudes coming from Marcus; he slammed the office door behind him and stormed out of the building. His final hope – dashed.

Standing there on Dean Street, alone, watching the busy life of Soho rushing around him, Nathan knew he wanted a drink. For a brief moment, he considered the Brave Trader, but he knew what sort of a welcome he would receive there: the same welcome Marcus had given him. The same welcome he would get anywhere that he went.

Although it was a warm spring day, Nathan started to shiver . . .

'Earth to Nathan, Earth to Nathan.' Nathan's attention returned to the present.

'Sorry, Sion – miles away.'

'There's at least one person in here who isn't worried by your reputation.' Sion gave a subtle nod towards the DJ's booth, about five feet away. A stocky man in his late twenties, wearing a plain white T-shirt and jeans, was standing there, staring over at Nathan. His hair was dark and slightly spiky, and he had a cheeky grin on his face. Nathan smiled back, captivated by that grin, imagining all of the possibilities . . . He suddenly realised that the man was walking over.

'Is your name Nathan? Nathan Dexter?'

Nathan swallowed. What was this? Another threat from the Elective? Another bar that would soon be barred to him? Unable to think of another reply, he simply nodded.

'I thought so, although the description didn't do you justice.' Another broad grin. 'This is for you. Er . . . happy birthday.' He handed Nathan a cream-coloured envelope.

Puzzled, Nathan opened it, half afraid of what it would contain. But there was nothing more threatening than a letter inside, the handwriting clear and classical. Nathan quickly scanned the words.

Dear Mr Dexter

They say that 'The enemy of my enemy is my friend'. You and I have a mutual enemy, Nathan, and I believe we can help one another. If you want to learn more, call on me tomorrow at the above address.

And a Happy Birthday. Enjoy your present.

Yours

A friend.

Mystified, Nathan looked at the address. It wasn't familiar: somewhere in Russell Square. But the address and the letter itself positively reeked of money. Who was this person? What did he want? And, more selfishly, what present? He put the letter back in the envelope and stuffed it in the pocket of his jeans, confused and puzzled.

'I'm Carl,' said the messenger quietly. Nathan looked round at him, and suddenly one thing became clear. The expectant expression on Carl's face meant that Nathan had at least one of his answers: he knew what the present was.

'I've been asked to take you out for dinner to celebrate,' he said. 'If you want, that is.'

This is all just too weird for words, thought Nathan. Things like this just don't happen. Still, he wasn't one to look a gift horse in the mouth, especially given the way that his luck had been going recently. He turned to Sion.

'I'll see you tomorrow – and we need to talk.'

Sion grinned, and gave Carl a fruity smile. 'Yes, I rather imagine that we do. Don't forget your presents, Nathan – all of them,' he added pointedly, nodding towards Carl.

Stifling a laugh, Nathan picked up the pyramid and cards, and led Carl out of the Crossed Swords. With everything falling apart around him, Carl was one bright spot in his life – and Nathan didn't intend to waste it. It may be only one night, but it was one that he could savour.

Sion watched as Nathan made his way through the busy throng of people and shook his head. Much as he cared for Nathan, he couldn't help thinking that he was as much to blame for his current predicament as the Elective. He took a sip of his quad vod and reflected on the situation.

Sion was very familiar with the workings of the Elective: his eye for detail and his observational and analytical skills had brought him to its attention on many occasions. However, he had always turned down the Elective's entreaties to join, explaining that he preferred to operate on the sidelines, outside of any restraints.

Which was *almost* true.

But perhaps now was one of those times to make his presence known to the Elective. To put a bit of stick about.

Nathan had hurt the Elective – badly. If Sion's sources were to be believed – and, unsurprisingly, his sources were beyond reproach – the Elective was haemorrhaging money, as Adrian Delancey's sinister Syndicate methodically assaulted the holding companies that provided the Elective's financial base. If left unchecked, the Elective would undoubtedly collapse by the end of the year – all because Nathan had given Delancey the Director's Codes, and the means to put the Elective out of business.

However, Sion knew that Nathan had been set up. He knew that Delancey had lured Nathan into a trap in Gran Canaria, misleading him so he would unwittingly betray the Elective. He knew, and he believed Nathan. End of story.

So, there had to be some way of forcing the Elective to see the truth, and to stop its relentless assault on Nathan Dexter. There had to be! The Elective wasn't stupid – it could recognise the truth when it saw it.

Draining his quad vod, Sion came to a decision. Tomorrow night, he would beard the Elective in its own den. His name counted for a lot on the gay scene; tomorrow, he would confront the Brave Trader's unofficial ruling council, the Royal Enclosure – and, through the Royal Enclosure, he would make sure that the Elective came to its senses regarding Nathan Dexter.

Because, if it didn't, Sion knew how to make it. Despite all the evidence, neither the Elective nor the Syndicate was all-powerful. But Sion knew who was.

Nathan's fingers were having difficulty getting the key into the door. Then again, after the meal that he had just eaten – or rather the two bottles of wine that they had drunk – that wasn't surprising. He looked round at Carl, giving him a shamefaced grin, but Carl was grinning as well. Oh well, thought Nathan, it *is* my birthday.

Carl had taken him to Nathan's favourite restaurant, Zilli Fish on Brewer Street, where the crab-and-avocado cocktail and the lobster spaghetti had been as wonderful as always. The two bottles of Soave had been chilled and delicious, and Nathan's recommendation of the espresso crème brulée had been appreciated by both of them. Sitting there, nursing their liqueurs and watching the crowds mill around the corner of Lexington Street and Brewer Street, Nathan decided to chance his arm.

'What's all this about, Carl?'

Carl shrugged. So far, all that Nathan knew was that Carl was a city trader by day, who acted as an escort by night. The fact that he appeared to genuinely fancy Nathan was a bonus, as far as

Nathan was concerned. However, although Nathan appreciated a present as much as the next man, a well-muscled hunk wasn't a normal gift. It was more like something the Elective would bestow on you. If it was the Elective, what were they playing at?

Carl shrugged. 'I'll be honest with you. I got a phone call yesterday, offering me about ten times what I normally get paid. All I had to do was deliver that letter, take you for dinner, and then . . .' He grinned. 'Well, that's up to you, Nathan.'

'This new "friend" of mine is certainly mysterious.' He sipped his amaretto. 'And I'd be a liar if I said I didn't want to drag you home with me,' he added with a smile.

'And, as I said earlier, I'd be more than happy. You're a nice bloke, Nathan.'

Was he being honest, or was this flattery all part of the service? For this one moment, Nathan just didn't care. Delancey, the Elective, the Syndicate, Scott . . . all of it could be forgotten for this one moment of perfection.

'I'll get the bill,' said Carl, reaching into his back pocket for his wallet.

That had been half an hour ago. Now the two of them stumbled into Nathan's house, laughing like schoolboys. Slamming the door shut behind them, Nathan dropped Sion's present, grabbed Carl and drew him towards him in a heartfelt hug.

'Easy, tiger,' said Carl, but he didn't resist. His own strong, muscular arms enfolded Nathan, making him feel safe, wanted. Carl's cheek brushed Nathan's, and the sensation of that dark stubble colliding with Nathan's own went straight to Nathan's cock.

Carl started to nibble on Nathan's ear, and Nathan could feel his hot breath on his neck. His cock was already hard: it had been weeks since he had been this close to another man, since someone had been in his house, wanting him, wanting to have sex with him. Reaching down, Nathan tugged on Carl's T-shirt, extracting it from his jeans and pulling it over his head.

Carl's body was just as Nathan had imagined: tanned, fit without being too muscular, with a light dusting of hair over his nipples. Nathan laid his hands on Carl's tits, squeezing them, first softly, then harder, relishing the groan of pleasure/pain that it caused.

Carl grabbed Nathan's belt and hurriedly undid it, before pulling open the fly buttons and allowing the jeans to fall to the ground. Nathan's dick was now so hard that the helmet was poking over the top of his boxers; Carl wet a finger with his lips and rubbed it over the sensitive red skin. Nathan gasped, and squeezed Carl's tits even harder, before roughly tugging at Carl's jeans until they dropped to the floor. Carl wasn't wearing any pants: an impressive seven-inch cock bobbed upright, thick and cut, a drop of pre-come glistening in the slit.

Falling to the carpet, Nathan cupped Carl's balls in one hand, while the other hand clasped the warm flesh of Carl's cock. Without hesitating, he took all of its length into his mouth, tasting the pre-come, smelling the musky odour of Carl's hairy groin. His own cock was still restrained by his boxers, and he was desperate to release it, desperate for Carl to suck it, to take it into his arse. But he was going to wait – because Carl was worth waiting for.

He continued to slide his lips up and down the shaft, moving his hand so that he was now stroking the hairy crack of Carl's arse. A single finger reached upward, probing, finding the hot hole of Carl's arse and gently playing with the rim. Carl growled, his hands roughly massaging Nathan's shoulders, but he made no move for Nathan to stop.

Nathan climbed to his feet and gently pushed Carl backwards on to the leather sofa, and manoeuvred him so that he was lying lengthways along the black leather. Then Nathan lifted Carl's legs up, revealing his arse, even with his ankles constrained by his pulled-down jeans.

Squeezing himself into the gap on the sofa, Nathan pulled Carl's arse cheeks apart, before burying his mouth in the warmth, scent and taste of Carl's ring. He forced his tongue into the hairy crack, licking the rim before burrowing deeper and deeper into Carl's arse. From the sounds that Carl was making, it was clear that Nathan had uncovered one of his weak spots, and rimming just happened to be one of Nathan's as well. He knew that he could have spent hours tasting Carl, fucking him with his tongue, going deeper and deeper before making Carl shoot his come. But his own needs were growing ever more desperate: his cock was now so stiff and so sensitive, rubbing against the leather of the sofa, that he knew that he would soon come of his own accord.

And he wanted his birthday present to have that honour.

'Let's go upstairs,' he whispered, before getting off the sofa and grabbing Carl's hand. They went up the stairs in expectant silence.

Switching on the bedside lamp, Nathan gave Carl a broad grin. 'Take off your jeans,' he ordered, perhaps a little more forcefully than he had intended. But Carl's response was sufficient to bring his cock back to full hardness.

'Yes, sir.' *Yes. Obedience.* Carl complied, pulling off his boots and jeans before standing there naked, his cock jutting upward.

'You want to be fucked, don't you?' When Carl didn't respond immediately, Nathan slapped him around the face, not too hard, but hard enough for Carl to know who was in charge here. 'Don't you?'

'Yes, sir,' said Carl. 'I want to feel you inside me, sir.'

'Get on the bed. On your back,' he ordered.

Carl complied, his well-honed body lying on the bed. Nathan took off his own boots and jeans. Then he got on to the bed, his cock now desperate to bury itself inside Carl's inviting arse. Grabbing a condom and the lube bottle from next to the bed, Nathan urgently rolled the latex over his cock, an action that brought him even closer to orgasm. He smeared the white lube over the condom, and rubbed even more into Carl's arse, making sure that he inserted first one, then two fingers inside him, loosening him up, relaxing him.

'Ready for this, boy?'

'Yes sir,' came the reply. 'Please, sir.'

That was all Nathan needed to hear. Hoisting Carl's legs upward, he brought his arse up and in front of him, just the right position for Nathan to enter him. With one hand, Nathan kept Carl's legs up; with the other, he guided his cock inside him.

After the faintest resistance, Nathan's cock slid inside, deep inside, right up to his balls. Carl gave a deep guttural groan, which turned Nathan on even more. He withdrew slightly, about half of his thick eight inches, before driving it back in with all the force he could muster. His hand strayed to Carl's nipples before squeezing them tightly. Carl's hand had moved down to his own cock; Nathan watched for a second as he started to wank himself.

'Did I say you could touch yourself?' he bellowed. 'I'm going to punish you for that.' He slapped Carl's arse, once, then again, hard slaps which left the red imprint of his hand on Carl's cheek. Seeing that, Nathan felt even more turned on, even more desperate to fill this hunk up. He started to pump his cock into him faster and faster, harder and harder, while one hand sought out Carl's cock and wanked him in time to his own thrusts.

'What do you say?' cried Nathan, riding Carl.

'Thank you, sir,' Carl gasped, as Nathan drove his dick into him, pulled on Carl's own thick cock, wet with pre-come. He could feel his shaft brushing against Carl's prostate with each fuck, his helmet touching the little nut again and again. The sensations were overwhelming: he was inside this guy, taking this guy, forcing this guy to do what he wanted. And he wanted this guy to come.

'Sir . . .' gasped Carl. Before he could say anything else, the first shot of come sprayed over Carl's chest, his stomach. Nathan knew that he should have been angry, angry that his slave hadn't held off until his master's release, but the sight of that hot white fluid over Carl's tanned, fit body, with more and more of it shooting from that thick length as Nathan carried on wanking, was too much.

Yelling with the indescribable explosion that burst from his groin, Nathan started to pump his own come into Carl's arse, wave after wave of pleasure that got better and better with each driving thrust. Finally, he was drained, empty, but unimaginably satisfied. Gently, he withdrew his still stiff cock from Carl's arse and pulled off the condom. Then he climbed on top of Carl, feeling the come rubbing into the thick hair of his chest and stomach. He placed an arm around Carl's neck and hugged him.

'Thanks,' he whispered.

Carl smiled. 'Happy Birthday.'

Nathan knew that he should be worried, worried about what would happen tomorrow, worried about the mysterious friend who had sent Carl. But, at this moment, he didn't care about anything, apart from the horny man he was cuddled up to.

And, given his current circumstances, that was more than enough to satisfy Nathan.

Two

      —————

Leigh watched from the open doorway as Scott James slammed
the empty Hooch bottle on the bar of the Brave Trader and
asked for another, ignoring the sympathetic yet slightly critical
look from Kevin the head barman. Everyone knew why Scott
was there, but no one wanted to talk about it. Nathan was a
forbidden subject in the Brave Trader – and his birthday doubly
so.

Scott was sitting on a stool at the corner of the bar, dressed in
a white T-shirt which showed off his well-muscled body. It was
clear that Scott was well on the way to getting drunk, but Leigh
wasn't surprised. It was Nathan's birthday, and, like Leigh and
Marco, Scott should have been with him, not standing alone in
the Brave Trader, propping up the bar and wallowing in self pity.

Enough of that! Still feeling pretty proud of himself for getting
Marco to consider contacting Nathan, and pleased to see Scott,
Leigh decided to see whether he could do the same for his friend.

Leigh sidled up to Scott. 'I thought I might find you here,' he
said, nodding at Kevin's silent enquiry as to whether he wanted a
drink. He looked beyond Kevin to the far end of the pub, to the
Royal Enclosure, the enclave of movers and shakers that stood in
the gap between the bar and the kitchen. All of the regulars were

there, and Leigh couldn't help wondering how many of them had turned up, just on the off chance that Nathan might brazen it out and actually set foot in the Brave Trader. To them, it would have the same allure as a car crash.

'Where else, Leigh?' said Scott with a shrug and a slur. 'Where else would I be tonight?'

Leigh didn't really have an answer to that. He picked up his pint of cider and looked around the rest of the familiar environment. Although it was in the heart of Soho, the Brave Trader was more of a local's pub, a community unto itself in an olde-worlde environment of wooden beams and dark-panelled walls. The regulars looked out for one another, creating a tight-knit group that resisted any outside intervention. 'The Brave Trader looks after its own,' somebody had once said.

Until recently.

Although the Elective had no direct influence over the Brave Trader, the pub's regular clientele contained a number of people who were senior members of the organisation: enough for Nathan to effectively be blackballed from the pub that he had virtually treated as a second home. Leigh remembered hearing about Nathan standing at the bar, never being served; old friends cutting him dead; Nathan being left alone all night, with no one to talk to him.

Steve, the previous landlord, had been helpless to act: as soon as word had got out, Nathan had simply been ignored. He would be served – eventually. But no one would speak to him.

Willie and Ron, the new landlords, had tried to welcome Nathan back, but the might of the Brave Trader was nothing compared with the Elective, even in its current, weakened state. As far as Nathan Dexter was concerned, the Brave Trader was a quarantined pub, and he was a forbidden subject.

Despite that, both Leigh and Scott had continued to visit it, without a word – openly. But Leigh knew that things were being said.

The Brave Trader wasn't that busy, but Thursdays were always a little on the quiet side. Even so, Leigh couldn't help imagining what it would have been like, if Nathan's party had gone ahead. Cabaret, a buffet, Nathan holding court in the Royal Enclosure . . . It would have been wonderful, a night to remember. Instead, there was an atmosphere of complete anticlimax, a feeling of what might have been. Everyone in the pub must have been thinking exactly the same as Leigh was, wondering about what it *might* have been like, what sort of a party it *would* have been.

And, if *they* were all wondering that, how the hell was Scott feeling? Leigh patted him affectionately on the shoulder. 'It's no use dwelling, mate. What's done is done.' *Oh, very sympathetic.*

Scott shrugged, and picked up the new bottle of Hooch like an old friend. 'I know. Everything's fine, Leigh. Absolutely fine. Couldn't be better.' But it was clear that he didn't mean a word of it.

Scott wasn't really Leigh's type, although he had to admit that there was something almost animalistic about him. Whether it was his muscular, hairy build, or the stubbly, thuglike face with its dopey yet aggressive expression, Leigh didn't know. He did know that he was exactly the type that Nathan went for, though. That was something that Leigh and Scott shared: they had both been out with Nathan. But, while Leigh's relationship had been fairly casual, he knew that Nathan thought the world of Scott. After years of looking for someone special, Nathan had believed that he had found it in Scott, found something that would last.

Until the Elective.

There had to be something that Leigh could do to help the situation. Oh well, time to state the bleeding obvious, he thought, and see what reaction that gets. 'Is it because of Nathan's birthday?'

Scott gave him a disbelieving look. 'That – and everything else.' He sighed. 'Where did it all go wrong, Leigh? A couple of months ago, everything was great –'

'Not that great,' countered Leigh, regretting it as soon as he said it. But he couldn't stop now. He picked up his cider. 'Unless I'm mistaken, you were the one who decided to get out. You left Nathan, Scott. If things had been that great, you would never have gone. Something was wrong, or have you forgotten that night we were all in the Crossed Swords, when Nathan was in Gran Canaria?'

Hard words, but necessary ones: if there was one thing Leigh just wasn't in the mood for, it was self-pity. If he wanted that, he could have stayed at home with Marco.

Scott's voice was quiet when he answered, the words slow and full of pain. 'I know, I know – but he didn't exactly leave me much choice, did he? It was either me or the Elective.'

'We all have choices,' muttered Leigh, thinking more about his current situation than Scott's recent past. How close was he to following Scott's course of action, of simply getting out of Marco's life, and leaving all this Elective stuff far behind?

Nowhere near, he decided. True, Scott had left Nathan, but Leigh knew how much this was tearing Scott apart. Scott would do anything to get back with Nathan – but his pride, his stubborn pride, wouldn't let him. Leigh didn't relish going through the pain that Scott was going through. Despite everything, he knew he would stick with Marco.

Suddenly, a plan began to form in Leigh's mind, something that would take them away from all of this wallowing. A change of scenery . . . 'You need cheering up,' he said. And so did Leigh. As much as he loved Marco, the last few weeks had been difficult. Getting out of London – especially if Nathan and Marco were about to have their long-overdue summit meeting – was probably the best idea.

'Really?' said Scott sarcastically. 'I would never have guessed.'

I deserved that, thought Leigh. Anna Raeburn I'm not. 'At least you smiled. Anyway, what are you doing for the next couple of days?'

Scott frowned before replying: he'd rather overdone the Hooches, and he clearly wasn't firing on all cylinders. 'Nothing in particular. Got a couple of essays to write, but nothing urgent. Nothing's *that* urgent any more.'

An idea had occurred to Leigh. Something that might just work. With Marco's current mood, Leigh was feeling a bit redundant. Why not get out of town for a couple of nights? It wasn't as if money were a problem: although the Elective's finances were in a downward spiral, Leigh felt sure that there was still enough in the petty cash to finance a holiday on the coast. 'How do you fancy a trip to Brighton for a couple of nights?'

'Brighton?' Leigh could have sworn that there was a slight flicker of enthusiasm in Scott's voice. Perhaps he could cheer his friend up after all.

Leigh continued his sales pitch. 'I haven't been there for a couple of years, so I thought it would be a chance to catch up on what's been going on. The weather forecast's quite good, so what do you say? Sun, sand, sea . . . and whatever else you fancy?'

Scott smiled. Definite enthusiasm. *Success!* 'Why not? It might do me some good to get out of London.'

'Exactly what I was thinking. It's a deal then. I'll pick you up tomorrow at twelve.' Then he thought of something. 'Where are you staying at the moment?' After Scott and Nathan had split up, Scott had briefly moved in with someone, but that had been only temporary, until Scott could sort his head out. Leigh realised that he had no idea where Scott was living at the moment.

'Back in halls, like the good little student I am,' he said miserably. 'Back where I started.' He held up the half-full Hooch bottle and stared at it blearily. 'Suppose it's my own fault. Thought I was better than I was.'

After partially cheering up his friend, seeing him start to slide back into depression and self-pity was the last thing that Leigh wanted this evening. He looked at the antique clock that kept time in the Brave Trader: only a few minutes to last orders. But Leigh really didn't feel like going home and suffering Marco's bad mood. Nor did he want to go home knowing that Scott was still upset.

He glanced over at the far wall and saw the poster pinned there. It showed a group of stylised Tom-of-Finland types in harnesses, leather caps and little else, advertising yet another charity night. Leigh smiled. Just the thing. 'Come on – let's go for it. How do you fancy going to the Collective? They've got a bar extension tonight.' He gave a wicked smile. 'Fancy a bit of sleaze?'

For a second, he was worried that Scott was going to say no. Then the familiar devil-may-care expression came over his friend, the old Scott resurfacing at last. 'Why not?' He drained his Hooch bottle and put it on the bar. 'Haven't seen the place since the refit.'

'It's a deal,' he repeated, finishing off his cider. 'Grab your jacket.'

Saying their goodnights to Kevin, Leigh and Scott made their way out of the Brave Trader, ready for a night at the Collective. But even Leigh had to admit: wouldn't it have been better if Nathan had been with them? Wouldn't everything have been better if Nathan had been with them?

Adrian Delancey stood in the garden on the huge, black and white, marble chessboard, watching the parrots fly among the trees. But he wasn't paying attention to them: his mind was elsewhere.

Was this all worth it? he wondered. All of the sacrifices, all of the games . . . was it worth it?

He turned from the garden and looked into his villa. Andy Burroughs was chained to the wall, a dog bowl of water in front of him. Powerless, dependent . . .

In that moment, Delancey knew that it was all worth it.

Whatever it took, he would have that power.

Scott and Leigh arrived at the Collective about midnight, after enduring a harrowing Tube journey to Earl's Court, dodging the drunks and tramps that appeared to have converged on the District Line.

By the time they reached the notorious leather bar, the place was absolutely packed. This was the first time that Scott had been there since its refit earlier in the year, and he had to admit that he was impressed. The old Collective had been dark and seedy, with lots of shadowy corners and the accumulated sleaze that came with being London's oldest leather bar. Many people had been horrified to learn that the Collective was to be refitted, afraid that it would lose every trace of its unique atmosphere, but all those fears had been allayed on its gala opening night.

The new décor of the Collective could only be described as 'industrial': it was still mainly black, but this was now edged with steel. Steel pillars, steel rails, and a steel staircase that led up to the so-called 'viewing gallery' that now encircled the downstairs bar, silver and black contrasting everywhere. But the legendary atmosphere was definitely still there – the refit hadn't destroyed it at all. It was almost as if it were imprinted in the very fabric of the bar, there for ever.

And, within seconds of entering, Scott loved it.

As Leigh forced his way to the bar to get some drinks, Scott looked around for any familiar faces. He saw one immediately: that of the famous grandfather clock, which now stood in the far corner of the bar. That clock had counted down to more last orders than Scott could imagine, and it was reassuring to see that a place had been found for it in the refurbishment.

And next to it was another familiar face: Eddie. As soon as Scott spotted him, he couldn't draw his attention away. Eddie was legendary on the London gay scene – the living, breathing definition of sex on legs. Six foot five, he was heavily muscled and extremely broad – the result of working out at the gym that he owned round the corner from the Collective. He was clean shaven with cropped hair and bore a cheeky grin and wicked eyes, a face that could pull anyone.

Tonight he was wearing jeans and a grey T-shirt, which showed off his thick, hairy arms, his tattoos just visible under the sleeves. The thought of that big, muscled, hairy body was enough to give Scott a hard-on, but he knew that it would never happen. Eddie could take his pick from the entire scene, so what chance did Scott James have?

'Here you go.' Leigh handed Scott a bottle of mineral water. 'Thought it best if we slowed down a little.'

Scott nodded. 'Good idea.' Trying to forget about Eddie, he gestured around the bar. 'Busy, isn't it?'

'Isn't that Nigel?' Leigh pointed across the bar at a tall, ginger-haired figure with a bushy moustache. Nigel had been the landlord of the Brave Trader before moving back up North to the Dutch Master in Manchester. Scott hadn't seen him since he and Mike Bury had visited Manchester in February, looking for the elusive Andy Burroughs. Not one of Scott's proudest moments.

Nigel saw them at the same moment they saw him. Waving, he came over. Scott was pleased to see that his dress sense was the same as ever: a red Levi shirt, leather chaps and a studded jockstrap, all set off with a pair of Doc Martens.

'Well, well, well,' Nigel said warmly, kissing them both on the cheek. Nigel was in his early thirties, and famous for his legendary rudeness to his customers. His bitchy asides and acid comments had livened up many a night in the Brave Trader, but Scott knew that it was nothing more than a front. Actually, he was very fond of him. Many was the time that Nigel had stood by him.

'What's this?' said Nigel with one of his customary snorts. 'The Nathan Dexter Appreciation Society?'

'Nathan and I have split up,' said Scott quietly. Correction: he *had* been very fond of Nigel. But, to be fair, Nigel might not have known.

'So I heard,' said Nigel with a snort. Scratch that, thought Scott. He's just being a bitch. Sensitivity wasn't his strong suit, but even he was hitting below the belt with that one. 'So, out for a bit of fun?'

'I remember the last bit of fun you sorted out for me,' said Scott with a trace of bitterness.

'Oh yes, our Andy. I don't suppose you know where he is, do you? He hasn't been seen since he met you.' Nigel raised an eyebrow. 'Never had you down as a serial killer, Scott. Where did you put him – under the patio?'

Scott ignored the slight – mainly because he didn't want to get involved: Andy Burroughs *had* vanished – and the only answer was Adrian Delancey. 'Anyway,' Scott said heavily, 'what brings you to London?'

Nigel shrugged. 'Felt like a bit of a change. I'd booked the time off to come to Nathan's birthday party, but . . .' He left the rest unsaid, in a rare display of diplomacy. 'I thought I'd revisit an old haunt. So, do want me to sort you out with someone?'

Scott thought about Eddie, but knew that that was an impossible dream. Eddie was a wank fantasy, nothing more. Before he could answer, someone else joined the conversation.

'Evening, Nigel.' Scott turned to see who had spoken and froze on the spot. Eddie was standing there, pint in hand. 'Haven't seen you for a while,' he continued in his thick East End accent. He gave Leigh and Scott considered glances. 'Don't pay any attention to him,' he said with the sort of grin that made Scott feel weak. 'He'll only get you into trouble.' Then he stared at Scott. 'Didn't you used to be with Nathan? Nathan Dexter?'

On today of all days, why did everyone have to keep going on about Nathan? But there was no way Scott could be angry with Eddie. 'A while ago, yes,' he replied.

Eddie nodded. 'Thought so. Scott, isn't it?'

Scott was speechless. Eddie knew his name. *Eddie!*

With one of his usual displays of social engineering, Nigel turned to Leigh. 'Leigh, a friend of mine is desperate to meet you. See you all later.' Scott watched as Nigel virtually dragged Leigh away, throwing a final wave at Scott as they vanished into the throng. Oh well, Scott thought, Leigh could look after himself.

Suddenly, Scott realised that he was alone with Eddie. And that Eddie wasn't making any move to leave. Did he want to talk to him?

'So, how's it going?' asked Eddie.

Scott had to drag his attention away from Eddie's fit body, the sculpted muscles standing out beneath the plain grey T-shirt. Scott's ultimate fantasy, engaging him in small talk. 'Fine,' he eventually replied, trying not to sound too nervous. 'My friend

Leigh thought I could do with some cheering up.' Oh God, Scott, he thought. Could you sound any more feeble?

'Nate's birthday,' said Eddie in his East End growl. 'I remember. So, what are you up to for the rest of the evening?'

Was this a come on? It couldn't be. Not Eddie. Scott decided that he was misinterpreting the situation, letting his fantasies run away with him. 'Oh, nothing really,' he answered, trying not to sound flustered. 'Just seeing who's about.'

Eddie put a big hand on Scott's shoulder. 'I've just had some new equipment delivered to my gym. Haven't had a chance to look at it yet. Fancy helping me give it the once-over?'

Scott opened his mouth to speak, but nothing came out. Eddie, *the* Eddie, had invited him home – his flat was above the gym – and Scott was standing there with his mouth open like a landed fish. After what seemed like an eternity, he managed to stammer out, 'I'd love to.'

Eddie grinned. Scott knew that he had seen countless blokes have the same reaction, but he was still embarrassed.

Yet Eddie didn't seem bothered. 'Good. Ready to go?'

Scott nodded, draining his mineral water and following Eddie out of the Collective, unable to believe his luck, and well aware of the envious looks that were being shot in his direction. As he passed Leigh, the look of pure shock on his friend's face made the moment even sweeter – Leigh knew all about Scott's hero-worship of Eddie.

Marco looked at his watch and sighed. It was well after midnight, and Leigh wasn't home yet. Then again, considering the mood that Marco had been in earlier, he couldn't exactly blame his boyfriend for staying away.

Sighing, he put the last report on top of the pile and sank back in his chair. It was late, he was tired, and, moreover, he was thoroughly pissed off.

But not just because it was Nathan's birthday. He stood up and walked over to the bookshelf that stood against the far side of the room. Reaching down, he plucked a leather-bound volume from the lowest shelf and read the opening words: 'It was the best of times, it was the worst of times.' How true. Dickens, *A Tale of Two Cities*.

But that was irrelevant. What was important was the single photograph that was secreted within the pages. He took the photo out and looked at it sadly. It showed Marco, slightly younger, slightly thinner, with his arm around a good-looking, dark-haired man. Lawrence, his ex-boyfriend. It was on nights like this – when everything was getting on top of him, when nothing seemed to work – that he remembered his old lover, remembered what it had been like.

Could we have done things differently? he silently asked the picture – the only picture of Lawrence that he had. Could we have made it last? But there was no reply – how could there have been? Lawrence was history, the dead past.

Marco just wished that he believed it.

With memory weighing heavily upon him, Marco replaced the picture, replaced the book, and went to bed.

Alone.

For a second, he wondered what Leigh was up to, but dismissed it. Tonight, Marco was happy to be on his own.

As he opened the door to his bedroom, he just wanted to go to sleep, to put the seventh of May behind him. It had been a day that he desperately wanted to forget, and not just because it was Nathan's birthday. Because it was Lawrence's as well.

With that thought in his head, Marco got undressed and climbed under the duvet.

Eddie unlocked the plain grey front door and stepped inside, switching on the light as he did so. They were standing in what appeared to be the reception area of Eddie's gym, but that was only a guess: Scott had never been there, and knew it only by reputation. But what a reputation!

'Drink?' Before Scott could reply, Eddie had opened a small fridge and extracted two beers. He threw one at Scott, who was amazed that he was able to catch it. He was more nervous than he could remember, and was surprised that he could hold the can without shaking.

'Thanks,' said Scott, opening the can and taking a swig.

'I spotted you looking at me earlier,' said Eddie. 'Actually, I've seen you looking at me on quite a few occasions. I gather you're a bit of a fan of mine.'

Scott felt himself blushing. 'Yes, I . . . I mean . . .' He just couldn't think of anything to say. In the end, he simply shrugged.

'So why didn't you say anything?' said Eddie. He walked over and threw his big, muscular arm around Scott's shoulders, pulling him towards him. 'I've seen you around quite a lot, Scott,' he said, hugging him. 'Actually, I was quite pissed off when I realised that Nate had nabbed you.'

Scott didn't know how to react. The man he had fantasised about was admitting that he had noticed Scott. He didn't even feel the familiar pain at the mention of Nathan's name: the pressure of Eddie's arm around his shoulder, of his big hand squeezing his biceps, ensured that everything else was forgotten. Scott's hard-on came back with a vengeance, and he could see Eddie casting a look towards the bulge in his jeans.

Eddie grinned. 'Anyway, I can see that you and me have wasted enough time. Let me show you around.'

Pulling Scott with him, he walked over to the door opposite and opened it, revealing the gym itself.

'Well, here it is,' said Eddie, pride in his voice.

He had every reason to be proud: Scott was impressed. Compared with his university gym, this was in a different league altogether. Everything looked new, rather than the tired old equipment that Scott normally had to make do with. Every type of exercise machine – each one top-of-the-range – was evenly spaced around the walls, which were completely mirrored. An exercise mat and a complete set of weights were at the far end, next to the water cooler.

'Fancy a bit of circuit training?' asked Eddie.

Without waiting for a reply, he threw Scott a singlet and a pair of shorts, which landed on the floor in front of him. 'I'll give you a hand warming up – once you've changed.'

Knowing that he had no choice – but not exactly bothered by it – Scott pulled off his T-shirt and undid his jeans, aware that Eddie was watching him closely. But Scott was watching Eddie as well: he couldn't stop looking as Eddie removed his own T-shirt and revealed his well-built chest and arms, the thick covering of hair, and the tattoos on his shoulders. Eddie pulled down his own jeans and boxer shorts in one easy motion, showing off impressively solid legs and a semi-hard cock which was even bigger than Scott had ever imagined, bigger than he had ever wanked over in his dreams.

Scott knew that Eddie was teasing him, but he didn't care. Two could play at that game. He unlaced his shoes and took off his jeans, standing there naked just longer than he needed to, showing Eddie what was on offer, before he picked up the shorts and singlet that Eddie had provided and put them on. Eddie simply stood there, watching, until Scott had dressed; then he put on his own shorts and singlet. For a moment, they stood there, dressed identically, with identical thoughts on their minds.

'Right – warm up first.' Eddie came over to Scott and stood behind him. 'I want to make sure that every muscle of yours is relaxed.' He laid his big hands on Scott's arms, and moved him into the correct position. 'Now, lean this way and stretch,' he ordered, and Scott obeyed. Obeyed because he wanted to, obeyed because this was just too good to be true.

For ten minutes, ten long minutes with his cock stiff inside his shorts, he did what Eddie told him to do. He stretched and leant over, obeying every instruction, each exercise making him even more excited. He could see that Eddie was just as aroused: that massive dick was visible beneath the thin grey fabric, and Scott would have done anything to rip off those shorts and bury his face in that cock, suck it and play with it and drink Eddie's come. But he knew he had to be patient; he knew he daren't do anything to break the spell, to ruin the moment.

Finally, the warm-up stopped. Eddie led Scott over to the

pressing bench at the far side of the gym and motioned for him to lie on it. Scott didn't hesitate.

Lying there, looking up at the big muscular frame of his favourite wet dream, Scott was almost overwhelmed. It doesn't get any better than this, he decided.

Eddie looked down at him and grinned, before pulling off his shorts and allowing his erection to bob stiffly below the shining chrome of the barbell that rested across the bench. Eddie's foreskin was drawn back, revealing the glistening helmet, only inches away from Scott's face. Then he lowered himself slightly, so that the big red helmet was resting on Scott's lips.

'Go on, suck it,' Eddie implored. 'I've wanted you to do this ever since I first saw you.' His voice was rough yet quiet. 'If you only knew the number of times I've lain in bed and wanked over you . . .'

The knowledge that the big man leaning over him was as much into Scott as Scott was into him burnt inside him as Scott reached out with his tongue and licked the warm helmet, tasting the sweat, smelling the scent of exercise and hard work. He ran his tongue around the ridge, then up, into the slit.

Eddie stepped back and moved so that he was next to Scott, before straddling the bench – and Scott. He ripped off Scott's T-shirt and pulled off the shorts, tantalising Scott by stroking his cock before sitting over him, his thick hairy thighs resting on Scott's own muscular, hairy chest. Moving forward, Eddie drove his dick into Scott's mouth, fucking it with the smooth rhythm that Scott had always fantasised about – although in the fantasies it had been Eddie's length driving into Scott's waiting arse.

As Scott fought not to choke on eight inches of thick hot dick driving down his throat, Eddie reached down to the floor and grabbed something. Scott realised that he was holding his own discarded shorts; seconds later, Eddie was rubbing them into Scott's face, forcing Scott to smell the sweat and man scent that Eddie had ground into them. The smell was overwhelming: this wasn't just the smell of their warm-up session. These shorts had been worn time and time again, and Scott could almost taste the fresh sweat mingling with older sweat, with the tang of come, lots of come, Eddie's come . . .

He had to force himself not to touch his cock, not to hasten the moment of inevitable release. Even though the sensation of Eddie's dick, pumping away at Scott's eager mouth, was better than Scott could ever have imagined, that wasn't what he wanted. He wanted to feel Eddie inside him, forcing his arse apart, hurting him.

Without warning, Eddie removed his cock from Scott's mouth, and swivelled round. All of his weight was on Scott's chest and stomach, and Scott found it difficult to breathe for a second, until Eddie had turned a hundred and eighty degrees.

With his knees supporting his weight on the bench, Eddie lowered his head and took Scott's cock in his mouth. Scott shuddered, both with the reality of the situation and the idea of it: lying on a pressing bench in Eddie's gym, the huge man himself licking and sucking at his dick. And Eddie knew how to do it: his mouth squeezed on Scott's shaft, while his tongue played with his helmet, toyed with it, licked it.

Scott strained his head forward so he could reach Eddie's dick; he was able to take about half of Eddie's length into his mouth. The shorts were next to him on the bench, having fallen off his face, but he could still smell them, and that smell was turning him on, turning him on as much as the man straddling him, sucking him, pleasuring him.

He wanted more of that smell, he wanted the taste of Eddie in his mouth. He pulled away from Eddie's dick, and moved his attention to his arse, his big solid arse, the cheeks covered with curly dark hair. Grabbing the cheeks with his hands, he opened Eddie's arse so he could get at the taste and smell of his ring, his tongue licking at the hairy crack, unable to get enough of the sweat and musk that awaited within. He assaulted Eddie's arse with fingers and tongue, opening it with his fingers, then plunging his tongue into the relaxed hole, driving it inside, tasting Eddie's ring, tasting Eddie himself. This appeared to drive Eddie wild: his bulk squirmed with pleasure above Scott, his mouth sucking more and more urgently on Scott's sensitive cock.

'I want to fuck you,' Eddie gasped. 'I've lain in bed at night and wanked over you, Scott,' he repeated, 'thought about what it would be like, what we could do together.'

'Oh yes,' said Scott, all his birthdays coming at once. Eddie, big, bulky Eddie, fucking him . . . He had to concentrate, to hold back, in case that image made him come there and then.

'Grab the bar,' Eddie hissed. Scott obeyed, grasping the metal of the resting barbell.

'Now, pull yourself up – pull your legs up,' he ordered, as he produced a condom from somewhere and put it on. 'Let me see your arse.'

Scott strained a little, but Eddie wasn't the only person who worked out. He hefted his legs into the air, offering his arse to Eddie like a sacrament. He wanted Eddie to take him, he wanted Eddie inside him. He was Eddie's, body and soul.

Eddie's arms reached over Scott, his hands landing on top of Scott's. Supporting himself, he guided his cock closer and closer to Scott's hole until it was finally touching. Scott shivered with anticipation, so very desperate to draw Eddie into him. Then, with a gentleness that Scott would never have guessed, he penetrated him. Inch by inch, he pushed his dick inside Scott. Scott was having a little trouble taking it all – Eddie was slightly thicker than Nathan – but he forced himself to relax, forced himself to take all of it. It was what he had always wanted: Eddie, big hairy muscular Eddie, on top of him, inside him.

Eddie finally drove the last part of his meat into Scott, and let it rest there, giving Scott a chance to get used to the feeling. Scott looked up at him, examining every inch of his dream lover. The thick solid arms, covered in hair and tattoos, the broad chest, the evil-looking face with its cropped hair and wicked eyes. It was heaven to him, especially when Eddie lowered his head and kissed Scott, full on the lips, his tongue violating his mouth as his dick was violating Scott's arse. Eddie's hands squeezed Scott's as he kissed him passionately, forcefully.

Scott was so involved, he hadn't felt Eddie withdraw, and was momentarily shocked to feel Eddie drive himself back inside, his heavy balls slamming into Scott's arse. Again and again, Eddie fucked him, fucked him but didn't stop kissing him, his tongue playing with Scott's tongue, his cock filling up Scott's arse.

Scott couldn't make a sound, but he wanted to groan, he wanted to scream with pleasure as Eddie rammed his arse again and again and again, faster and faster, each stroke bringing Scott closer and closer to orgasm. And each time Eddie was totally inside, Scott squeezed his arse around the invading cock, his rhythm matching Eddie's. It was like some great machine of flesh and sweat and cock, the parts interlocking with an almost mechanical perfection.

Even though they were kissing, Scott could tell that Eddie was close, his breathing rough and irregular. Scott wanted this to last for ever, but he knew it couldn't. This was a dream, this was fantasy, and the churning in his balls told him it would soon be over.

Just as he knew he was going to come, Eddie pulled his mouth away from Scott's and let out a bellow, a scream of release as his cock pumped come into Scott's arse. Scott could feel that meat shooting, could feel it pulsing inside him, and that was enough. Without even touching himself, a jet of come shot from his cock and landed on his chest, on his face, on the bench. Another, and another, as Scott experienced the deepest orgasm he could ever remember. It felt like something was being torn from him, part of him and part of Eddie, something special that they had created.

Scott didn't know how long it lasted. Seconds, minutes, hours . . . it didn't matter. He cherished the moment, knowing that it would be something he would always, always remember.

Sated, Eddie withdrew and sat next to Scott on the bench, his fingers playing with the hairs on Scott's chest.

'Thanks,' he said quietly. 'It was better than I could have imagined.'

Scott smiled, but reality was beginning to reassert itself, break-ing through like a tidal wave. 'It was great,' he replied. But in his heart he knew something else, with just as much certainty. It was Nathan's birthday. And he would have given anything for it to have been Nathan sitting next to him.

Nathan shut the door behind Carl, and watched him through the window blinds as he sauntered down the street.

'Nice present,' he muttered to himself as he went into the kitchen and poured himself a large tumbler of Laphroaig, dropping a single ice cube into it to crack open the flavour. Carl had given him his number – perhaps they could meet again. Then he sighed: who was he kidding? Carl had been a one-night stand, nothing more, nothing less. He was still on his own. He glanced at the picture standing on the table next to the living-room door: he and Scott, arms around each other. Better times. He would have given anything for it to have been Scott.

But it hadn't been. It had been a one-night stand.

But Carl hadn't been just any old one-night stand. He had been a gift – a birthday present. Nathan reached over to his discarded jeans and pulled out the mysterious letter. In the gloom of the Crossed Swords, he hadn't really been able to examine it.

The paper quality was excellent: good, creamy stock. He held it up to the light: there was an obscure watermark that looked like a coat of arms, but not one that Nathan recognised. The handwriting was elegant, bold, and formed of confident strokes with a fountain pen. The address was embossed into the paper . . .

Nathan shook his head and tossed the letter aside. Nothing. Not a clue as to the identity of his mysterious benefactor. He might as well read some tea leaves or consult the entrails of a sheep . . .

Of course! Sion's present!

The pyramid and cards were where Nathan had left them on the floor, dropped and forgotten in the excitement of Carl. Nathan had no intention of using them to find out who had written the letter – even he had to admit the stupidity of that idea – but what harm could it do to look into the future? It wasn't as if he had much to look forward to, was it?

47

He swigged back the single-malt whisky, and poured himself another. Then he grabbed the two parcels and took them to the table, before carefully unwrapping the black silk that enshrouded the cards. If he remembered correctly, the black silk was important: it protected the cards from outside forces, whatever that meant. And it wasn't enough to buy your own Tarot pack: the cards had to be given as a present. Perhaps it was all superstition, but what did he have to lose? He picked up the pack and started to shuffle it. *This is daft*, said his inner voice. But what did he have to lose?

As Nathan shuffled the deck, he remembered what Sion had said: 'You might want to give it a go this evening. It is your birthday – that should be significant.'

A glance at the clock confirmed what Nathan had suspected – at half-one, it was well past his birthday. But Nathan wasn't without a few superstitions of his own. His birthday celebrations always started at midnight and carried on until he went to bed – whenever that was. So, in the world according to Nathan Dexter, it was still his birthday, and any special forces that might just be floating around his house in Docklands should still be around. He grinned: the only spirit he knew was in the glass of Laphroaig in front of him.

Without looking at the results, Nathan placed the shuffled deck on the black silk, and then set the crystal pyramid on top of it. Then he concentrated. What did he want from his future? Did he want his final revenge on Delancey? Did he want Scott?

The answer was simple.

Nathan Dexter wanted his life back.

As he left the living room, he cast one last look back at the pyramid, laughed at the ridiculousness of it all, and switched off the light.

Scott stood on Earl's Court Road, trying to hail a taxi and trying to make sense of the evening. Sex with Eddie had been better than he could have imagined, the culmination of years of fantasy made real. And Eddie's parting words – 'See you again?' – made it clear that he was definitely game for a rematch. But however good the sex had been, however gorgeous Eddie had been . . .

He wasn't Nathan.

And that was all that Scott could think about.

Nathan never used an alarm clock: years of habit meant that he always woke at 7.30 a.m., whatever the time of year, whatever he had been up to the night before. And this morning was no exception. Rubbing his eyes, he tried to ignore the slight hangover that throbbed in his head and wrapped himself in his blue towelling dressing gown.

As he made his way downstairs, he thought about what he had to do today, and the familiar weight of his worries began to descend. His birthday over, it was back to the grind that was now his daily existence: trying to find a job, trying to get some sort of structure into his life. But first things first: a cup of coffee and a couple of paracetamols to kick-start himself into action.

As he reached the kitchen, a stray thought made him stop. He turned round and looked at the table, seeing the crystal pyramid as if for the first time. Last night it had seemed a good idea, but now, with reality sinking in, Nathan was actually rather embarrassed. Tarot cards? Really! Still, it wouldn't do any harm to have a look, would it?

He sat at the table and lifted the pyramid off the black silk. The Tarot deck sat there, waiting for him to take the first card, but Nathan suddenly felt a shiver of nervousness – fear, even. Did he really want to know that things were going to get even worse?

Brave and fearless Nathan Dexter, frightened of a bit of mumbo jumbo, a little voice chastised. *You'll be jumping at shadows next.*

He reached out and took the top card from the pack and turned it over. And frowned. He hadn't been sure what to expect: he wasn't that familiar with the Tarot and how to read it, but even he knew the significance of the card he was currently holding.

The picture was of a regal figure atop a white steed, a sword held high. The King of Swords.

The answer was suddenly, terrifyingly, clear. In the Tarot, the King of Swords had a specific meaning. It represented the antithesis of all the enquirer represented. His archenemy, the person who would destroy his life.

And in Nathan Dexter's life that could be only one person. The person who had cost him his career, his relationship, his friends . . . his life.

Adrian Delancey.

Nathan let the card flutter to the table and faced the final truth, the one that he had been ignoring, hiding from since his fall from grace at Delancey's hand.

The only way that Nathan was going to re-establish himself, the only way that he would repair the damage, the hurt, the pain that had been done to him, would be to face his final fear. He stood up and retrieved the letter and once again read the words: 'You and I have a mutual enemy, Nathan.'

Who else could the mysterious friend be referring to?

All of Nathan's other plans went out of the window. It was time to stop being afraid of shadows, it was time to stop allowing others to dictate his destiny. He was going to see this 'friend', was going to uncover the truth.

And then Nathan Dexter was going to start fighting back.

Three

_____

Marco had been awake for a couple of hours when Leigh finally surfaced, his bleary eyes and unsteady walk proof of the good night he had undoubtedly had. Wherever that had been. Marco had no idea what time Leigh had got home – diplomatically, Leigh had slept in the spare room last night.

'It lives, then,' said Marco. The words were light, but there was a thread of coldness running through them that Marco just couldn't help. For the last hour, he had been trying to make sense of the stack of reports from Elective HQs across the world; the last thing he wanted to do now was have another argument. But, given the nature of his relationship with Leigh at the moment, that seemed virtually inevitable.

'If you can call it that,' said Leigh quietly. 'Scott and I went to the Collective – it was a charity night.'

'Looks like you're the one in need of charity,' said Marco. He looked at his boyfriend, hung over, looking like death, and his anger vanished. Leigh could be irritating and unreliable, but Marco still loved him. 'Sit down – I'll make you a coffee.'

Two minutes later, they were sitting together on the sofa, two steaming mugs on the table in front of them. 'So, how's Scott?'

Leigh shrugged. 'Exactly as you'd expect. Nathan should stop having birthdays and start having days of official mourning. The way everyone was moping about yesterday, I half expected people to start laying flowers outside Nathan's front door.' He picked up his mug and sipped the strong coffee.

Marco laughed, but it was hollow. He had other things on his mind. He had made Leigh a promise, and he intended to keep to it. 'I'm going to see him this afternoon,' he said flatly. It wasn't something that he was looking forward to, but he knew that it had to be done.

Leigh immediately brightened. 'You are? That's great!'

'Don't expect too much, Leigh. Nate's got a lot of explaining to do. But it might be a start.' Or an end. What if Marco learnt the truth and it wasn't to his liking? What if Nathan Dexter really was a bastard, prepared to hurt his closest friends in return for a quick buck? Marco had the evidence to prove that a substantial sum of money had been transferred into Nathan's current account after the Gran Canaria fiasco.

But he also had proof that the money had been immediately transferred out of Nathan's account and into another, which almost certainly belonged to Delancey's complex web of Syndicate businesses. Why would Nathan do that? None of it made sense. Hopefully, by finally bringing himself to talk to Nathan, Marco might be able to understand.

'Er . . . there's something I need to tell you as well,' said Leigh, breaking Marco's chain of thought.

A brief chill ran through Marco. What had happened last night at the Collective? Marco and Leigh were both adult enough to overlook and forgive the odd sexual infidelity, but that didn't mean that Marco had to like it, did it?

'OK: what was his name?'

Leigh laughed, and gave Marco a playful punch. 'Nothing like that. Well, not me, anyway. It's just that . . . well, Scott and I are going away for a couple of days. To Brighton.'

'Are you now?' Marco didn't know what to make of that particular news item. 'When? Come to that, why?'

Leigh put his mug down on the coffee table and grabbed

Marco's big paws. 'This afternoon. Marco. We've been living in one another's pockets for too long. I need some time on my own – I need to have some fun.'

That hurt. A lot. But, then again, the truth often did. 'So, I'm not fun any more?' Even Marco had to admit that he hadn't exactly been the life and soul of the party recently, and he had no one to blame for that but himself.

'It's not that. I just want to let my hair down.' He rubbed his short crop. 'If I had any, that is.'

Marco sighed. As much as it pained him to admit it, Leigh was right. He thought of the promises he had made to Leigh when they had been in Las Vegas: '*Nathan and I think that we'll have completed the audit for the Director in about two months' time. Once we've done it, I'll resign. OK?*'

And here they were, three months later – and, if anything, Marco was even more involved than ever. For a moment, he considered restating the promise, but knew that there was no way that he could keep it at the moment. He had to help save the Elective – he owed that to Lawrence. The organisation that had crippled his ex-lover had been bought to book; now Marco had to ensure that it continued to live up to its original ideals.

'How long were you thinking of staying?' Even though Marco wasn't entirely keen on the idea – he could just imagine what Leigh and Scott would be getting up to in one of Britain's gay capitals – it did give him a chance to concentrate on what he was going to say to Nathan.

'A couple of nights. I was wondering . . .' Leigh put on his little lost puppy look.

'You were wondering whether I'd help you out.' Marco laughed.

'Not you – the Elective. I could say I was going on Elective business.'

Marco laughed at his boyfriend's audacity. 'The Elective isn't a travel agency.' But what would a couple of hundred pounds matter to an organisation that was currently losing about a hundred thousand a day?

'OK, use your Amex card.' As Adjutants of the Elective – a position that had given them freedom to investigate the Elective's many operations – both Leigh and Scott had been given American Express cards with unlimited credit. Scott's had been cancelled – Marco had really had no choice – but Leigh still had his. 'But don't break the bank,' he ordered, leaning over and giving Leigh a peck on the lips. As he pulled away, he gave Leigh a wry smile. 'The Elective's not exactly rolling in it at the moment.'

Standing up, Leigh grinned, a fraction of his former self resurfacing. 'I'll try not to. Anyway, I'd better get ready. I'm meeting Scott at twelve.' With that, he finished his coffee and went upstairs.

Marco looked at his watch. It was coming up to 10 a.m. Knowing Nathan, he would have found some way to celebrate his birthday, and Marco was loathe to open negotiations with a hung-over Nathan Dexter. 'I'll give him another hour,' Marco muttered, before getting up and going to his desk to continue the endless paperwork: it seemed that, for every pound the Elective lost, it generated at least two official reports. Sighing, he picked up the next one from the pile and started reading.

By eleven o'clock, Nathan had managed to get rid of his hangover and was preparing to leave. Time was when he would have phoned for a cab, but, with his current financial situation, that just wasn't sensible. For a second, he regretted having handed back the 'gift' that Adrian Delancey had given him: to implicate Nathan even further in his plans, Delancey had deposited £50,000 in Nathan's account. Even though Nathan had immediately transferred the money back into the account from which it had come, he was sure that the damage had been done. The Elective would undoubtedly have seen it and come to the obvious conclusion.

But Nathan knew that he could never have accepted it. It just wasn't in Nathan's nature – he couldn't have spent it, knowing that it carried Delancey's taint. But that didn't stop him from wishing that his bank account were just a little healthier.

As he locked the front door behind him, he was suddenly aware that something felt different. Walking off towards the tube station, he looked around with a sense of . . . well, almost wonder. It was as if he were seeing everything for the first time. Canary Wharf Tower; the cranes surrounding the Millennium Dome, the Thames . . . Things he saw every day of the week all seemed clearer and new.

Because he was actually doing something. For the last three months, it had been like the Red Queen's race in *Alice Through the Looking Glass*: he had been running faster and faster just to stay in the same place. Every move he made, every attempt to pull himself out of the downward spiral, had met with the machinations of either the Elective or Delancey's Syndicate. This time, with the arrival of the mysterious letter, there was a chance that he could break that spiral, enlist the help of somebody who would understand. Someone who had the power to back Nathan up.

He wished he could have confided in Marco, but there was no way that he could approach his former friend. The evidence against Nathan was damning: he had given Delancey the means to destroy the Elective. That he had been misled was simply Nathan's word against what appeared to be hard facts on paper.

As he turned the corner on to the main road, he sighed. He doubted that Marco would ever want to speak to him again.

He was too far away to hear his phone ringing.

Marco slammed the receiver down in frustration. After all the build-up, after hours of plucking up the courage, the bastard wasn't even at home. For a second, he considered just leaving it. He'd explain to Leigh that Nathan wasn't around . . . Who was he kidding? Leigh wouldn't let it rest until Marco and Nathan met. He quickly tried Nathan's mobile, but that was going straight through to voice mail: obviously Nathan Dexter didn't want to be found.

There was only one thing for it. If the mountain wouldn't come to Mahomet . . .

Leigh suddenly appeared in the doorway, holding his rucksack. 'Well?' he asked, eyeing the phone quizzically.

'He wasn't in.'

'That's hardly an excuse,' Leigh countered.

'I know. Which is why I'm going in person. I'll wait outside his front door all day if I have to. Happy?'

Leigh grinned. 'I suppose so. Anyway, I'd better get going. Don't want to keep Scott waiting. This is for his benefit.'

'Really?' said Marco laughingly. 'I suppose the thought of spending a couple of nights in Brighton is totally repellent to you, then?'

'It's a bit of a hardship, but I'm sure I'll cope.' Dropping the rucksack on the floor, he went over to Marco and gave him a hug.

Marco enfolded Leigh in his arms and squeezed him tightly. 'Look after yourself. And look after Scott – he needs it.'

'I will. And Marco . . .' Leigh looked up at him 'Thanks for this. All of it.' Then the doorbell rang. 'That'll be the taxi.' Leigh pulled himself away from Marco's hug and retrieved his rucksack. 'I'll give you a ring when I get the chance,' he said cheerfully, before letting himself out of the flat.

'*If* you get the chance,' Marco muttered. Knowing Scott and Leigh, he had two hopes: Bob Hope and no hope. Smiling to himself, he began to prepare himself for a confrontation he was dreading.

It took Nathan nearly an hour to reach the address in Russell Square: the newly reopened East London line took an age to reach Whitechapel, and waiting for the District Line was even worse. Nathan was feeling distinctly irritable as he pushed past the dithering tourists in the ticket office and came out into the May sunshine, blinking in the daylight.

Quite apart from the lingering effects of his hangover, this whole 'mystery' thing was getting to him. Nathan had been a journalist for the better part of a decade, and was used to anonymous tip-offs and informants. But this was something different. There were two types of informer: those that did it for the money, and those that did it for revenge. Given the address, the former seemed unlikely. So, if it was the latter, why? What had Adrian Delancey done to earn the enmity of this 'friend'?

Assuming that it wasn't a trap. Sending an escort for his birthday wasn't the sort of thing that you did unless you were rolling in money, and Nathan knew of only two organisations like that: the Elective and the Syndicate. Was his 'friend' nothing more than a lure?

Pulling out the letter for the umpteenth time, he checked the address once more. He couldn't give up now. After a quick glance at the Square itself – Nathan had more than a couple of very happy memories of Russell Square after dark – he got his bearings and headed towards the address.

It took him a couple of minutes to be certain that he'd found the right place. The problem with the houses of the rich and famous was that their owners were often so full of their self-importance that they saw house numbers as an unnecessary evil, and this address was no different. Nathan had to calculate his destination from the numbers of the houses on either side.

Standing outside, he was impressed. Most of the neighbouring houses were no longer residential: he had lost count of the number of accountants, solicitors and doctors who had set up shop around the Square. But this was definitely a residential address: there was no brass plaque, just a solid blue door with a big brass knocker in the centre. Oh well, he wasn't going to get any answers standing outside like a lemon, was he?

Mounting the three terracotta steps, he grasped the knocker and gave it three decent raps. Thirty seconds later, the door was opened by a short, slightly tubby man dressed in a formal morning suit. He was in his early forties.

'Can I help you?' he said with a faint but untraceable accent. Nathan knew immediately that the man standing in front of him wasn't the master of the house: his almost period costume and stiff bearing made Nathan think of Hudson from *Upstairs Downstairs*. So, Nathan's 'friend' had a butler. Nathan instantly corrected himself: it was quite possible that the butler himself was the 'friend'. One of Nathan's earliest investigations had come about when the cleaning lady had finally had enough of her employer's ill-treatment of her, and had come to Nathan with evidence that had put five people in prison for crimes ranging from drug-dealing to prostitution. Perhaps the butler did it, thought Nathan with a smile.

But, if that were the case, the letter would have indicated that; otherwise, Nathan would have put the butler at risk by just turning up on the doorstep. No, Nathan had to assume that the 'friend' was the master of the house.

'Hello – my name's Nathan Dexter.'

'Ah yes, sir. The master is expecting you,' he said, almost disdainfully. 'Do come in.' The butler held the door open and gestured for Nathan to enter.

The hallway simply dripped money. Nathan wasn't the world's greatest art critic, but he could recognise a work of art when he saw it. The paintings that lined the long hallway were either genuine or incredible reproductions. A number of long low tables stood against the walls, their tops crowded with vases and statuettes. Nathan guessed that he could have bought his house in Docklands outright for the cost of just one of those tables.

As he followed the butler down the hallway, he was desperately looking for signs towards the identity of his 'friend', but there was nothing to indicate anything about him. There were no photographs, no portraits, nothing. Nathan knew only one thing: his 'friend' was loaded.

Finally, after passing enough antiques to buy a small Third World country, they reached a staircase. Nathan followed the butler up three flights, until they reached a small landing. The butler opened the door opposite and stood in the doorway, annoyingly blocking any chance Nathan had to see inside. But it didn't really matter: in a few moments, all would hopefully be revealed.

'Mr Dexter is here to see you, sir,' the butler intoned.

'Thank you, Hadleigh. That will be all.' The voice was deep

58

and resonant, but not as upper-class as Nathan would have expected, given the trappings of the house. Then the butler – Hadleigh – stood aside and ushered Nathan into the room.

It was not what he'd expected. Instead of a continuation of *The Antiques Roadshow*, this room was the exact opposite. The walls and ceiling were white, with a deep cream carpet on the floor. One wall was taken up with an entertainment centre that must have cost tens of thousands of pounds: you didn't just go out and buy a Bang and Olufsen setup like that on a whim. The widescreen television next to it was bigger than anything Nathan had ever seen before, and speakers were strategically placed around the room: Nathan guessed that it was probably acoustically perfect. Definitely loaded.

'Welcome to my playroom, Nathan. I can call you Nathan?'

Nathan had been so overawed by God's own hi-fi that he had momentarily forgotten the reason for being there. He turned to catch his first look at his mysterious new 'friend'. He was sitting at a chrome and glass desk, which was occupied by a very serious-looking PC. He was dressed in a plain white T-shirt and jeans, the T-shirt showing off a broad solid body. He had a pleasant, attractive face: a square jaw covered in a day's growth of thick stubble, and a short flat-top. Nathan guessed that he was in his mid-thirties. But the oddest thing of all was, he looked familiar. Had Nathan met him before? He couldn't think where. Not only that, but there was something . . . different about him.

'You have me at a disadvantage,' said Nathan. Wasn't that the understatement of the year?

'I know,' came the reply, and Nathan felt a chill run up his spine. That was exactly the dialogue that had been spoken the first time he had met Adrian Delancey. For one second, he wondered once again whether the whole thing was a trap. But if it was, it was too late for regrets.

'I'm sorry,' said the man warmly, registering Nathan's discomfort. 'Didn't mean to sound so melodramatic. My name's Lawrence, Lawrence Dashwood. You might have heard of me, Nathan.'

For a moment, Nathan's mind went blank. Then it all came together in a leap of deduction that impressed even Nathan.

Of course he recognised him. He had seen a photograph of him. And that was why he seemed different. In that picture – the only one Marco had, and taken over five years ago – he had been standing up. But today he wasn't sitting on an ordinary chair. He was sitting in a wheelchair, the wheelchair to which he had been consigned by Adrian Delancey's hired thugs.

Lawrence Dashwood was Marco Cappiello's ex-boyfriend, and the reason for Marco's involvement with the Elective.

What the hell did he want with Nathan?

As the taxi pulled up outside Scott's halls of residence, Leigh could already see his friend waiting for him, a holdall on the pavement in front of him. Leigh instructed the driver to stop, opened the door and allowed Scott to get in.

'How are you feeling this morning?' said Leigh.

Scott gave a wry grin. 'I've felt better. I had the hangover from hell this morning.'

'Me too.' He leant forward. 'Victoria Station, please,' he said, before settling back into the plush leather seat. It was a taxi in the way that Concorde was a plane. Marco had arranged for one of the Elective's private fleet of limos to take Scott and Leigh to Victoria. Leigh had considered asking whether it could take them all the way to Brighton, but decided that was pushing it just a little bit. He didn't want to abuse Marco's hospitality any more than was necessary.

'How was it, then? Eddie?'

The smile on Scott's face was all the answer that Leigh needed.

'So, how was Marco?' asked Scott.

'Not exactly happy. Then again, he's got a lot on his mind.'

'The Elective, presumably.' Scott's grin faded as he spat the words out, and it was obvious that he blamed the organisation for his current problems. Despite being more than happy to accept their hospitality of a holiday in Brighton, thought Leigh.

'That, and . . .' Should he tell him? Should he tell Scott that

Marco was off to see Nathan? As far as Leigh knew, Scott hadn't seen Nathan since the afternoon he had walked out on him in February. But keeping quiet, especially on a matter this sensitive, would only lead to troubles further down the line, he decided.

'He's seeing Nathan today,' said Leigh quietly.

'What?' Scott went pale. 'He's not going to hurt him, is he?'

'Don't be stupid. Marco's not like that: straightforward revenge isn't his style. Look, this whole Elective business is his way of avenging his ex-boyfriend, Lawrence. Roughing somebody up just isn't him, Scott. No, Marco just wants to talk to him, to find out what really happened.'

Scott sighed. 'I hope they can sort something out.'

'If they do . . . well, what will you do?'

'What do you mean?' But Scott knew exactly what Leigh meant – and, given Leigh's expression, was forced to admit it. 'Would I go back out with him? Of course. Like a shot. It's just that . . . well, he's not exactly popular at the moment, is he?'

Leigh glanced out of the window as they sped down the Embankment towards Victoria and considered what Scott had said. Unpopular: that was the understatement of the century. Nathan Dexter had been blacklisted across the city: pubs, clubs, even employment denied him. All at the demands of the Elective, the Elective that Marco was desperately trying to save. A sudden wave of anger swelled in Leigh.

'You selfish bastard!' he snapped. 'I know Nathan. Sometimes I think I know him better than you do. Last night, while you were drowning your sorrows in the pub, while you were getting your arse fucked by Eddie, what do you think Nathan was doing, eh? It was his fucking birthday, for Christ's sake!'

Scott deflated, his expression contrite. 'I'm scared, Leigh. Scared of what's going to happen to Nathan, and scared what would happen to me if I went out with him again. I'm scared of what he's going to say to me if I saw him again.'

All his anger drained, Leigh put his hand on Scott's knee. 'I know, I know.' They sat there in silence as the car approached Victoria, swinging past the Monarch of the Glen, Victoria's newest gay pub. Steve, the former landlord of the Brave Trader, was now in residence there, and Leigh knew how much Nathan had been looking forward to the opening night. Of course, he hadn't been able to go. Another loss. How much more could Nathan take?

The problem with Nathan was, he didn't know when to give up. Leigh had a horrible feeling that, before too long, Nathan would decide to fight back. And, when that happened, all hell was going to break loose. He couldn't shake that thought as the car drew up outside the station.

As they watched the car drive away, Leigh momentarily wondered whether going away really was such a good idea. What if things did get out of hand between Nathan and Marco? Shouldn't Leigh be on hand to help?

No. This was something that Marco and Nathan had to do alone. If there was one thing that Leigh knew about Nathan, it was that, when the chips were down, he could be guaranteed to perform a miracle.

With that, they made their way towards the train.

Brighton was waiting.

'I've heard a lot about you,' said Nathan, as he sat down in the chair opposite Lawrence. Suddenly, a lot of things were beginning to make sense.

'All good, I hope,' said Lawrence with a warm, easy smile. Nathan had to admit that he was extremely good-looking; he could see why Marco had been so much in love with him. 'Anyway, I'm being rude.' He made a couple of movements with his mouse, and the door opened almost immediately. Hadleigh was standing there with a tray bearing two glasses and a bottle of red wine. The hi-tech equivalent of the bell rope, Nathan supposed.

'Just set it down on the table, Hadleigh,' said Lawrence. As his butler laid down the tray on the low table between Nathan and Lawrence, Lawrence continued: 'Similarly, I've heard a lot about you. And not all good, I'm afraid to say.' He picked up the bottle and examined the label. 'A '64 Pétrus. I hope you like it,' he added as he poured two generous glasses.

Nathan fought hard not to be impressed, but failed miserably. That one bottle alone was worth thousands! Marco had said a few things about Lawrence, but had failed to mention the fact that he was a multimillionaire. It wasn't the sort of thing you usually left out of conversations, was it?

'I'll admit that I don't have the best reputation at the moment.' Nathan took his glass and stared into its ruby depths.

'You could say that.' Lawrence raised his glass. 'Which is why you're here, Nathan. It's time to repair all of that. Anyway, a toast: to the future.'

As the glasses clinked together with the tinkling that comes only from the finest lead crystal, Nathan had to admit that he was still at a complete loss as to why he was there. 'What future? The Elective's made sure I'm unemployable, unshaggable, and unable to get a drink anywhere in town.'

Lawrence raised an eyebrow. 'Unshaggable? Hardly, Nathan. Carl was most impressed by your . . . actions last night. But I see your point.' He sipped the wine and smiled. 'The '64 is my favourite. Other people might rave about the '61, but I find it a little too . . . tart for my tastes.' Coming from another, that would have sounded pretentious, but from Lawrence it was a simple statement of fact. Here was a man who was comfortable with the finer – the finest – things in life.

Which was all well and good, but it didn't explain why Nathan was sitting there with Marco's ex, drinking a glass of wine that cost a small fortune. 'Lawrence, why am I here?'

Lawrence's tone was calm as he replied. 'It's simple. I want Delancey brought down. And you're the best man to do it.'

Nathan wasn't surprised that Delancey was involved. Indeed, he would have been surprised if he hadn't been. 'Me? Why?'

Lawrence turned in his wheelchair. 'Because you hate him, Nathan. He has systematically taken everything that really matters away from you, piece by piece. Your reputation, your friendships, Scott. He set you up so that the Elective would believe that you had betrayed them. He's driven a wedge between you and everything that you ever held dear. Admit it, Nathan: wouldn't you like to destroy him?'

The idea was tempting. But impossible. 'How can I? Not only is the Syndicate after me, but the Elective is, too. I can't move in London without either organisation finding out where I am. Their people are everywhere.'

'Not quite everywhere, Nathan.' Lawrence wheeled himself over to a huge bay window which overlooked Russell Square. He beckoned Nathan over.

'My room has one hell of a view.'

And it was impressive. The whole of Russell Square was laid out beneath them. Nathan imagined that, at night, things could be quite . . . interesting.

'Not just the Square, although that does provide the occasional distraction. From here –' Lawrence indicated the entertainment centre '– my eyes and ears watch and listen across the whole of the city. At any given time, I know exactly where everyone concerned with either the Elective or the Syndicate is. Every person, every club, every safe house . . . All monitored and recorded.'

Nathan was astounded. 'But that sort of surveillance would cost –'

Lawrence smiled. 'Millions. One hundred and seventy million pounds, to be precise.' He threw his arms open. 'And, at this moment, neither the Elective nor the Syndicate has the faintest idea that you are here. Part of my investment makes my presence here undetectable. In fact, it makes me undetectable, full stop. Neither organisation even realises that I exist. Or realises that it isn't a two-horse race at all. It never has been.'

Nathan's mind was working overtime. 'You're saying . . .' It couldn't be. After all this time, all of his investigations, had he totally failed to notice another shadowy organisation? 'Another Elective?'

'Not quite. I represent the original, you might say.'

Of course. 'You were there first!'

'Clever boy,' said Lawrence, clapping his hands. 'I'm the head of something far, far bigger and far, far older than anything the Syndicate or the Elective can even begin to comprehend. Indeed, bigger and older than anything they *could* comprehend. Have you ever heard of the Hellfire Club?'

Nathan narrowed his eyes, trying to place the reference. Then he remembered – he had happened across the name when he was researching secret organisations as part of his investigation into the Elective. 'It's the name given to a number of organisations in the eighteenth century, devoted to political intrigue, debauchery and pleasures of the flesh.' He paused. 'But what has that got to do with anything?'

'Do you know what happened to these Hellfire Clubs, Nathan?' said Lawrence mysteriously. It was obvious that he was enjoying this game of Twenty Questions.

Nathan shook his head. Lawrence was playing a game with him, but it was in Nathan's best interests to take part. 'I assumed that they just faded away as people lost interest. But that was hundreds of years ago. I'm not sure I understand.'

'Lost interest? Lost interest? How can anyone ever lose interest in political intrigue or pleasures of the flesh? Have you?'

Nathan could see his point. Then it hit him. It couldn't be . . . could it?

'Forgive me if I'm wrong, Lawrence, but wasn't the founder of the most famous Hellfire Club called Sir Francis Dashwood?'

Lawrence positively beamed. 'Well done. My great, great, great . . . something or other uncle, as a matter of fact. And I'm a chip off the old block, so to speak. Figuring it all out now, are we, Nathan?'

Nathan shook his head. 'That isn't possible. You're saying that the Hellfire Club's been around for two hundred years, and no one's noticed?'

Lawrence took a sip of his Pétrus. 'That's exactly what I'm saying. When mad old Frankie died, control of the Hellfire Club fell to his nephew, Alistair. Alistair realised that the Hellfire Club could be a force for good for people of his . . . persuasion, but he also knew that the only way for it to be truly successful would be for it to fall out of sight. He spent a considerable part of the family fortune hiding the Club. Within a couple of years, everyone assumed that the Club had simply faded away, as you put it.

'But nothing could be further from the truth. The Hellfire Club has influence across the globe, Nathan. Governments, the money markets, everything.'

Nathan was confused. 'But that's exactly what the Elective claims. How can you both exist? Come to that, if you're operating in the same spheres of influence . . . how come the Elective doesn't know about you?'

Lawrence laughed. 'Nathan, you still don't follow, do you? The Hellfire Club *owns* the Elective. It's ours – bought and paid for.'

Marco looked at his watch and sighed. Where the hell was Nathan? He'd been to his house, but no one had been there. For a while, he had hung around, waiting, but the curtain twitchers were out in force, and the last thing Marco wanted was for the police to be called: he could do without the inconvenience.

So, what next? He had to see Nathan – he'd promised Leigh. He knew that Nathan wasn't working: the Elective had seen to that. Their revenge had been swift and terrible, and, once Marco had realised what they were doing, he had tried to rein them back in. But the Elective blamed Nathan for their downfall, and there was a price to be paid. A price they intended Nathan to pay for in his dearest blood. Once they had started, they weren't going to stop.

Perhaps Nathan was having a drink somewhere. It was too early for the Crossed Swords, but there were precious few other gay places left that would welcome him. Then Marco remembered something: although Nathan rarely drank in straight pubs, there was one place that he used to frequent, not far from the British Museum. Something to do with real ale and cask-conditioning, apparently. Perhaps that was where he was hiding.

Oh well – even if he wasn't there, Marco fancied a drink. He just hoped that they served a decent pint of lager.

The train was about ten minutes late leaving Victoria. Scott and Leigh were sitting in one of the standard–class carriages, watching London speed past them.

'I remember the last time I was on a train,' said Scott. 'It was when Mike Bury and I went up to Manchester.'

And what a trip that had been! They had gone to find Andy Burroughs, the man who had designed the security system for the Elective's communications network. Although Scott had been successful, Delancey had got there first: Andy had been kidnapped and Scott had been framed for drug possession and thrown into the cells for the night. Then again, that hadn't been too bad. The big hairy straight bloke he'd shared the cell with had been more than happy to forget his principles for one night and keep Scott entertained. But Andy Burroughs hadn't been seen since.

'Have you seen anything of Mike recently?' asked Leigh.

Scott shook his head. 'No, but I'm not sure that I want to. The last I heard, he was keeping Nathan company. We wouldn't exactly have a lot to say to one another, would we?' Fair enough, so Scott had left Nathan, but that wasn't any reason for him not to feel jealous, was it?

'Scott . . .' The tone of Leigh's voice made it clear that Scott wasn't going to like this at all. 'When we get back from Brighton, why don't you at least talk to Nathan? Try to sort things out?'

After his earlier outburst, a lot of Scott's anger had gone. It was only because he knew that Leigh was right that he had reacted that way. 'I suppose I could ring him. What harm could it do?' He smiled at Leigh. 'Nathan means a lot to you, doesn't he?'

Leigh shrugged. 'He saved my life, remember.'

The train hurried past the suburbs towards Brighton

'Let me get this straight: you own the Elective?'

Lawrence drained his glass. 'Perhaps the '66, next. Or do you fancy a drop of Dom Perignon? Sorry – I'm going off at a tangent. Of course the Hellfire Club owns the Elective. Do you really think that that bunch of millionaires could have set up the Elective without the Club being aware of them? After that, it was simplicity itself to take control, while still allowing them to believe that they were the biggest fishes in the pond.'

'And they have no idea that the Hellfire Club exists?'

'None. And, in an ideal world, we would have wanted it to remain that way. Then Delancey appeared.'

'That's what I don't understand. According to Marco, you refused to let Delancey take over your club in Bermondsey, and the Elective broke both of your legs. The whole reason that Marco is involved with the Elective is to somehow make amends for that.' Was Nathan missing something here?

Lawrence sighed. 'Yes, it does all sound rather paradoxical, doesn't it? Unfortunately, that's because Marco doesn't know the entire truth. You see, I had to mislead him somewhat.'

'I would have thought he would have noticed that you were a millionaire, at the very least.' These sorts of trappings weren't that easy to hide, were they?

'A millionaire?' Lawrence laughed, a deep laugh of true amusement. 'My dear Nathan, I'm not a millionaire. I'm a *billionaire*,' he announced. 'But Marco wouldn't have mentioned that, because I wasn't when I knew him. OK, I was loaded, but it was nothing like this. Traditionally, the Black King of the Hellfire Club takes office upon the death of the predecessor: usually his father. Until then, we firstborn are kept in the dark about the Hellfire Club. When I was going out with Marco, he knew that my family had money, but even I didn't know that there were a few billion pounds stashed away. When Delancey made his move, I had no idea about the Hellfire Club.'

'But surely your father would have realised? Surely he would have taken steps to stop Delancey?'

Lawrence closed his eyes, and an expression of pain briefly crossed his face. 'My father and I weren't particularly close. But, even so, if he *could* have done something, he would have done,

I'm sure. But, by the rules of the Hellfire Club, his hands were tied.'

Nathan frowned. 'But if the Hellfire Club owns the Elective –'

'Nathan, Nathan, Nathan – that's the whole point. That's the reason why I asked you here in the first place.

'The hand of the Hellfire Club cannot be detected. To do so would jeopardise everything we've worked for. Don't you think I wanted revenge against that bastard Delancey? From the moment I learnt of my birthright, I tried to find ways to pay him back.' He indicated the wheelchair, his useless legs. 'You see, Delancey's thugs didn't just break my legs: they caused severe nerve damage. I'm been undergoing the best therapy that money can buy – and by God, with my fortune, that's the best – but there's a good chance I might never walk properly again. I'm the Black King of the Hellfire Club, and I want to see Delancey burn in hell for what he did to me. But I can't. It was made quite clear to me by the Club's Inner Circle that I couldn't do a thing.

'Until now.'

'The Syndicate!'

'Exactly. By moving against the Elective, Delancey has placed the Elective in danger. Unless he's stopped, the Elective will cease to exist by the end of the year. And, if that happens, there is a good chance that it will reveal the existence of the Hellfire Club.'

Nathan felt a sudden surge of righteous anger. 'So, now that it's all about money, the Hellfire Club's willing to act. Seeing its next Black King crippled just wasn't enough, was it?'

Lawrence placed a firm hand on Nathan's knee, and Nathan was shocked to feel himself respond to the touch. 'Nathan, my family has been nurturing the Hellfire Club for two hundred years. If you knew the good we've done in that time, you would understand that I had no choice but to accept the counsel of the Inner Circle. But now . . .' The smile on Lawrence's face was wild, feral. 'Delancey has become a liability. And I now have the authority to have him brought down, by any means necessary – as long as the Hellfire Club is kept out of it,' he added.

OK, so it was all making some sense, now. But why him? Why Nathan Dexter? 'So, where do I fit into this? If the Hellfire Club wants Delancey out of the way, why not choose a professional?' This was all getting too bizarre for words. Nathan was a journalist, not some mercenary assassin. If he had understood Lawrence correctly, he wanted Delancey silenced permanently. Could Nathan do it? Even after everything that Delancey had done, could he undo the final moral restraint and kill him?

'I chose you, Nathan, because you have as much reason to see Delancey stopped as I do. I need someone who will act as an extension of me: and you are the perfect candidate. You would be my avatar, so to speak.' He squeezed Nathan's knee and his eyes bored into Nathan's. At that point, Nathan felt helpless.

'Will you do it, Nathan? Will you put Adrian Delancey out of my misery?'

Marco downed the last of his Foster's and stood up. Fair enough, it was nice pub, but it wasn't really his scene. He'd been waiting for nearly an hour, but it was becoming increasingly clear that Nathan wasn't going to show. Oh well, he'd done his best. Marco decided to return to his flat and carry on phoning him. One way or other, he would track down the elusive Nathan Dexter.

Having stepped out into the glorious May afternoon, he found himself taking the scenic route back to the nearest Tube, through the greenery of Russell Square. Not for the first time, he thought about the duality of the little park laid out around him. By day, it catered to families, happy playing children running around without a care in the world. Nannies wheeled their charges in pushchairs and prams, while students sat on the benches and soaked up the sunshine as they revised for their exams.

But by night it was a very different story. Marco had visited Russell Square many, many times under the cover of darkness, and had never failed to have a good time. He remembered the first time he had been there, soon after moving to London. Standing by the brick-built toilets, he looked around nonchalantly at the dozen or so other men who were waiting. But waiting for what? It was as if they were expecting some cue, some signal. How different from the cruising he had enjoyed in Melbourne, where everyone just pitched in the moment they reached the cruising grounds.

Suddenly, the signal must have been given. The man to the left of him, a clone in leather jacket and jeans, pulled out his cock, an impressive, thick semi-erection that he quickly wanked into its full glory. The skinhead next to him reached out and took over, pulling on the man's cock with leisurely strokes. Watching the scene, Marco felt his own cock stirring, and decided to do something about it. He unbuttoned his jeans, releasing his cock from its restraint and letting it stand free. He looked around, hoping that someone would notice him, someone would want to be with him. Seconds later, his wish was granted: a man detached himself from the shadows and sauntered over to him.

Marco was impressed: he was about six feet tall, and well muscled, his Ben Sherman shirt unbuttoned to show an impressively hairy chest. He smiled at Marco, and Marco was instantly drawn to the cheeky grin and the deep, penetrating eyes.

'Hi,' he muttered, before taking Marco's cock in his hand and pulling on the thick seven inches. Marco groaned as the man tightened his grip and increased his speed. Then he stopped. 'Don't want this to be over before we get started, do we?' Sinking to his knees, he pulled Marco's jeans and boxers down, before nuzzling into Marco's groin, his tongue flicking at Marco's balls. He drew his tongue upward, licking the long shaft with teasing strokes until he reached the thick red helmet. One hand started to rub the dense covering of hair on Marco's stomach, while the other squeezed Marco's shaft, forcing a single pearl of pre-come out of his dick slit. The man lapped up the droplet before engulfing Marco's cock in his mouth, sliding his lips up and down the shaft.

Marco didn't know how much longer he could hold on, especially when he looked over at the clone and skinhead and saw that they had stripped off: the clone was bent over, leaning against the brick wall of the toilet, while the skinhead had his hands on his shoulders and was sliding his impressive cock in and out of the clone's firm arse. A few feet beyond them, two bears were on the grass, fully clothed but with their cocks in each other's mouth, sucking and pleasuring each other.

Marco felt the familiar build-up, the tightening of his balls, the warm glow that was beginning to burn in his groin. The man continued to suck him, his mouth pulling on Marco's cock, his tongue flicking around Marco's dick slit and the sensitive ridge of his helmet.

Suddenly, Marco could no longer hold back. With a loud groan, he pumped his cock deep inside the man's mouth, shooting his come, filling up the man's mouth with his hot spunk. The man swallowed, taking every last drop, still sucking, still wanking, taking everything that Marco could give him. Finally, Marco pulled away. The man looked up at him, his eyes gleaming, a broad grin on his face.

'Now it's my turn,' he said. 'Do you fancy going somewhere a bit more comfortable, though?'

Marco thought about it. OK, so he didn't know this bloke from Adam, but there was something about him that made Marco want to know more.

'Where were you thinking?'

The man got to his feet. 'My house. I only live over there.' He pointed at one of the big houses that surrounded the Square. 'What do you say?' The pleading look in his eyes was difficult to ignore. So Marco didn't.

'OK, you're on.' He held out his hand. 'My name's Marco.'

The man took the outstretched hand and shook it warmly. 'Hello, Marco. I'm Lawrence.'

Marco couldn't help smiling at the memory. His years with Lawrence had been the happiest time of his life. Not that he didn't love Leigh, but with Lawrence it had been something different, something deeper. If only Lawrence could have seen that he was doing all of this for him! All he had ever wanted had been Lawrence's forgiveness. Deep inside, Marco just couldn't help believing that it had all been his fault.

He hadn't seen Lawrence for years, but hardly a day ever went past without Marco thinking about him. As he reached the edge of the Square, he looked over at the house, wondering whether Lawrence still lived there. Part of him wanted to run over there, to knock on the door, allow Hadleigh to show him into Lawrence's playroom . . . But part of him knew that he just couldn't. If Leigh had thought that seeing Nathan again would be hard, he had no idea of what seeing Lawrence again would have been like.

Suddenly, the front door opened. Marco froze, not knowing what to expect.

But what he saw was the last thing he could ever have expected. It just wasn't possible. Nathan was standing there, saying his goodbyes to Hadleigh.

What the hell was going on? Unable to move, unable to think clearly, Marco watched as Nathan walked off, deep in thought. Nathan and Lawrence? What was Marco going to do now?

As Hadleigh showed him out, Nathan's mind was reeling. Lawrence hadn't asked him to decide immediately: he had a day or so to think about it. Could he do it? Should he do it? Delancey was evil, that was true: between them, Lawrence and Nathan had more than enough reasons to want him dead. But could Nathan do it? Historical evidence showed that simply defeating Delancey wasn't enough: he always found a way to return. Lawrence meant business, and Nathan just didn't know whether he was up to it.

But it hadn't been as simple as that. Not only did Delancey have to be stopped, but so did the Syndicate. And for that Lawrence needed information: specifically, he needed to know the location of Delancey's headquarters. If Nathan accepted Lawrence's proposal, he would be leaving the country on a quest to find that information. And, if Lawrence was to be believed, he wouldn't be returning for a very long time. Perhaps that would be the best idea – to put Britain behind him and start all over again.

Pondering his decision, he set off for Russell Square Tube. Preoccupied, he didn't see the person watching him from the other side of the Square.

From his vantage point, Lawrence watched as Nathan left the house. Lawrence was almost certain that Nathan would accept his offer: not only would he get his revenge, but it would give him a chance to rebuild his life. Either was reason enough for him to say yes. And Nathan deserved it. Lawrence had done his research: he was a good man, well liked and reliable. How much longer could he put up with the Elective's witch-hunt before he cracked? Lawrence didn't like to see one of life's decent people dealt such a shitty hand.

Suddenly, Lawrence's eyes were drawn to the Square itself. There was a figure standing there, watching the house . . . no, watching Nathan. One of the Elective's agents? One of Delancey's paid thugs? No – that wasn't possible: Lawrence had taken too many precautions. As Lawrence looked more carefully, he recognised the stocky figure in the Square. And froze.

It was Marco.

Lawrence felt his stomach tighten. To see him now, after all these years . . . All the feelings came flooding back, the need, the desire, the love. The reason why he wanted Delancey to pay for what he'd done.

Losing his legs was one thing, but Delancey had cost him far, far more than that.

He had cost him his soul. Once Marco had decided to throw his lot in with the Elective, there had been nothing that Lawrence could do. There was no way that the worlds of the Hellfire Club and the Elective could be allowed to collide in Lawrence and Marco's relationship. Reluctantly, Lawrence had had to say goodbye to the warm, friendly Australian.

It was a pain he could never forget.

But, if this all worked out, perhaps there was a chance. Perhaps something could be done to recapture his previous happiness.

Who was he kidding? Marco was happy with Leigh now. Why would he take a backward step? Why would he return to something that had hurt him as badly as it had hurt Lawrence? Lawrence moved away from the window, over to the table, and picked up his wineglass. And threw it against the wall, watching antique lead crystal smash into a thousand shards.

Like his heart.

Four

——————

Nathan didn't feel like going home. An empty house wasn't what he wanted at the moment. He wanted company. He knew that he wouldn't be able to talk about his meeting with Lawrence – that much had been made abundantly clear – but he did need a distraction for an hour or two, time enough for him to come to some sort of a decision. Standing outside the entrance to the Tube, he suddenly knew where he wanted to be. And with whom.

Mike Bury.

Mike now lived in Hampstead, about five minutes' walk from the Heath – very convenient for him. Nathan hadn't seen him for a couple of weeks, but he had spoken to him the other day: the open invitation still stood. Mike represented a kind of safe haven, someone who would listen and lend emotional support.

When Scott had walked out on Nathan, Mike had been there for him, one of the few allies he had on an increasingly hostile gay scene. They had started a clumsy, almost teenage relationship, but they soon both realised that it wasn't going to work. They functioned best as mates who occasionally had sex – especially when they had taken advantage of the playroom that had been set up in the cellar of Mike's old lodgings. Nathan smiled as he remembered it: indeed, he had been really disappointed when Mike had bought his own house and left the playroom behind.

But Nathan's dealings with the Bury family went back further than Mike. Last year, just before Nathan's initial encounter with Adrian Delancey, he and Scott had met John Bury, Mike's twin brother. However, John had been anything but a casual shag: he had been sent by Delancey to crack into Nathan's computer and ransack his files. Nathan had discovered him, forcing him to flee . . . only to find that Adrian Delancey did not take failure lightly. John had been murdered, and Mike had come to London to unearth the truth.

Yet another victim of Delancey's evil schemes, thought Nathan. And he was still having doubts! If he told Mike about Lawrence, he knew that Mike would tell him to accept the assignment without hesitation. But Lawrence couldn't risk compromising the Hellfire Club any further. Even letting Nathan in on its existence was an unprecedented step.

Even so, a couple of hours with Mike Bury would be just what the doctor ordered. With that thought in mind, he showed his travel pass to the station attendant. He was a big blond bear with a goatee beard and a warm, knowing smile. Nathan glanced at his name badge – Simon, apparently – smiled back, and headed towards the lifts. As he reached them, he looked back, and received a bit of an ego boost when he saw that Simon was still looking at him.

Have to visit Russell Square again, he decided, as the lift arrived.

'I'm afraid the master isn't seeing anyone today,' said Hadleigh calmly. 'If you would care to leave your card, I will make sure that he gets it, sir.'

'For Christ's sake, Hadleigh, it's me. Marco! You must remember me.' Marco didn't know why he had done it, but he had. Something had possessed him, taken control of him. Marco had suddenly found himself standing in front of that oh-so-familiar door. Once, he had had a key. Now he had to wait for

Hadleigh to answer. And the more difficult task: persuading Hadleigh to let him in.

'I'm a butler, sir. I'm not paid to remember. Quite the opposite, in fact.'

Marco groaned. He had to see Lawrence. He wasn't going to leave without doing one of the most difficult things in his life. Not having come so far.

'Is there a problem, Hadleigh?' The voice, the familiar voice, echoed down the long hallway. Marco felt the breath freeze in his throat. For a second, it all came back to him, all of it.

'Lawrence?' he said, the words almost a whisper.

Hadleigh stood aside, and, for the first time in five years, Marco came face to face with his beloved Lawrence.

'Marco.' The weight behind that single name, the emotions, the depth of feeling and passion, all of it struck Marco like a punch in the stomach. 'Well? Are you going to stand there all day, or are you going to come in?' And then, to Hadleigh: 'Bring a bottle of Yarra Yering Pinot Noir – a 1980, I think – to the Summer Room.'

Hadleigh raised an eyebrow. 'The Summer Room, Your Lordship?'

'You may not be paid to remember, but you are paid to listen.' Marco almost applauded. He had always got a kick out of watching Hadleigh get his comeuppance.

As Marco stepped back into the house that had once been his home – and back in time to when he had been truly fulfilled – he couldn't help but be touched by Lawrence's gesture. That had been their wine, the grapes grown in a vineyard not far from Melbourne. That had been the wine they had drunk on every anniversary, on every special occasion. And it had been the wine they had shared when their first joint venture with a club had been a success.

It was a wine that Marco hadn't touched since.

Not a word was said as Marco followed Lawrence's wheelchair down the hall towards the Summer Room. Another gesture: the

Summer Room had always been Marco's favourite room in the house: he always claimed it felt less 'historical' than the rest of the place.

Lawrence pushed open the door and wheeled himself in. Marco looked around the spacious Summer Room, and smiled at the wave of memories that washed over him. The Summer Room was a vast conservatory at the back of the house, with a huge glass ceiling. The walls were painted the faintest shade of lemon, and hung with tasteful, summery scenes that Marco himself had chosen. Indeed, this had been the one room in the house that Marco had considered exclusively his. Something about the sunshine and the openness reminded him of Australia.

Then it hit him: the room was exactly as it had been on that cold, painful day five years ago, when Marco had walked out of the house and out of Lawrence's life. The magazines, the books, the papers . . . everything in exactly the same place.

Lawrence must have understood his expression. 'Yes, Marco: nothing's changed. In fact, this is the first time I've set foot in here – as it were – since you left. I couldn't bear the memories.'

Lawrence had hardly aged since they had split up. Still that cheeky grin, the square jaw, the short dark hair. Marco felt his heart pounding as he looked at the one person he had thought he would never see again. If only there was some way . . . He caught himself. Nothing could be achieved with what-ifs. But something *had* changed.

'Hadleigh called you "Your Lordship",' said Marco. 'So – it eventually happened, then?'

Lawrence nodded. 'The old man died soon after you left. So, here I am, the new Duke. Bit more money, seat in the House . . . nothing special.'

To someone who didn't know Lawrence, he might have sounded arrogant, but Marco knew that Lawrence cared very little for monetary wealth *per se*. To him, the money was merely a means for him to surround himself with the best toys that money could buy. 'Anyway, enough of that. I'd love to reminisce, but that's not why you're here, is it? You want to know what Nathan Dexter was doing here. I've been expecting a visit for the last half-hour, Marco – ever since I saw you out of the window.'

'Checking the Square for trade, no doubt,' said Marco warmly. He sighed, and slumped into his favourite chair, an overstuffed, comfortable armchair. It felt like an old friend. 'But yes – that's part of the reason I'm here. I wasn't aware that you and Nathan even knew one another. But also . . . happy birthday for yesterday.'

Standing there in the Square, Marco had finally known that he had no choice. And now, seeing Lawrence again was like a dream come true. The last five years, the pain, the loss . . . all gone. For a moment, he could persuade himself that everything was just how it had been . . . But he knew that it wasn't.

And that hurt more than anything.

Lawrence shrugged. 'Thank you. Another year older. Anyway, regarding Nathan . . . we didn't know one another. Until today, that is.' At that point, the door opened and Hadleigh entered, bearing the tray. He set it down without a word and departed. Still sulking, no doubt. As Lawrence poured two glasses, Marco thought about the spectacular rows that he and Hadleigh had had over the years, when they disagreed about what was best for the 'young master'. Marco guessed that Hadleigh had read too many *Batman* comics as a kid: he saw himself as Alfred to Lawrence's Bruce Wayne. But this was the town house in Russell Square, not Wayne Mansion, and Lawrence Dashwood was not a mysterious billionaire with a secret identity, was he?

The glasses filled, Lawrence leant forward in his wheelchair and transfixed Marco with those deep eyes of his.

'The time has come for complete honesty between us, Marco. There's an awful lot that you don't know – an awful lot that I just couldn't tell you when we split up.

'But you deserve the truth, Marco. I just hope you're ready for it.'

★

Marco had recommended the Brighton Grand; as Scott and Leigh got out of the taxi they had taken at the station, they both had to admit that the white and gold façade was impressive.

'When you said we were staying in Brighton, I thought you meant some crappy B and B, not the bloody Grand,' said Scott as he hauled his holdall out of the taxi.

'We deserve a little luxury,' said Leigh, mounting the steps and entering through the big glass doors. 'It's not as if we're paying, is it?'

A flash of the Platinum Amex card later, the two of them were shown up to their rooms.

Throwing his rucksack on the bed, Leigh was impressed. It was a large room, elegantly furnished, with an enormous bed. From the window, he had a view of the Brighton seafront, the sea a gorgeous deep blue under the warm May sunshine. He just knew that he was going to enjoy himself.

Leigh was just finishing unpacking when there was a knock at the door. Assuming it to be Scott, he bounded over and opened it. But it wasn't Scott standing there. A stocky bear in his late twenties was in the doorway, wearing a rugby top and jeans. He had cropped hair and a full black beard, and was smiling.

God, he's cute, thought Leigh.

'Leigh Robertson?' asked the bear, smiling warmly.

Puzzled, Leigh nodded.

'Alex sent me. He wanted to make sure that you had a good time in Brighton.'

Alex was the regional administrator of the Elective responsible for Brighton. It was one of the more prestigious posts, second only to the administrators of London and Manchester. Leigh had met Alex a couple of times: he was a warm, amiable man, and sending someone to help Leigh 'settle in' was exactly the sort of gesture that he would think of.

'Come in,' said Leigh, closing the door behind him.

'I'm Pete, by the way,' said the bear. Then, without another word, he pulled off his rugby top. Leigh was impressed: Pete was slightly tubby, but that was disguised by the thick covering of

81

black hair that covered his stomach and chest. In a lot of ways, he reminded Leigh of Marco. For moment, Leigh felt a pang of guilt: it was obvious what Pete was offering. Should Leigh accept? But the sight of this hunky bear, with his beard and hairy chest, was too much to resist. Any lingering doubts vanished as Pete undid his jeans and let them drop to the floor. He wasn't wearing any underwear: Leigh was impressed by the fat, hard cock that bobbed up once released from the denim. He grinned, inviting Leigh to do whatever he wanted.

Without needing any prompting, Leigh moved closer to Pete and fell to his knees, nuzzling his groin, taking in the heady mixture of man and sweat. His tongue licked the thick black hairs of his thighs, first one leg, then the other, each time getting closer and closer to Pete's balls. Pete's big hands massaged Leigh's shoulders, both releasing the pent-up tension and building up Leigh's excitement.

Finally, Leigh couldn't hold out any longer. He took one of Pete's balls in his mouth and rolled it around, tasting the salty sweat, feeling the hot skin, the thick hairs. His own cock was so stiff that it was almost painful, constricted by his jeans. Part of him was desperate to release it, but another part enjoyed the dull pain, enjoyed the feeling that it was forbidden. Leigh's mouth took the other ball, and tasted that, while his hand reached up and started stroking Pete's body, his fingers clawing through the thick hair of his stomach, up to his chest and his big nipples. As he continued to mouth Pete's balls, he tugged and squeezed on the big bear's nipples, enjoying the groans and gasps that this caused.

Now he was ready: his tongue traced a line of spit up the underside of Pete's dick, up and up until he reached the impressive red helmet. Pulling away slightly, he grasped Pete's dick in his hand and squeezed, forcing a drop of pre-come to bead in the slit; with his other hand, he scooped it up with a finger and licked it off.

Pete smiled. 'You liked that, didn't you?'

'Was it that obvious?' There was something earthy, animalistic, about Pete. Leigh was desperate to take that stiff cock in his mouth, but, when he did, it would be mutual. He wanted to feel that bearded face grinding into his groin, that moustache scraping up and down his cock. He stood up.

'Time to get comfortable,' he muttered.

Guessing what he was about to do, Pete stepped forward. 'Let me.' With that, he pulled off Leigh's T-shirt. Leigh caught sight of himself in the mirror: his smooth, well-built body, his dragon tattoo on his shoulder. Indeed, if there was one benefit to Marco's frequent sulks, it was that it gave Leigh a chance to visit the gym more often.

Pete's hands were on Leigh's belt now, unbuckling it, then unzipping the jeans so that they slid to the carpeted floor. For a second, they stood like that: naked, hard, their jeans around their ankles. Then Pete hurriedly removed his boots to allow his jeans to come off, and Leigh did the same. Suddenly, there was a sense of urgency, a feeling that they both wanted each other, there, then.

As soon as Leigh was completely naked, Pete pulled him over to the king-size bed and gently pushed him on to it so that he bounced on the soft mattress. Leigh lay there as Pete climbed on top of him, his solid, hairy thighs astride Leigh's chest. His big hands played with Leigh's chest, pushing and pulling his firm pecs, as he leant forward and kissed Leigh on the mouth, his beard tickling as his tongue met Leigh's. Leigh's cock was hard, harder than it had felt for ages, and Leigh longed to feel Pete's mouth around it, sucking it, nibbling at it . . .

Pete stopped kissing Leigh and edged forward. Then, placing both hands on the wall, he slid his cock into Leigh's mouth, pushing the whole length inside him, his balls against Leigh's chin. He began to fuck Leigh's mouth, his cock touching the back of Leigh's throat before withdrawing. Leigh's hands were all over Pete's body, stroking that thick fur, touching the taut muscles of Pete's back. His cock was almost sore now, desperate for attention, but Leigh did nothing: he knew that, when the time came, it would be worth the wait.

Then Pete manoeuvred himself round; keeping his dick firmly inside Leigh's mouth, he turned so he could fulfil Leigh's needs. Leigh shuddered as his cock was engulfed by the hot wetness of Pete's mouth, the feeling of Pete's tongue as it flicked over the sensitive skin of his helmet. All the while, Pete continued to slide his own dick into Leigh, allowing Leigh to taste the sweetness of his pre-come. Leigh's hands moved from Pete's back to his hairy arse, rubbing his cheeks, wishing that his mouth was free so that his tongue could slide into the darkness of Pete's hole, licking at his ring, forcing its way inside, tasting Pete . . . The image was too vivid. This, coupled with the hypnotic rhythm that Pete was building up on Leigh's cock, made Leigh surrender himself, letting the fire that was raging in his groin take over. His groans were stifled by the fat dick that continued to pump away into his mouth as he let himself come into Pete's mouth. It was one of the most intense orgasms he had ever had: his back arched, his balls felt that they were going to explode as his come shot into Pete's grateful mouth. Pete swallowed every drop, but that seemed to be the trigger for him. Leigh tasted his salty warmth before he had even realised that Pete was coming.

Leigh almost choked as Pete filled his mouth with hot spunk, but he took every last bit, the taste, the taste that Leigh loved, making his own orgasm go on and on and on.

Drained, exhausted, Leigh just lay there, unwilling to move in case he spoilt the moment. It was Pete who moved first, turning and placing his hands on Leigh's shoulders.

'Welcome to Brighton,' he said with a smile. At that moment, there was a knock on the door. Leigh guessed it was Scott, but wasn't quite up to seeing him at the moment.

He grinned. *Wish you were here.*

When Mike opened the door, he was genuinely pleased to see Nathan, even though it was obvious that Nathan had woken him up: he was wearing a pair of boxer shorts and nothing else. With much of the mystery surrounding his brother's death now cleared up – albeit unsatisfactorily – Mike had given up his bar job at the

Brave Trader, which he had taken on to place himself at the centre of events, and was now concentrating on his full-time job as a computer analyst. And the reason why he hadn't been able to see Nathan last night had been because he'd been working.

Standing there in the doorway, Nathan could see why he found him so attractive. It wasn't just the height, although he was an impressive six foot five. He was broad-shouldered, with a light dusting of gingery-brown hair across his chest, turning into a thin blond line of fur which descended towards the hair that covered his stomach. His hair was currently cut in a short flat-top, and he wore a close-cropped full beard. When he smiled – as he was doing now – his whole face lit up with an eagerness and innocence which Nathan found irresistible.

'Come in – I'm really glad you're here,' said Mike. As the door shut behind them, he grabbed Nathan in a tight hug and squeezed him, while his mouth sought out Nathan's own, his tongue forcing Nathan's mouth open and entwining with Nathan's own tongue. His hands roughly caressed Nathan's back as Nathan's hands sank lower and lower, stroking his firm arse, sliding beneath the thin cotton of the boxers before seeking out the furry hole between his cheeks. His fingers probed further and deeper, reaching inside, sliding into that hot hole – before Mike grabbed his wrist and pulled away.

For a second, Nathan didn't know how to react. Surely things hadn't changed between him and Mike? Or had they? Had the hate campaign, the insidious whispers, reached even Mike?

'Not here. I've got your birthday present. I'd hate you to miss it.'

Puzzled, Nathan followed Mike down the long hallway that led to his bedroom. But before they reached it Mike stopped.

'I hope you like it. I had to pull in so many favours for this,' he said, before theatrically opening . . . a cupboard.

'Come on!' he urged, motioning for Nathan to go in first.

A cupboard? What's the present, then – a day trip to Narnia with Mister Tumnus and the other fauns? he thought wryly, but said nothing.

It was only when he reached the door that he realised that it wasn't a cupboard at all: it opened on to a flight of stairs.

'You first,' said Mike. Nathan gingerly grasped the stair rail and nervously edged into the darkness.

'Aren't there any lights?' he asked as he was engulfed.

'That would spoil it,' said Mike. 'I'll switch the lights on when you get to the bottom.'

Fumbling in the dark, he finally reached what he hoped was the bottom of the stairs and waited. He almost jumped out of his skin when Mike touched him.

'Sorry,' he mumbled. 'Anyway, happy birthday, Nathan.'

Nathan blinked in the sudden illumination. A single, dim bulb hung from the ceiling. But that was enough to show Nathan everything he wanted.

The floor was made from smooth flagstones, while the walls were unpainted concrete. A set of metal shelves stood to the left: each shelf was full of every sex toy Nathan could imagine, and a few that he couldn't. Dildos of every size and colour, vibrators, handcuffs of every variety . . . It was like being in a branch of Clone Zone.

To his right, the wall appeared bare – until Nathan spotted the manacles. For a second he thought back to Amsterdam, and Ruud, the Dutchman who had chained him up. He still thought about that particular experience.

The *pièce de résistance*, however, was in front of him. A sling – identical to the sling upon which Nathan and Mike had cemented their relationship months ago – was suspended from the ceiling, leather and chains inviting Nathan to sit in it, to use it to its fullest advantage. Indeed, this playroom was a virtual copy of the one that had been beneath Mike's old house.

'I don't understand . . .'

Mike grinned. 'I've always wanted a playroom – one of the reasons that I bought this place was because it had a cellar. I got Richard, my old landlord, to build a copy of his for me.' His grin turned evil. 'I haven't tried it out yet, though.'

There were a few differences: in the far right corner, a shower

86

nozzle was mounted on the wall; next to the sling was a chest, its lid open, full of leather chains and cock rings . . . But if this was Nathan's birthday present from Mike . . . he was happy. After the last few months, Nathan had learnt to enjoy moments like this when he could: there was no guarantee that there would be another.

'Mike . . . I just don't know what to say.'

'You don't have to say anything. Just help me road-test it.'

Nathan grinned. 'I don't know where to start.'

Mike nodded towards the far corner. 'Fancy a shower?'

Nathan needed no further encouragement. He turned to Mike and continued where he had left off, pulling down the boxer shorts to reveal Mike's cock, now semi-hard.

'My turn,' said Mike, unbuttoning Nathan's shirt and yanking it from his jeans, before throwing it into the corner. Hurried fingers undid the belt, before Mike dropped to his knees and untied Nathan's boots. Looking down, seeing Mike's head so close to his already stiff cock, Nathan was sorely tempted to grab Mike and grind his face into his groin. But he held back – this was going to be worth waiting for.

His boots removed, Nathan slipped out of his jeans. Mike dragged his boxers to the stone floor, allowing Nathan's cock its long-awaited freedom.

'Come on.' Mike led Nathan over to the corner, to the shower. He turned the tap beneath the nozzle and adjusted the temperature; within a few seconds, a warm spray cascaded down in front of them. Without a word being said, the two of them walked into the shower.

They embraced in the water, stroking each other's body, touching each other with the familiarity that they now had. In another life, perhaps things would have been different. Perhaps they really would have been lovers. But Nathan's heart was lost to Scott.

That didn't detract from the intimacy of the moment, though: his friendship with Mike, their mutual attraction, was more than sufficient to allow Nathan to enjoy their times together.

Mike whispered into Nathan's ear. 'There's something I've always wanted to try,' he said, with the faintest trace of hesitation.

'What?' Nathan replied as he kissed Mike's neck.

'I'd like you to piss on me.'

Nathan was a little surprised, but only because it was something that he and Mike had never done before. But it was definitely something that Nathan had done – done and thoroughly enjoyed on many occasions.

'That's why I had the shower installed,' Mike added.

Nathan stepped back. 'Actually, I'd like to do that. I'd like to piss all over you, like the little shit that you are.' Mike and Nathan found the roles of master and slave equally comfortable, and Nathan guessed that it was his turn to be master. Even if it wasn't, it was the role that he wanted to play.

'Yes, sir. I've been a bad boy, sir,' Mike muttered. 'I need to be punished.'

'Yes, you do. Kneel down,' Nathan instructed. Mike obeyed, kneeling on the wet stone of the floor, streams of water trickling down his broad back.

Sometimes, it was very difficult to piss on demand. However, the countless glasses of wine at Lawrence's were having their effect, and Nathan's bladder was full. Willing his stiff cock to subside slightly, he concentrated. Finally, the first drops of golden piss fell from his cock. Feeling the pressure build, he aimed his cock at Mike. And pissed.

A torrent of piss covered Mike, over his shoulders, over his back, over his chest. Nathan moved his cock slightly, allowing the strong stream to cover Mike's hair and his face. Mike looked up at him and opened his mouth, his eyes urging Nathan to fill him up with his piss.

'Wank yourself while I'm punishing you, boy,' Nathan ordered, as he pissed into Mike's mouth. Mike was swallowing every drop that Nathan could piss, drinking the golden urine with satisfaction in his eyes. His hand pulled furiously on his cock, and Nathan could see that it was turning Mike on more than either of them could have imagined.

'I want my boy to come,' he instructed, watching as Mike's wanking became faster and faster, his face reddening with the familiar flush that always overcame him this close to orgasm.

As the last drops of piss dripped from Nathan's cock, he roughly shoved it into Mike's mouth, allowing him to swallow all of it, to drink him dry. As Mike took Nathan's cock, he finally came: Nathan plugged Mike's mouth with his cock, forbidding him to cry out as come bubbled out of the end of Mike's dick, dripping over his hand as he forced every last white drop from his big balls.

Satisfied that Mike was finished, Nathan took his cock from his mouth and gave it a couple of strokes to bring it back to full hardness.

'Stand up,' he commanded. 'And give me your hand.' Mike offered his hand to Nathan. Despite the shower, there was still a considerable amount of come smeared over it. Nathan grabbed the hand and forced it to Mike's mouth. 'Lick that clean.'

Eagerly, Mike's tongue darted out and lapped up his own come.

'Don't swallow it.'

When he was satisfied that Mike had licked his hand clean, Nathan pulled him towards him and kissed him. Mike's mouth tasted of piss and come, a combination that made Nathan's cock even harder than it had been, bringing him dangerously close to orgasm. Nathan's tongue took the stored come from Mike's mouth and drank it, relishing the hot, salty taste as he swallowed it.

'Good boy,' he said quietly. 'It's your master's turn now. You've been a good boy, so you can piss over your master.'

'Thank you, sir,' said Mike, as Nathan fell to his knees.

'Go on – piss on me.'

Nathan knelt there expectantly, waiting for the first drops to wash over him. Unlike Mike, who had been forced to remain still, Nathan smeared the first yellow drops over his hairy chest with a mounting feeling of excitement. It was clear that Mike had needed to piss as much as Nathan had: a thick stream of it began to flow all over Nathan's body, glistening over his thick black body hair. Nathan washed in it, rubbing it over him, breathing the slightly acid smell and getting even more turned on.

Satisfied that he was wet with it, he pulled Mike towards him by his still-pissing cock, and took it in his mouth. Mike's stream showed no sign of abating, and Nathan swallowed it all with difficulty. The taste of Mike's piss was just what Nathan had hoped for: almost smoky, a rich oily taste. Nathan's other hand fell to his cock, almost painfully stiff now, and he started to wank himself, lubricated by the oil of Mike's piss. Nathan drank and drank, draining every last drop from Mike's dick as he wanked himself closer and closer to completion.

There! As the last squirt of piss entered his mouth, Nathan came, thick white streams of it that fell to the stone floor, defying the shower to wash it away. Another spasm, then another, as Nathan deposited his load. Finally, with a last shiver of pleasure, Nathan leant backwards, allowing the shower to wash away all traces of their lovemaking. He looked up at Mike, who was grinning like an idiot.

'Well?' he asked. 'Was that a suitable road test?'

Mike laughed. 'It's a start. I still need to check how the sling holds out.' He grabbed a bar of soap from the floor. 'Let's clean up. Then we can find out.'

As Mike started to soap Nathan's groin, Nathan felt his erection beginning to return. It was going to be a busy afternoon.

Adrian Delancey had dismissed everyone from his immediate vicinity. He sat alone in his study, mentally visualising the remaining moves before final victory. To him, it was a complex chessboard; the pieces were the various players in the game. Everything was in place, everything was predictable. The strong forces of the Syndicate against the weaker pieces of the Elective: checkmate was inevitable, everything was predictable . . .

Except the actions of the opposing King.

The irony was that Nathan was probably the best weapon that

the Elective had: he was probably the only person on Earth who could damage Delancey. The current situation – with Nathan and the Elective at loggerheads – suited Delancey perfectly.

But that didn't guarantee success: what was Nathan Dexter going to do? Delancey wasn't foolish enough to believe that he had completely defeated him. Nathan would do something – but what?

Until he took his place on the chessboard, until he made his opening move in this endgame, Nathan was a dangerous opponent, a wild card. And Delancey didn't like uncertainties.

He picked up the phone. 'I want to know where Nathan Dexter is,' he ordered. 'And I want him tailed from now on.'

He frowned. If Nathan was reluctant to act, then perhaps it was time to force him on to the board. He made another call . . . and made another move in the game.

Nathan lay on the bed, Mike's arm around him. He could have stayed like that for the rest of the day, but he had a decision to make. What should he do? Nathan was no closer to deciding than he had been a few hours ago. He stared at the ceiling, trying to come up with an answer. He felt sure that he should do it, but he still needed to overcome those lingering doubts. If he was going to have a final showdown with Delancey, he had to be one hundred per cent sure. There could be no room for indecision.

He remembered one of his first editors, the man who had helped to make Nathan the journalist he was. He was full of sayings and aphorisms, but there was one that currently stuck out in Nathan's mind. One of the first rules of reporting: 'The truth points to itself.' What truth?

'I still miss him, you know,' said Mike quietly. 'I can't help thinking that things might have been different if I'd been there.'

Nathan knew that Mike was talking about his late brother, John, murdered by one of Delancey's thugs. Suddenly, things started to come together in his mind. But it was Mike's next statement that finally crystallised everything in Nathan's thoughts.

'If only there was some way to stop Delancey,' he growled.

'To stop him from ever doing anything like this to anyone else . . .'

The truth points to itself. Nathan came to a decision.

'I have to go,' he said. 'Things to do, I'm afraid.'

Mike sat up in bed and smiled. 'It was good to see you, Nathan. Don't leave it so long next time.'

'I won't,' said Nathan as he pulled on his clothes. He had made his mind up. Now he needed to talk to Lawrence.

Marco sat back in the armchair and blew the air out through his lips. 'That's quite a story, Lawrence. Quite a story.'

Lawrence drained his glass and placed it on the table. His expression was one of understanding, of concern. Despite everything that had happened between them, Marco could tell that Lawrence must have hated the lies and deceptions that the Hellfire Club had required of him. 'It's all true, Marco. But you see why I couldn't tell you?'

Marco gave a bitter laugh. 'And I thought the *Elective* was secretive!' But to hear the truth, finally, after all this time . . .

Lawrence had told him all of it. The Hellfire Club, its relationship with the Elective, the truth about Nathan's so-called 'betrayal' . . . At this moment in time, all Marco wanted was to find Adrian Delancey and kill him. That bastard had taken everything. From Marco, from Lawrence, from Mike Bury, from Nathan . . .

'I'll do it for you, Lawrence. No need to involve Nathan. I'll find Delancey.' *I'll find that murdering bastard and I'll see him burn in hell for what he's done to you. To us.*

Lawrence shook his head. 'It has to be Nathan, Lawrence. For reasons that will eventually become clear, Nathan's the only one who can do this. However . . . now that you're here, I do want you to help. But in other ways, important ways. Anyway, all of this is moot unless Nathan agrees. And he is man of high moral principles, Marco. I'm not certain that he –' He broke off as his mobile phone rang.

The conversation was brief, but Marco could tell that it was

Nathan on the other end. Part of him desperately wanted to grab the phone from Lawrence and talk to Nathan, but he knew that would be a mistake. Marco now knew that he, Nathan and Lawrence were all part of something much bigger, much more important. In their relationship, Lawrence had always been the one in control, and, for once, Marco was more than happy to let that still be the case.

Finally, Lawrence put the phone on the table. 'As you've probably guessed, that was Nathan.'

'And?' Marco knew Nathan. Nathan wasn't a murderer. Despite everything that Delancey had done to him, Nathan wouldn't do *that*, surely?

Lawrence smiled, a triumphant smile. 'The game's afoot.

'He flies to Monte Carlo this evening.'

Five

_____

There wasn't really any reason to go back to the house in Docklands: Lawrence had assured Nathan that everything that he needed would be waiting for him when he reached the plane, and, given Lawrence's resources, Nathan believed him. But yet another of Nathan's superstitions was that, whenever he travelled abroad, he always set off from home. Many was the newspaper or magazine editor infuriated with Nathan because he insisted on going home, rather than travelling straight from the office.

But today it was even more important.

Lawrence had told him that the taxi would arrive at four o'clock, taking him on the half-hour journey to City Airport, where a private jet would fly him to Nice. From Nice, he would travel to Monaco – Monte Carlo, to be precise – and the Palais du Cypresse Hotel.

That gave him about half an hour. Nathan sat on the sofa with a tumbler of whisky and tried to collect his thoughts. He had thought that his life couldn't get any more bizarre, but this . . . To discover that Marco's ex wasn't just some footnote in his friend's history, but actually one of the most important players in this game of death and deceit that Nathan had unwittingly entered

... But, the way that things had been going, such a coincidence was nothing more than par for the course.

As the whisky burnt his throat and warmed his stomach, Nathan analysed his decision for the umpteenth time. Adrian Delancey had to be stopped: every life that he touched was damaged by the encounter, feelings and emotions ripped apart by his self-centred machinations. The man was pure poison, and Nathan had a responsibility to stop him.

He had started this: Nathan had started the investigation into the Elective. Who was to say that, had he left well enough alone, Delancey would have been stopped by the Elective itself? Marco had known what was going on; perhaps he could have managed to stop the man without the death of John Bury.

But no. Nathan would have met Scott, even if he hadn't been sniffing around the Elective. And Scott had been having sex with Delancey for months before Nathan had ever met him. Somehow, it had been Nathan's destiny to get involved – and now it was his responsibility to sort things out.

For once, Nathan didn't have to do much of the background research. Lawrence had located someone from Delancey's past who was finally more than willing to blow the whistle on him – for a price. Nathan's first assignment was to find this man and bring him safely back to London. Once the man was in London, Lawrence could ensure that he vanished into the folds and shadows of the Hellfire Club, safe from Delancey.

But what of Scott? Part of Nathan – a large part – wanted to talk to him, to confide in him. But Nathan knew that he couldn't do that. It was nothing to do with Lawrence's need for secrecy: if it came to a choice between his loyalty to the Hellfire Club – something that the Club still needed to earn, come to that – and his feelings for Scott, Scott would win hands down.

Nathan just didn't want to put Scott in any more danger. Perhaps Scott was safer out of the picture. The less he had to do with the situation, the better.

Besides, he didn't even knew where Scott was any more.

★

Scott was tired of waiting for Leigh – he had no idea why he wasn't answering his door, but, after an hour, he'd finally had enough. OK, so it was great to sit in the splendour of one of the hotel's best suites, raiding the minibar and surfing through the cable channels, but it didn't take too long for the place to become just as much a prison as his rooms in halls. Besides, the sound of the sea and the warmth of the sunshine through the patio windows were too good to ignore.

Changing into a pair of knee-length grey shorts and a green T-shirt, Scott decided to see what a Friday afternoon in Brighton had to offer.

Even though it was quite early in the season, there were quite a few people around, taking advantage of the good weather and the fact that it had been a Bank Holiday week. Scott crossed the road opposite the hotel and made his way to the beach. There was something about being this close to the sea that Scott found irresistible: perhaps it was because he originally came from Coventry, which was about as far away from the sea as you could get.

Standing on the mixture of sand and pebbles, he looked out across the virtually smooth sea as it reflected the cloudless blue sky. He ought to feel relaxed, happy – but happiness continued to elude him. Leigh's intentions were good, Scott knew that: Leigh had hoped that, by taking them both out of London, Scott could take his mind off Nathan for a while.

Some hope. Nathan was never far from his thoughts. Scott knew that he had made the wrong decision, he knew that he had left Nathan just at the point when he needed him most.

The problem was, he had never intended for it to go this far. By walking out, he had hoped to shock Nathan into realising where his priorities lay. Scott had had no idea of the trap that Nathan had walked into, no idea that Nathan's life was about to become a living nightmare.

And now he too was trapped, too ashamed to go back, too terrified to go forward. He walked towards the sea and picked up a pebble. Then, with an expertise that came from hours skimming stones as a kid, Scott hurled the pebble across the sea, watching as it bounced once, twice, three times – and then sank without trace.

Scott sighed. And came to a decision. When they got back to London, he would phone Nathan and see whether he felt the same way as Scott did.

Anything was better than dealing with the pain.

Hearing the car pull up, Nathan got to his feet and looked out of the window. A huge silver BMW was waiting outside – presumably his lift to City Airport. He glanced around the living room, almost for the last time. The last time, he thought. Given what I'm about to do, it might very well be.

Having locked the door behind him, he took one last look back before opening the car door and getting in.

If the truth be known, he thought, I don't actually care whether I come back or not. Without Scott, there isn't a lot to look forward to. And, if the cost of not returning is the final end of Adrian Delancey, it's a fair exchange.

'City Airport?'

He looked up at the driver. He was in his mid-thirties, dressed in a smart grey suit. He was even broader than Nathan, with short curly hair, longish sideburns and a wicked smile.

'That's right,' said Nathan, remembering the taxi driver who had taken him and Marco to the hotel in Amsterdam last year. I wonder if he offers the same service, he thought idly as the car drew off.

From what I know of the Hellfire Club, I wouldn't be surprised, he said silently to himself, smiling. And then he caught the smile from the driver.

This could be a very interesting journey.

Lawrence called for another bottle of wine. He knew that he and Marco had probably had far too much already, but what the hell: he had accomplished so much today that he deserved to celebrate.

'I've missed you, you know,' said Marco. He had definitely

had too much: his Australian accent was very strong. And he was saying things like that. The trouble was, it was exactly what Lawrence wanted to hear. Even so, he protested.

'Marco – it was over five years ago. I can't believe that you've been holding a candle for me all this time.' And yet he could believe. If Lawrence could for Marco, why couldn't Marco for him? But this was dangerous territory. The situation was critical: unless he could stop Delancey, everything for which his family had worked for the last two centuries would be destroyed. He couldn't allow that to happen. Nothing could get in the way. Nothing. Except . . .

Marco stood up and walked over to him, standing behind his wheelchair and placing his hands on Lawrence's shoulders. 'I never wanted to leave. Never wanted to leave this place, leave you.' His voice was thick with emotion.

'Marco, you have a new life now, a different life. You have the Elective, and I have the Hellfire Club. And you have Leigh, or had you forgotten?' Hard words, but this was a hard situation.

'I know, I know . . .' Marco moved round, sank to his knees in front of Lawrence's wheelchair and took his hands. 'But I still love you, Lawrence.'

Lawrence sighed. All he wanted to do was reach out and grab him, take Marco in his arms and tell him that he felt the same, that not a moment had gone by over the last five years that he hadn't thought about him. But he couldn't. He just couldn't. The Dashwoods stood for duty, loyalty. As much as he wanted it, Lawrence was bound by his birthright. His voice hardened slightly.

'Marco . . . do you want to help me or not?'

Marco pulled back. The moment, that moment that had hovered over them like a storm cloud, seemed to have ended.

'What do you want me to do?' The disappointment was clear in Marco's voice, but there was nothing that Lawrence could do about it. Not yet, anyway.

'That all depends on how things work out for Nathan in Monte Carlo. The itinerary I have planned for Nathan will eventually take him further into Europe, probably Germany, and that's going to be the difficult one – if there's one place that Delancey will be keeping an eye on, it's there. Don't ask me why, but Germany seems to be his secondary power base, as Nathan found out when he went to Munich a few months ago. That's when he's going to need help, Marco.'

'But what if he doesn't want to talk to me?' said Marco. 'We didn't exactly part as friends, did we?'

'You know the truth now. Tell him, explain. He's a reasonable man – you know that.'

'OK – sort out the details.' Then he frowned. 'Actually, there's a better way of doing it. I have some long-standing Elective business in Germany. That way, even if Delancey is watching, he won't suspect anything.'

'Delancey suspects everything,' said Lawrence bitterly. 'That's the problem. But that's a good idea: the longer we keep the Hellfire Club and the Elective separate, the better.'

Before they could continue, there was a discreet knock. The door opened to reveal Hadleigh with his tray.

'Ah, Hadleigh – just lay it on the table.'

As Hadleigh placed yet another bottle of the Australian Chardonnay on the table, Lawrence looked around. Seeing Marco in his favourite chair made it seem like old times. But it couldn't be. Too much had happened. There was no way that things could be as they were.

Was there?

Nathan reached City Airport without any delay, sadly. The thought of his chauffeur taking him in the back of the car had been an inviting one, but time was short. Nathan knew that they were only one step in front of Delancey at the moment; every second counted. And sex with chauffeurs was hardly conducive to good time-keeping, was it?

He got out of the car and waved a reluctant farewell to the chauffeur, who gave him an impish smile in return. Let's hope you're waiting when I get back, thought Nathan. If I get back.

As he stepped into the main concourse of City Airport, all marble and money, a man in a grey suit approached him from the direction of the checkout desks.

'Mr Dexter?' He was in his late twenties, with a short goatee beard and close-cropped hair. If anything, he looked like a slightly younger version of Nathan himself. Nathan couldn't help smiling: he could definitely detect the hand of the Hellfire Club in this one. Thank you, Lawrence.

'That's me,' Nathan replied.

'I'm Gary. I'm your PA for the next few days.'

'PA?' Nathan had never had a personal assistant. He wondered what his new PA's duties involved, but he suspected that they were whatever Nathan wanted. Sweet. 'Nice to meet you.' He shook Gary's hand warmly. 'When do we leave?'

'The plane's waiting for us. If you'd like to follow me?' Gary strode off towards the departure area. Nice arse, thought Nathan.

A silver-grey Learjet was standing on the tarmac, devoid of any external markings. Nathan remembered the last time he had been in a Learjet: when he and Marco had gone to Gran Canaria, unaware that they were flying into a trap. Nathan shook his head. No time for memories: he had a job to do.

He stepped across the tarmac bathed in the late-summer sun, mounted the steps and entered the plane, not sure what to expect.

Whatever he had been expecting, this plane surpassed all of it.

If he hadn't known that he was in a plane, he would never have suspected. The interior designers had been busy: it looked more like a gentlemen's club than a plane. The walls were wood-panelled, and hung with paintings. Huge leather armchairs were dotted about, and he spotted a widescreen TV at one end. The floor was so thickly carpeted that his Caterpillar boots sank into the pile. Luxury bordering on decadence . . . It was like being in an episode of *Dynasty*. And Nathan loved it. After months of being treated like dirt, it was a lovely feeling to be cosseted. Even though he knew that it was a dangerous indulgence, he felt sure that it wouldn't do him any harm – for a while.

Besides – there was no guarantee that he would ever walk away from this, was there?

'Take a seat, Mr Dexter. We'll be taking off soon.' Gary closed the door behind him and locked it shut. 'Once we're airborne, I'll get you a drink.'

As Nathan sank into the soft leather of the armchair, he looked out of the window and tried to make some sense out of the day's events. When he had left his house this morning, he had only had some vague clue that there was someone out there who could help him to clear his name and put paid to Adrian Delancey. And now? Now he was working for an organisation so secretive that it made the Elective look like a public institution, backed by more money than he could possibly imagine, headed by Marco's ex-boyfriend.

But he knew he had made the right decision. He wouldn't let anyone else get hurt by Delancey. Ever.

'Buckle up, please, Mr Dexter.' Nathan did as he was told, as the plane began to taxi along the runway. As the jets fired up and he was pushed back into his seat, he craned his neck to look out of the window. This was his favourite part of flying: the feeling of power as the jet took to the air, the sensation of being pushed back into your seat. Nathan smiled: when he had been a little kid, he'd always wanted to be an astronaut. This was as close as he was going to get.

It took only a few seconds after full burn for the aircraft to lift off; in moments they were airborne. He watched as the ground fell away. It didn't take long for them to fly over the half-built Millennium Dome, and Nathan had to admit to being impressed by its sheer size: the idea that you could fit all of Trafalgar Square inside – and Nelson's Column – was staggering. The plane then banked slightly and passed very close to the chrome and glass of his favourite building, Canary Wharf Tower, before heading over the Thames and out of London, out of England . . .

'Care for a drink, Mr Dexter?' said Gary, unbuckling his seat belt and getting up.

Nathan nodded. 'I'd love one. And please . . . Don't call me Mr Dexter. Makes me feel like my dad!'

Gary laughed, an easy chuckle which lightened the ominous atmosphere considerably. Wandering over to a beautiful polished wooden cabinet, Gary pulled down the front to reveal a collection of bottles and decanters.

'You drink whisky, don't you? A single-malt? Either that or Foster's.'

Lawrence had obviously done his research, but that was hardly surprising – Nathan would have been more surprised if he hadn't. Nathan thought that he was meticulous, but he didn't have billions of pounds and a two-hundred-year-old network of informants to take advantage of, did he?

Gary handed him a heavy tumbler of amber liquid, and Nathan gave it an appreciative sniff. Unless he was mistaken, it was Laphroaig. Very nice.

'Is that OK, Nathan?'

'Perfect, Gary.' He grinned. 'Why don't you make yourself a bit more comfortable?' He was assuming that Gary was there to assist him in all situations, and was pleased to see his assumption proved correct as Gary took off his jacket and hung it over his chair. He undid his top button, loosened his tie, and rolled up his sleeves. Nathan wasn't disappointed by the slight visual clues: Gary's arms were covered with thick brown hair, while a small tuft of the same peeked out from his collar. Just the way that Nathan liked it.

You *have* done your research, Lawrence.

'Perhaps you'd like to get even more comfortable?' urged Nathan, now desperate to see more of his assistant. Gary complied without comment: standing up, he unbuttoned his shirt, letting it hang free as he took off his shoes and removed his trousers.

Nathan was enthralled. Gary was a perfect example of the sort of bloke that Nathan fancied. Broad-shouldered, not too muscular, and absolutely covered in hair. Arms, legs, chest, back, all of him . . . Just looking at him gave Nathan an instant hard-on.

'Is there anything else I can do for you, Nathan?'

Feeling as randy as hell, Nathan didn't hesitate. 'Take my clothes off.'

Standing there, Nathan could feel the pressure of his cock against his jeans, and couldn't wait for Gary to release it, to suck it, to take it inside him . . .

The sensation of Gary's hands, undoing his Levi shirt, stroking Nathan's own chest hair, made Nathan shudder with anticipation. As Gary's hands dropped to the waistband of his jeans, he leant forward and kissed Nathan, a deep kiss, his tongue probing Nathan's mouth. Nathan's hands slipped round to Gary's back, his fingers running through the thick dark hair, as his tongue met Gary's, slid past and entered Gary's mouth. Their goatee beards rubbed against each other, and all Nathan wanted was to be closer to Gary, inside Gary, feeling Gary's arse draw his cock inside him, tight around him.

As his jeans fell to the carpet, Gary stopped kissing Nathan and fell to his knees. As his fingers undid the laces of Nathan's boots, his mouth came closer, closer to Nathan's groin. Nathan could feel Gary's beard scratching at his thighs, his tongue licking his balls. He let out a grunt as Gary took first one, then the other ball in his mouth and played with it, sucking and squeezing it until Nathan didn't think he could take much more. Gary stopped, and turned his attention to Nathan's cock, its eight inches so hard that it was almost flat against his hairy stomach. His tongue traced its way up the shaft, finishing with a teasing flick to Nathan's helmet. Then his mouth engulfed it, taking all of Nathan's shaft, the tongue still playing with the ridge of his helmet, his dick slit . . .

Nathan gently pushed him away. The way Nathan felt at the moment, too much of that would make him come. And he didn't want that. Not yet.

'Is there something else you'd like, sir?'

Sir. That one word alone was enough to turn Nathan on even more.

'I want to fuck you, Gary. I want to feel my dick inside you.'

Gary grinned. 'My pleasure, sir.' He took Nathan's hand and

guided him over to the white rug in the centre of the cabin. It was even thicker than the carpet that it lay on. Gary placed his hands on Nathan's shoulders and urged him on to the rug, so that he was lying down.

'You just lie there, sir. Let me take care of you.' Gary squatted over Nathan, his seven-inch cock stiff and proud, his balls heavy and almost touching Nathan's stomach. He produced a condom, seemingly from nowhere, and carefully rolled it over Nathan's sensitive dick. Even that was almost too much: Gary's fingers, stroking Nathan's thick shaft, made Nathan gasp with pleasure.

Gary completed his task, and gave Nathan a broad grin. 'Is that OK, sir?'

'Oh yes,' groaned Nathan. He could feel his helmet brushing against Gary's arse, and knew that all he wanted was to ram it inside the guy, force his way into his hot ring and slide it in and out until Gary brought him off . . .

Gary lowered himself, one hand between his legs, guiding Nathan until all of his shaft was buried inside Gary's arse. Nathan felt Gary squeeze himself around Nathan, eliciting a satisfied sigh from him. Nathan reached out and took Gary's cock in his hand, feeling the warm meat. He moved his thumb so it was resting on the wetness of Gary's slit, before rubbing it in small, circular movements. Now it was Gary's turn to gasp; the action drove Gary on, making him lift himself off Nathan's dick and then sit back on to it, faster and faster.

As Gary drew Nathan inside, Nathan carried on stroking the end of his cock, his other hand playing with Gary's balls, cupping them and squeezing them as they hit his stomach with each downward movement. Gary was grinning, his eyes closed with the pleasure that Nathan was causing. Nathan started to wank Gary, pulling on that thick cock, drawing the foreskin back and forth over Gary's hot, wet helmet.

'Oh yes, sir, yes sir . . .' said Gary breathlessly, as Nathan's other hand moved to his hairy chest, stroking it, scratching it, watching as this bear of a man took Nathan inside him, pulled

Nathan's dick inside him, faster and faster until Nathan knew he couldn't take any more.

He couldn't hear Gary's groans over his own shout of release as his come pumped from his dick, load after load of it inside Gary's hungry arse. Gary was shooting as well, hot gouts of white come raining over Nathan's chest, his beard, everywhere. Nathan carried on wanking, determined to get every last drop from Gary's pumping hardness, watching as the come continued to flow, over Nathan's hands, his stomach, as Nathan kept on shooting and shooting inside the man's arse.

With a heartfelt groan of total satisfaction, Nathan slumped back on to the rug, beaming with pleasure. Gary looked down at him, his own smile rivalling Nathan's.

'We've still got another hour before we reach Nice,' he said cheekily.

And Nathan could think of better ways of passing the time than reading the in-flight magazine.

Adrian Delancey read the report for the fourth time, still trying to make sense of what it meant. If it meant anything. If there was one thing that Delancey had learnt, it was that all information was a matter of interpretation.

And he had no idea how to interpret this.

Turning away from the PC monitor, he looked out of the patio doors, but the brilliant sunshine and birdsong did nothing to ease his mood. Something was going on – and he was determined to find out who was behind it. And why.

Even though Delancey was pretty certain that he had clipped Nathan Dexter's wings, he didn't like to leave anything to chance. Ever since that business in Gran Canaria, he had been occasionally following his erstwhile adversary's movements, just in case he suicidally tried to take on the Syndicate. Ironically, this was where the Elective had come to Delancey's aid: their revenge had been swift and brutal, effectively barring poor Nathan from every pub, bar and club in London and ensuring that he was virtually unemployable. Nathan had become predictable – boring, even.

But was that such a bad thing? Delancey had enjoyed their little game, enjoyed taking someone as insufferably good as Nathan Dexter and tearing his life apart, but that was exactly what it had been.

A game.

There was no time for games any more. With the Syndicate so close to final success, it was taking all of Delancey's skill to ensure victory. Almost with regret, Delancey had had to put his games to one side – all except this, the endgame. However, he had always made sure that he knew exactly what Dexter was up to.

But now . . . now he appeared to have simply vanished. And he wasn't the only one. Over the last few months, a number of the key people whom Delancey kept a close eye on had dropped out of sight. Some of them – like that two-faced bastard Marco Capiello – were gone only for the odd afternoon. But others had apparently simply . . . vanished.

Another man, a less vigilant man, might have assumed that this was the result of stupidity or inefficiency on the part of those paid to watch these people, but Delancey knew that he had assigned his best people to this task. This just wasn't possible . . .

Unless he was up against somebody else, somebody with the same type of resources as the Syndicate.

The obvious answer was the Elective, but Delancey knew that organisation too well: even at its height, it wasn't *that* good. God knew, he himself had tried to use its resources to make people disappear, to no avail.

No, there was another player in the game, a player who was on a par with Delancey and the Syndicate, a player who had chosen to use Nathan Dexter as their weapon.

So they would have to be stopped. Delancey would identify them and confront them, persuade them to step aside or be crushed underfoot by the relentless advance of the Syndicate –

He stopped. Another message had just come through, and the subject line showed it to be urgent. Of course, it could be nothing – his agents in the field were only too fond of seeing everything as being urgent – but he supposed that he ought to read it.

He was very glad that he did.

Picking up the phone, he dialled a number.

'David, it's Adrian. I want you to get yourself the next flight to Nice.' No, that would be too late. Far too late. This needed to be headed off at the pass. If the other player was showing his hand . . . 'Scratch that – I'll have one of the Learjets standing by at City Airport. Once you reach Nice, get a helicopter to Monte Carlo.

'One of the pieces has decided to jump back on to the board. So it's time to show him the meaning of checkmate.'

Putting down the phone, Delancey studied the message again, with one question paramount.

Nathan Dexter didn't have the resources to go to Monte Carlo. Not any more.

So who did?

Six

————

'I was beginning to wonder where you were,' said Scott, trying to peer over Leigh's shoulder into the room. There wasn't anything to see – Pete had left about an hour ago, and Leigh had meticulously remade the bed to hide any evidence – but the pang of guilt that Leigh was feeling was making him extremely paranoid.

And if you carry on like this, Scott's going to guess something's up, he chided himself.

'I . . . I fell asleep. Sorry, have you been knocking?'

Scott barged into the room; the way he was looking around, it was clear that he didn't believe a word of it. Then Leigh realised that Scott's attention was focused on the carpet next to the bed – and the crumpled towel that he and Pete had used to clean up with. He gave Scott an abashed smile. 'I'll tell you about it later.'

'Don't worry – whatever it was, your secret's safe with me. Anyway, I've been out for a walk. And I've come to a few decisions. When we get back, I'm going to see if Nathan wants to make another go of it.'

'Scott – that's great!' Then he thought of something. 'You weren't thinking of going back now, were you?'

'No – I still want to see what Brighton's got to offer.' He gave a wicked grin. 'For all I know, this could be my last night of freedom.'

The sun was just getting low on the horizon as the Learjet approached Nice; the city lights were glittering in the impending twilight, and Nathan found the whole thing quite alluring.

He had fleetingly visited Nice a couple of years ago, but that had been on a press trip to Cannes, and he had just been passing through. It had been nothing like this, though: fair enough, it was BA Business Class, but that still wasn't a Learjet, was it? And BA doesn't offer you your own personal Gary, either, he thought.

As the plane approached the airport, Nathan suddenly realised that this was the first time he had been outside the country since Gran Canaria. A trap for Adrian Delancey. Like this was.

He just hoped that he was more successful this time.

Nathan swigged the last of his whisky as the plane touched the runway in one of the gentlest landings Nathan had ever experienced. I could get used to this, he decided.

'I suppose this is where we part company,' he said to Gary, not without a trace of regret. The little bear cub had been the epitome of hospitality, and Nathan couldn't remember when he had enjoyed himself so much. Certainly not since the first time he had heard the name Adrian Delancey.

'Oh no, Nathan. I've been assigned to help you on every step of the journey.' He grinned impishly. 'I'm going all the way.'

Nathan cocked an eyebrow. 'I don't doubt that.'

At that moment, the plane reached its final resting place on the runway and stopped. Nathan unbuckled his seat belt.

'How are we getting to Monte Carlo?' When he had visited Cannes, he and his fellow journalists had piled into a people carrier for the short journey to the gambling capital of Europe. 'Road?'

Gary shook his head. 'You'll see,' he answered mysteriously.

'You're kidding.' Nathan stood on the tarmac, his eyes wide in surprise. After leaving the Learjet, he had expected to follow

Gary through the airport to their mode of transport. Fair enough, he hadn't expected a people carrier – this *was* the Hellfire Club. It'll probably be a limo, or a Rolls, he had decided.

He hadn't expected a helicopter.

Dressed in the silver-grey livery that Nathan was beginning to recognise as the Hellfire Club's colours, the small helicopter sat on the tarmac next to the Learjet, its blades a blur above it.

'Next stop, Le Palais du Cypresse, Monte Carlo.' Gary obviously found Nathan's expression of shock highly amusing. 'Or does sir find this too ostentatious?'

'I'll get you for this,' Nathan hissed.

'Can't wait,' said Gary, ducking beneath the spinning blades and opening the door. 'After you.'

As Nathan buckled himself in and placed the comms headset over his head, he felt the faintest trace of unease. Although he had travelled by plane more times than he cared to remember, this was the first time he had ever been in a helicopter. Planes were easy: you could just about forget that you were a mile in the sky, surrounded by nothing more than a few thousand tons of metal – especially with Gary to distract you. But this: the large windows meant that there was no way you could ignore the fact that you were dependent on a couple of spinning blades and the laws of physics for your safety.

'I've never been in one of these before,' he explained into the microphone of the headset.

'Don't worry about it.' Gary placed a reassuring hand on Nathan's knee, and squeezed. Nathan smiled.

'I hadn't been in a helicopter until about two years ago,' Gary continued. 'And now . . . well, I even learnt how to fly one.'

'Thanks. We'll know what to do if the pilot falls out.' Having Gary there was a great reassurance. But it was more than that: there was something about Gary that Nathan found comforting. It was as if they had known each other for years, had been part of each other's life for ages. It was really odd feeling – and the trouble was, Nathan found it frighteningly familiar. Wonderfully familiar.

He was falling for Gary.

What the hell was he going to do about it?

But that line of thought was swept away by the sudden sensation of movement, as the helicopter lifted itself off the runway in a series of small jerks, hovering there for a couple of seconds before heading off into the dusk.

Nathan's initial trepidation vanished – this was great! The helicopter sped over the airport; in seconds they were over the ocean. It felt strange: the helicopter's nose was pointed downward, but they were travelling forwards. It was nothing like being in a plane: every slight movement, every turn, every bank, was amplified. Every part of his body moved in time with the helicopter. This really *was* flying!

'You'll have about an hour to freshen up and get changed before the meeting, Nathan,' said Gary, checking his Psion Organiser.

As the helicopter left the coast and started to fly over the serene blue of the Mediterranean, Nathan suddenly realised that he had been so caught up in the adventure that he actually had no real idea what he was doing, or what he was expected to do. The very fact that he was doing *something*, compared with the aimless drifting of the last few months, had been almost intoxicating. But now, as the helicopter flew over the picturesque bay of Nice, the time had come for a few answers.

'Since you seem to know a lot more about this than I do, care to fill in a few details?' he asked.

Gary shrugged. 'There isn't a lot to tell – I only know what we've got planned for this evening.' And then, a little sheepishly, he added 'You're not the only one that Lawrence keeps in the dark.'

Nathan was beginning to realise that Lawrence was every bit as calculating as Delancey. He just hoped that he was siding with the guys in the white hats – and not even bigger bastards. 'So, tonight's dinner. Who's it with?'

'I don't actually know. Apparently, Lawrence has been in touch with him, but he won't make himself known until we get to the hotel. He's terrified that Delancey will locate him.'

Delancey again. But the fact that this mysterious person was afraid of Delancey suggested that he knew something, something important, something that might help them to bring Delancey down.

'Do you know, for someone who doesn't like mysteries, I seem to find myself at the centre of rather too many of them,' Nathan muttered.

'I bet you wouldn't have it any other way,' said Gary.

Watching the smooth waters of the Mediterranean pass beneath them, the tantalising lights of Monte Carlo growing ever closer, Nathan knew that Gary was absolutely right.

Lawrence had insisted that Marco stay for dinner, and Marco had been unable to refuse. Quite apart from what he knew would be an unsurpassable meal – Mrs Clarke was an excellent cook – he just didn't want to go. Not now, not ever. If this was all he was going to get, all the time that he was going to spend with Lawrence, he wanted it to last.

Now, with the remains of the meal heaped in front of them – scallops and smoked salmon, followed by venison that Marco would have died for – sitting there nursing an enormous brandy balloon full of Louis XIII, Marco felt a contentment that had eluded him for nearly five years.

'When do I leave for Germany?' he asked, well aware that he was starting to slur.

Lawrence gave him a lopsided smile, and Marco had to smile to himself. During their relationship, it had been Lawrence who had always chastised Marco for drinking too much: seeing Lawrence even slightly worse for wear was highly amusing.

'Oh, not until tomorrow at the earliest.' He glanced at the grandfather clock in the corner of the dining room, and once again Marco was overawed by the sheer display of wealth, especially since he knew that all of the antiques in the town house were simply the overspill from Dashwood Hall, Lawrence's ancestral home.

'Nathan should just be arriving in Monaco. If he makes contact with Brett, he should have the first bit of information that we need.'

'Who's Brett?'

Lawrence steepled his fingers. 'You and Nathan have been fighting Delancey the wrong way, Marco. You've been using the mechanics of the Elective against him, forgetting that he's the past master of political intrigue.' Lawrence smiled. 'Apparently it's in the blood. Sir Henry Delancey almost ruined the Hellfire Club in the middle of the last century thanks to his machinations. That, and an indiscretion with a minor royal in a homosexual brothel in Spitalfields.

'Anyway, you've been forgetting one thing. An easy thing to forget, I'll grant you, but something very, very important. Delancey's a person.'

Marco frowned. He knew that he had drunk far too much, but Lawrence wasn't making much sense. 'What do you mean?'

'He has a past, Marco. Discarded lovers, badly treated one-night stands, betrayed business partners . . . A whole catalogue of enemies that you haven't even heard of. Individually, they're all too frightened of Delancey to act. But together, working for a common cause . . .'

'And this Brett? Where does he fit into all of this?'

'Brett McMasters was Adrian Delancey's first business partner, when they were young city traders in the eighties. Thatcher's boys to a T, without morals, without conscience. Unfortunately for Brett, he developed both morals and a conscience. He refused to stand by when Delancey raided a pension fund to buy some Far East securities. But, before he could act, Delancey got wind of it and stitched him up, had him fired and made him unemployable.'

'Sounds familiar.' But Marco wasn't thinking of Delancey – he was thinking about Nathan. That was exactly what the Elective had done to him. Perhaps the taint of Delancey hadn't been cleansed from the Elective. Perhaps his cancer was too insidious, too deeply ingrained.

'For the last ten years, Brett's been working in Germany. He set up his own business, far away from Delancey, and was becoming very successful. Then, about three years ago, Delancey found out about it. He mobilised the Elective to shut Brett's business down.

'But I got there first. The Hellfire Club bought Brett's business and helped him to vanish. And now . . .'

'He wants revenge,' Marco completed. Was that what all of this was about? Revenge?

Lawrence frowned. 'He wants justice, Marco.'

'Justice is nothing more than civilised revenge.' Then he laughed at just how pretentious that had sounded. 'Perhaps I've had too much to drink. Perhaps I ought to go.' Where did *that* come from? Marco heard the words slip out, but he didn't mean them.

'I don't want you to go,' said Lawrence softly. 'I want you to stay the night.'

'With me.'

The Aquarium down Steine Street was packed to the rafters with a mixture of all types: Muscle Marys, clones, pretty boys . . . all determined to have a good time. And that included Scott and Leigh. Leigh drained his cider and ordered another round of drinks.

'Well?'

'Well, what? If someone had sent me a bear for the afternoon, I would have done exactly the same thing,' said Scott reassuringly. 'What are you worried about?'

'I . . .' Leigh actually wasn't sure. Yes, he had slept with someone else, but that was part of the agreement that he and Marco had. As long as they didn't get involved, that was the cardinal rule . . . As he handed over the money, he tried to pinpoint it, but could come up with only one answer.

He had enjoyed it too much. He wanted to get involved.

After handing over Scott's drink, Leigh held out his hands. 'I don't know, and I don't care.' Tonight wasn't a time for heavy emotional baggage: they both needed a break from everything.

114

And Brighton was going to give it to them. 'Where shall we go later?'

Scott frowned. 'I'm not sure. I've never been to Brighton before, remember?' He looked over Leigh's shoulder. 'Actually, I'll go wherever he's going.'

Leigh turned to see what had attracted Scott's attention – and felt his heart miss a beat when he realised who it was.

Pete. His pet bear.

Scott must have spotted the look of shock on Leigh's face. 'You know him, don't you?' This was reinforced when Pete started pushing his way towards them. Scott broke into a grin. 'It's that bloke, isn't it? The bear?'

Before Leigh could answer, Pete was standing next to them. He grabbed Leigh in an affectionate hug and kissed him on the lips.

'Hi. Thought you might be in here. I've got tickets for the three of us to go to the VIP night at Club Extreme. Interested?' He turned to Scott. 'You must be Scott – heard a lot about you from Nathan. I'm Pete.'

At the mention of Nathan, Scott shivered, but tried not to let it show. He shook Pete's hand, desperately trying not to imagine Pete standing in front of him, naked. He was wearing a white shirt and jeans, with the sleeves of the shirt rolled up to reveal beefy, hairy arms. Leigh's description hadn't come close to the gorgeous hairy bear standing there. You lucky bastard, thought Scott. I wouldn't mind, but we came here to cheer me up. I'm the one who's single!

Then he realised what he had just heard. 'Club Extreme? You're kidding.' Club Extreme was the most exclusive nightclub in Brighton, and the VIP night doubly so.

Pete grinned. 'Not at all.' He reached into his back pocket and pulled out three black tickets.

'Sounds great,' said Leigh, enthusiastically. 'We were just trying to decide where to go.'

'Then that's sorted,' said Pete. 'Drink, anyone?'

As Pete leant over the bar, Scott started to wonder about

Leigh. Was his relationship with Marco as strong as he made out? Or were they about to go the same way as Scott and Nathan?

He hoped not.

'Just a second,' Nathan called out in response to the knock at the door, as he adjusted his bow tie for the umpteenth time. Despite all the galas and award ceremonies he had attended over the years, he had never got the hang of tying a bow tie, and was beginning to doubt that he ever would. Giving it one last check in the mirror, he strode over to the door and opened it. Gary was standing there, dressed exactly the same as Nathan: black dinner suit and bow tie. 'Exactly' was just the right word: the two, in their suits, with their similar haircuts and goatee beards.

You make a good couple, said his inner voice. Did they? Or was he just desperate for another relationship? He just didn't know any more, which was why it was all the more important to concentrate on the here and now. On the fight against Delancey.

'Thought I'd see if you were ready.'

Nathan beckoned him in. 'Just about. It's been over a year since I last had to squeeze myself into one of these. How do I look? I feel like a nightclub bouncer.'

'Have to see if we can find you one, then.' Gary enfolded Nathan in a hug and gave him a deep, passionate kiss. He finally pulled away. 'Anyway, does that answer your question?'

Nathan didn't know what to say. Their feelings appeared to be mutual, but Nathan just didn't know how to proceed. What about Scott? What about Delancey? No – he wasn't even going to think about it. He had a job to do. Patting his jacket to check that he had everything, he cast a last look around the room and ushered Gary out into the corridor.

Nathan had stayed in more hotels than he cared to remember. Some had been nothing more than a bed for the night, but others had been luxury. He thought of the places he had stayed either as a journalist or on Elective business, such as his all-time favourite, the Senator in Munich, or the opulent Garden Palace in Marrakech. But nothing could have prepared him for Le Palais du Cypresse.

His room was enormous, and simply dripped money and style. The bed was about three times the size of his king-size back in Docklands, while the antique furniture and ornaments would have given Lawrence's town house a run for its money. Nathan didn't even want to think what this was costing the Hellfire Club, but he was determined to make the most of it. After months of being treated as a nonperson, the way that the staff behaved towards him, the knowledge that everything he wanted was simply a phone call away, was almost intoxicating. Then he looked at Gary, and another emotion stirred inside him. Gary must have sensed that Nathan was staring at him, and gave him a warm grin.

Money, respect, love.

It was all too good to be true. With that cynical thought buzzing round his head, Nathan followed Gary down the corridor towards the Imperial Suite.

Towards the first step in putting paid to Adrian Delancey.

Club Extreme was legendary. It was the living embodiment of the old nightclub joke: 'If you're not on the list, you're not coming in.' And getting on the list was about as likely as winning the lottery.

Somehow, Scott and Leigh were on the list.

Club Extreme was based in a converted hotel. The façade was still in the ever-present Georgian style that was so common in Brighton, but the new owners had painted it entirely black. Nestled between two more conventionally white hotels, it looked like a pool of darkness, a void.

It was a void that Leigh was really looking forward to seeing. The rumours about the clientele and the goings-on at Club Extreme were as varied as the descriptions of its interior, and he couldn't wait to boast about it when he got back to London.

Pete led the way to the main entrance, although one rumour asserted that there was another entrance, specifically for those who didn't want their presence to be advertised. Once inside, it didn't matter – nothing mattered. Beyond the doors of Club Extreme, everything was rumour and hearsay, nothing could be proved.

Having handed over the three tickets, Pete waited as the bouncer checked on the famous list. Satisfied, he ushered the three of them inside.

The entrance hall was anything but black: from the thickly carpeted floor to the high, domed ceiling, everything was mirrored, making it very difficult to get a true impression of its size. Leigh guessed that it was about twenty feet across, leading to two doorways, dark arches in the mirrored walls.

'Dance floor and main bar to the left,' Pete explained, 'quiet bar to the right. There are a few other bars, but I'm sure you'll find them.'

'Isn't there a VIP bar or something?' asked Scott. 'Somewhere forbidden to us lesser mortals?'

Pete shook his head. 'Tonight, Scott, we're all VIPs. Or all lesser mortals. Anything goes at Club Extreme,' he said ominously.

'I fancy a quiet drink before the evening gets going,' said Leigh. 'Any other takers?'

Pete nodded. 'Sounds good to me.' With that, the three of them walked through the darkened archway.

The 'quiet bar' wasn't quite what Leigh had expected. It was huge – about the size of the Collective. Indeed, it had the same sort of circular bar in the centre. But that was where the similarity ended. The floor was thickly carpeted in deep blue, and the distant walls were rag-washed in a complementary but lighter shade of the same colour. The walls were straight – every few feet two of the walls met at an angle, marked with an ionic column that met the ceiling high above them. In front of the walls, leather sofas and armchairs were dotted about.

Even this early in the evening – Club Extreme didn't close until the next morning – there were quite a few people in the bar.

'Smart,' whispered Scott. 'Bet the drinks don't come cheap,' he added ruefully.

'No money ever changes hands in here,' said Pete, stroking his beard. 'Who do you reckon runs the place?'

You didn't have to be a rocket scientist to work out the answer to that one. 'The Elective,' Scott replied.

'Exactly. Right – sit yourselves down, and I'll get us some drinks.'

As Pete walked over to the bar, Scott shook his head. 'I don't like this at all. It just doesn't feel right.'

'Why?'

'Leigh, Nathan can't move in London thanks to the Elective. And we're getting pissed and partying at the Elective's expense.'

Leigh's voice was hard when he replied. 'Look, Scott, my boyfriend happens to be the Comptroller of the Elective – at least for the time being.' Even as he said the words, Leigh wondered whether he had said more than he intended. Did he mean that Marco was planning to leave the Elective soon? Or that Marco wouldn't be his boyfriend for much longer? Watching the stocky figure of Pete as he stood at the bar, Leigh just wasn't sure.

He continued, 'Like it or not, I'm part of the Elective. If you don't like it . . . well, piss off to Revenge or something.' Hard words, but the whole point of this weekend was to cheer Scott up. If he wanted to whinge and mope, then Leigh would rather he do it elsewhere.

Scott sighed. 'I'm sorry. I promise I'll enjoy myself, OK?'

Leigh grinned. 'OK – truce. Let's find somewhere to sit.' He looked around. As he did so, somebody knocked into him.

'Sorry,' said the culprit before moving off.

Leigh's voice was hushed as he spoke to Scott. 'Was that who I thought it was?'

Scott shrugged, looking as surprised as Leigh felt. 'I didn't even know that he was gay.' As they watched the celebrity walk to the bar, Leigh knew that it was going to an interesting night.

★

Marco sank back into the plush blue leather of the couch and sighed with contentment. Dinner was over, and he and Lawrence had retired to yet another of the town house's many rooms. This one, the Blue Room, had been Marco's favourite after the Summer Room. Everything was decked out in shades of blue: the carpet, the walls, the furniture – even the paintings on the walls were predominantly blue. But it wasn't a cold blue: it was a refreshing blue, the blue of a Mediterranean evening, the blue you looked up into when you were sitting by the pool savouring the first cocktail of the night.

The blue that made Marco feel that everything was going to be all right.

Once they had reached the Blue Room, Marco had helped Lawrence from his wheelchair and guided him to the couch, both surprised and delighted that Lawrence had regained some movement in his legs. He was never going to run the London Marathon, but he wasn't a cripple any more.

'How do you feel?' asked Lawrence softly. 'If this makes you feel uncomfortable . . .'

Uncomfortable? Quite the opposite: this just seemed so . . . so right. Marco winked at Lawrence and squeezed his arm tighter around his shoulders. 'I feel alive,' Marco whispered. 'I feel . . . young.'

Lawrence snuggled up closer to him. 'Just for tonight, it would be good to just forget about all of it. The Elective, the Syndicate, the Hellfire Club . . . and Leigh.'

Marco frowned. 'You know about Leigh?'

'Of course I do. I know where you met him, how you met him . . . the lot.'

'I . . . I don't know what to say.'

'Don't say anything, Marco. I'm not asking for a life-long commitment from you. I'm just asking for one night.' His tone was almost pleading.

Marco stared into those penetrating blue eyes, those eyes that had captivated him so long ago, those eyes that had drawn him into the greatest, deepest love of his life.

'It won't be just one night,' he said quietly. 'Not now. I love you, Lawrence.'

'And I love you, Marco.' Lawrence kissed him on the cheek, first gently, then harder, with more passion. His lips moved round to Marco's jaw, to his mouth, forcing themselves on him, assaulting him. But there wasn't any resistance. It was everything that Marco wanted, everything that he had dreamt of for the last five years.

His hands tugged at Lawrence's shirt, a pale blue one that he had changed into for dinner. Marco wanted to rip it off his back – he was that desperate to feel his body against Lawrence's once again. But he wouldn't. Their lovemaking had always been a gentle matter, and, even though Marco had waited years for this moment, he wanted it to be just like it had been.

Undoing the last button, he eased the shirt off Lawrence, and was pleased to see that his body was exactly how he remembered it. Fit, but not too muscular, with a broad, hairy chest. Without hesitating, he nuzzled up against the thick fur, the smell of Lawrence bringing back all the memories, even the ones that he had locked away because they were too painful. But they weren't painful any more.

Lawrence continued to kiss him, his hands pulling at Marco's T-shirt. Freeing it from his jeans, he paused from kissing him for a second as he drew it over Marco's head, revealing Marco's thickset, hairy body. Lawrence had always called him his pet gorilla, which was apt – his chest hair spilt over his shoulders and back. Some people found that a turn-off, but Lawrence loved it. Had loved it. Would love it . . . Marco decided not to look for reasons or explanations. He wanted to enjoy the moment.

'My pet gorilla,' whispered Lawrence, and Marco felt his cock stiffen even more at the old nickname. 'Fancy giving me a hand upstairs. I'm not as good on my feet as I used to be,' he said lightly.

Marco got to his feet, and helped Lawrence up. As he had noticed earlier, Lawrence was no longer entirely wheelchair-bound, but he was still a bit shaky.

'Put your arm round me,' he said softly.

Complying, Lawrence leant into him for support. 'This makes a change,' he whispered. 'I've lost count of the number of nights I've had to carry you up to bed after one too many.' He paused. 'Does Leigh have to carry you to bed?'

The mention of Leigh's name hurt, but not for the reason that Marco would have expected. Marco didn't miss him, and didn't even feel hurt by that. It was as if the last five years had been nothing but a dream, like Bobby coming out of the shower in *Dallas*.

With that thought buzzing round his head, he supported Lawrence as they mounted the stairs.

Marco remembered which door led to Lawrence's bedroom – indeed, how could he forget? He had lost count of the number of mornings he had woken up in his flat in St John's Wood after a particularly vivid dream about Lawrence, only to be crucified with disappointment when he realised that it hadn't happened. Lawrence pushed open the door and walked in first.

Reaching the bed, Lawrence lowered himself on to the black duvet. Looking up at Marco, he grinned. 'Just like old times,' he said quietly.

If only. Marco immediately stopped himself. All that mattered was this evening, nothing else. He wouldn't – couldn't – think about tomorrow. It hurt too much.

With Lawrence so close, Marco didn't hesitate: he pulled him even closer, desperate to feel the warmth of his body next to his. They started to kiss again, but there, with his arm around Lawrence's shoulders, their mouths pressed together, Marco froze.

Lawrence gave him a puzzled look. 'What's wrong, Marco?' he asked, moving round so that his body was facing Marco's.

Marco shrugged. 'I'm worried. After all this time –'

'After all this time, you're worried that you're going to be a disappointment, that this could never live up to what you've thought about, night after night?'

Marco gave an embarrassed smile. Either Lawrence was an exceptional mind reader, or he was also describing how he felt.

'Well let me tell you something,' said Lawrence. 'You never have been and never could be a disappointment.'

Marco sighed. Relieved that Lawrence understood, Marco's eyes dropped to Lawrence's groin, his trousers barely restraining the bulge inside. A small patch of wetness was growing on the beige material – that was enough to force Marco's stumbling fingers to undo the belt and unzip the fly.

Marco couldn't keep his eyes off Lawrence's hard-on, the thick, eight-inch dick which Marco had sucked and wanked and allowed into him for five long years, a time that he had thought would never end.

Lawrence had been everything that Marco could have had hoped for – and more than he could ever have dreamt of. Deep, deep inside, Marco could feel that familiar aching pain growing dull as it healed, and yet there were alarm bells ringing: Marco had been hurt before, and the last thing he wanted was to go through that pain again. Not with Lawrence.

Marco's hand gripped Lawrence's dick, pulling the thick foreskin up and down over his moist helmet in a gentle rhythm. Lawrence groaned softly, his own hand reaching out and stroking Marco's erection. It was Marco's turn to groan. 'Let me get your trousers off,' Marco hissed. It took him a couple of seconds to pull them around his legs. Marco had been worried that years of being in a wheelchair would have affected Lawrence physically as well as mentally, but he was pleased to see that his legs were still well muscled.

Lawrence must have caught the admiring glance. 'I can still exercise,' he explained. 'But my favourite exercise . . . well, I haven't done that for a while,' he said mischievously. He placed a hand on Marco's groin and pressed, making Marco shudder.

Marco cuffed Lawrence affectionately around the ear with his free hand, but didn't break his stride. His hand squeezed Lawrence's cock and wanked it, but then Marco remembered what Lawrence really liked. He brought his thumb to his mouth and wet it, before returning his attentions to Lawrence's cock. He began to wank it once again, but with his wet thumb rubbing Lawrence's hot helmet with small circular movements. It didn't take long for Marco's spit to be joined by Lawrence's own pre-come. Lawrence gasped, unzipping Marco's jeans and freeing his own thick cock.

'I'd forgotten what this was like,' Lawrence whispered.

'I hadn't,' said Marco. Then, before he could help himself, he found himself whispering something that he'd been trying to keep to himself.

'I love you, Laz.' *Damn!* Marco could have hit himself. That's it, Marco, he thought: ruin the moment. And use the pet name, just to really rub it in. But Lawrence didn't say anything: he didn't have to. The look in his eyes, those deep brown eyes . . .

'Gorilla,' he hissed. Then he slid across the duvet to get even closer to Marco and put his free hand around his shoulders, massaging the sensitive region at the base of Marco's neck.

He remembered my soft spot, thought Marco, shuddering with pleasure. Even as that sent wave after wave of almost electrical excitement through him, Lawrence started to nibble at Marco's beard, tiny sharp bites that started at his throat and continued upward, reaching his chin before moving round to his moustache, biting and nibbling all the time.

Neither of them was silent during this: they had never been silent when making love. Marco grunted with each tiny bite, while Lawrence growled like a wild animal, low guttural sounds in Marco's ear – familiar sounds. Words no longer mattered: everything had been reduced to its lowest, basest level.

Or its highest level, thought Marco.

He neither knew nor cared how long this moment lasted. Lawrence was virtually clamped around his neck, kissing and biting, while one hand continued to play with Marco's erection, the other with Marco's nipples, seeking them out through the thick black mat of hair. Marco's hand was around Lawrence's dick, stroking, wanking, rubbing the helmet; together, they were reaching levels of ecstasy that he had thought he had forgotten about. Marco pulled at Lawrence's chest, tugging at the hair, running his fingers through it.

As Lawrence pleasured him, Marco began to groan, getting so close to orgasm that he was sorely tempted to push Lawrence away.

I want this to last for ever, he thought desperately. Lawrence finally found Marco's mouth and kissed him deeply once more, and Marco responded immediately, moving his other arm so that it was around Lawrence's strong, smooth back. He pulled him even closer, but he didn't want them to be close: he wanted them to be one, closer than two people could be. All the time, the two of them continued to wank each other, their rhythms matching. The sounds of their frantic actions became louder and louder, groans and gasps, their strokes in perfect time, their mouths locked together.

'I'm not far off,' sighed Lawrence, a flush coming to his face as he stiffened while Marco continued to wank him off. But Lawrence didn't try to pull away: neither of them wanted to hold off, and he wasn't going to stop – not when he was so close as well. He carried on, wanking faster and faster, knowing exactly what strokes would bring him off. He took his arm from around Lawrence's shoulders and felt his way through the chest hair, grabbing Lawrence's right nipple and squeezing it, squeezing it hard, just as Lawrence liked.

Marco knew what the result would be. With a yell of abandon, Lawrence came, spunk gushing out in thick white gouts that splashed on to his stomach hair and covered Marco's hand. But Marco wasn't concerned: even as Lawrence was shooting his load, he didn't stop wanking Marco; Marco realised that he had been holding himself back, and let Lawrence's actions take control. It took only a few seconds: Marco's cock flexed and tensed in Lawrence's grip, and Marco pulled Lawrence closer, feeling Lawrence's body touching his, the damp chest hair, mingled with sweat and come, rubbing against his own . . . He grunted as come shot from his cock, hitting his stomach and chest again and again. He let Lawrence jerk the last few drops of come out of him as he sighed.

Finally, panting with exertion, the two of them lay – although perhaps 'collapsed' would have been a better word – on their backs, ignoring the warm dampness of the black duvet. Lawrence turned to look at Marco.

'All right?' he asked.

Marco grinned, but he couldn't think of the words, couldn't turn his churning emotions into anything useful.

He didn't have to. The expression on Lawrence's face, the way he hugged Marco towards him, was enough.

As sleep began to take over, Marco's last thoughts were not of himself, or even of Lawrence.

They were of Leigh.

I'm sorry, mate, he thought. I'm sorry.

Seven

Nathan stood in the doorway of the Imperial Suite, momentarily taken aback by the sheer concentration of wealth that
confronted him.

As far as he could see, the room was full of gambling tables.
And, since the room was as big as a football pitch, that was a lot
of gambling tables, each one a centre of action and excitement.

'I feel so out of place,' he hissed to Gary. But how out of place
was he? Looking at the gamblers, he realised one thing. They
were all men. Men laughing together, gambling together – and
more. Open displays of affection, men kissing, touching one
another . . .

'This is a gay hotel?' He found it hard to believe that a gay
hotel could exist in Monte Carlo without Nathan's having heard
of it.

Gary shook his head. 'Not entirely. The Elective hires the
Imperial Suite once a month.'

Nathan shot Gary a shocked look, although he knew that he
shouldn't have been surprised: when wealth and homosexuality
met, the Elective wasn't going to far behind, was it? 'The
Elective? Oh God, I'm going to be popular, aren't I?'

'Calm down,' said Gary, putting his hand on Nathan's arm.

PAUL C. ALEXANDER

'No one knows who you are. These are the French and German arms of the Elective. They've never heard of Nathan Dexter.'

Famous last words! But he was here now, and had no choice but to act out the role that Lawrence had created for him. 'I hope not. Anyway, where are we supposed to be meeting our "friend"?'

'He said he'd be playing roulette next to the fountain.'

Nathan scanned the room. The decoration was ornate but not fussy: gold and white, with lots of cherubs. The green baize of the tables stood out clearly. Where was the fountain?

About halfway down the room, to the side, a tall fountain of white marble was shooting a spray of water into the air. A roulette table stood next to it, with six men watching the wheel intently.

'I suppose we'd better locate our quarry,' said Nathan, leading the way. 'This is just so melodramatic,' he whispered.

Gary laughed. 'You love it.'

As they reached the table, the men were cheering. One of the party had just won – three red, apparently – and was adding his spoils to the large pile of chips in front of him. Nathan took an opening at the table and surreptitiously tried to study the six men. Which of them was it?

In this environment, it was difficult to judge them. In a club, they might have been in leather or rubber, or combat gear. But, dressed in their ubiquitous dinner suits, they displayed little to distinguish them.

Number one was shorter than Nathan, mid-thirties, clean-shaven, with swept-back blond hair. His watery blue eyes suggested that he was German.

Number two was dark-haired, with a full beard, and again looked very Germanic – about forty, Nathan guessed. Three and four could have been twins: cloned from the Dolph Lundgren gene pool, they looked as if they had been poured into their dinner suits, which bulged with their muscles. Five was a possibility: he too was furtively glancing around the table. He was quite sweet: much shorter than Nathan, he had a bushy moustache and a stocky build. In his suit, he really did look like a nightclub bouncer.

The final suspect was about thirty-five, with an almost geometrically perfect, blond flat-top, square jaw, and his attention firmly on the table. Which wasn't surprising. He was the one who was winning.

For a moment, Nathan was at a loss as to what to do. It was Gary – wonderful, indispensable Gary – who came to his rescue: he placed a pile of chips on the table. Nathan had to rein in his shock: there must have been over ten thousand pounds there!

'What's this for?' he hissed.

'Nathan: every single person in this casino is a millionaire. So, even if you're not, you've got to act like one. Have you ever played roulette before?'

'A long time ago.' Nathan remembered a very drunken evening, many years ago, when he and his then partner had lost about five hundred pounds in a casino in Portsmouth. The next day, nursing his hangover and his overdraft, Nathan had sworn never to repeat the experience.

Until now, obviously.

'Your bet, sir?' The heavy accent of the croupier brought him back to the present. The man had the dark skin and hair of a Monégasque, with an engaging smile that Nathan found enticing, especially since he knew the rules of the Elective: everything was on offer, everything could be bought. But he was here for a purpose.

'A thousand dollars on thirteen red,' he instructed, and watched as the croupier moved his chips, before repeating the question to the Dolph Lundgren twins.

'You're English.' The statement came from the man with the blond flat top. The one who was winning.

Nathan nodded. 'I'm . . .' He hesitated. What if he gave his name, only to be unmasked as the archenemy of the Elective?

'Nathan Dexter?' The man held out his hand. 'Lawrence's description didn't do you justice. I'm Brett McMasters. Pleased to meet you.'

Nathan shook his hand. 'You appear to be winning, Brett.'

The other man shrugged. 'More luck than anything. This is the first time I've played roulette for years. I just thought it would be a good place to meet.'

'Thirteen red!' announced the croupier. It took Nathan a few seconds to register that he'd won, and he stared in shock at the pile of chips that was pushed towards him. Even though it wasn't his money, he could feel the intoxicating thrill of winning coursing through him.

'Seems like you're the lucky one,' said Brett. 'Shall we quit while we're ahead and get a drink?'

'Sounds like a good idea. Gary?'

'I'd prefer us to be alone, if you don't mind.' Brett looked around nervously. 'No offence,' he said to Gary, 'but I've learnt to be paranoid.'

Gary smiled, but Nathan could see he was put out. 'No problem. I've got things to attend to, anyway.' With that, he headed off to the far side of the casino. Nathan suddenly felt angry – why couldn't Gary join them? What the hell was so important, anyway? But he immediately realised that he was overreacting: Gary was here to help, and, if that meant leaving Nathan and Brett alone, well . . . that was what he was paid to do.

The only problem was, Nathan was already missing his company.

'The Silver Lounge is supposed to be quite good,' said Brett. 'Serves an excellent Margarita, apparently.'

'Lead the way,' said Nathan. But he still found himself looking across the casino for Gary.

After a few drinks in the quiet bar, Scott had decided to explore the rest of the Club Extreme. He was actually feeling a bit guilty: Leigh had gone to a lot of trouble over this weekend, and Scott was repaying him by being an absolute bastard. He was so preoccupied with his thoughts that he suddenly realised that he was completely lost: he wasn't sure that he could even have found his way back to the quiet bar.

Oh well, just keep going, he told himself. You'll soon end up somewhere.

The club seemed to be full of corridors. Then again, it had been a hotel. Scott harboured all sorts of suspicions about what was happening in the rooms above the ground floor, but this was Club Extreme – where everything goes.

The corridor ended with a solid metal door, studded with rivets. It reminded Scott of the front door of the Harness, but that reminded him of Nathan, so he left that thought well alone. Now rather nervous, he pushed the door open, and stepped inside.

It was black: walls, ceiling, floor. The only illumination came from some concealed spots above.

Scott wasn't the only person in the room. A muscular man with cropped hair and a goatee beard came over to him. He was wearing a pair of leather chaps and an upper body harness over his muscular, smooth body. For a second, Scott was convinced he was going to be thrown out: he remembered straying into the leather bar at Gavans in Wolverhampton once, dressed in a green Fred Perry, and being given his marching orders by the leather-man on the door.

'Hi,' said the man gruffly. 'I'm Gus.' He had a deep American accent. 'My friends and I were just about to start. You can watch if you want.' He grinned, his eyes narrowing as he looked Scott up and down like a piece of meat. 'You can join in if you want, but you'll have to change.'

Scott hesitated for a moment. What were they about to start? Did he want to join in? But then Gus nodded in the direction of the far wall. Two other men were standing there. One was wearing nothing but a leather jockstrap: he was thinner than Gus, with a full beard and a hairy chest. The second was a bear: tubby, with a full blond beard and a *very* hairy chest, the blond fur carrying on over his shoulders. He was wearing a full body harness, his erection enhanced by a metal cock ring.

'That's Larry and Greg,' Gus explained.

Scott didn't hesitate. The thought of having sex with the blond bear was far too tempting. 'I wouldn't mind joining in,' he asked.

'Fine by us,' said Gus. 'Put this on.' He handed Scott another jockstrap.

Undressing as quickly as possible, he just about managed to force his hard-on into the thong, aware of the admiring glances from the others. After what felt like an eternity, he was ready.

'OK – let's get started,' said Gus, leading him over to the others.

'This is Larry –' Gus introduced him to the dark-haired man '– and Greg.' Scott was getting more excited by the second, and he could feel his helmet pushing past the waistband of the jockstrap. He began to imagine the three of them together, Larry forcing his cock up Scott's arse, while Greg fucked his face. The fantasy was almost more than he could handle, and he could see Gus looking enviously at his erection.

Without even thinking, Scott found himself speaking. 'I'll do anything you want.'

Without saying anything, Greg grabbed Scott and kissed him. As his tongue probed Scott's mouth, Gus and Larry fell to the floor and started licking the leather jockstrap. Seeing Scott's red helmet poking out, they assaulted it with their tongues, kissing each other at the same time.

'Nice chest,' said Greg, reaching out and squeezing Scott's nipples. Scott groaned, but placed his hands over Greg's to urge him to continue. The pain was mixing with the pleasure being caused by Larry and Gus, and the recipe was overwhelming. But it got even better: Gus ripped off the jockstrap, and he and Larry started to take it in turns, engulfing Scott's thick, stiff cock in their warm mouths, sliding their lips along the shaft and massaging the sensitive helmet with their tongues. The feelings that were running through Scott's body were almost unbearable: he moved his hands and started massaging Greg's hairy chest, running his fingers through the thick blond hair, stroking his stomach before reaching his cock. Thanks to the cock ring, Greg's shaft was huge and red, the helmet wet with pre-come. Nathan grasped it and began to stroke it, firm wanks back and forth along the six-inch length. Greg responded by squeezing Scott's tits even harder.

Larry and Gus stood up as one. 'Now you're going to have all three of these cocks,' said Gus. 'Do you want that?' Scott nodded soundlessly. 'Come on, then.' They pulled Scott over to the other side of the room: an old vaulting horse stood against the wall.

'Lean over it,' Gus ordered.

Scott obeyed, feeling his cock rub against the rough material of the horse.

'Greg wants to fuck your arse, and Larry and me want to fuck your face. Is that what you want?' he repeated.

'Yes,' Scott hissed. 'Do whatever you want with me.' He wanted to be taken, to be treated like a bit of shit, a slave to do their bidding.

Larry and Gus stood in front of him, while Greg started playing with his arse, his fingers stroking his ring. Gus unzipped his chaps and brought out six inches of thick, veined dick, while Larry pulled off his jockstrap to reveal his own meat: longer but thinner than Gus's. Then they moved forward so that their cocks were just inches from his mouth. Their helmets rubbed against each other for a moment, and, when they moved apart, a strand of pre-come stretched between them.

'Suck them both,' Gus ordered.

Scott found it an effort not to choke as Gus and Larry forced their cocks into his waiting mouth. Gus's was thick but Scott could have coped with it on its own; but the width of Larry's as well meant that he could get only their helmets in his mouth. He took turns in flicking his tongue across each of their hard wet cocks, relishing the groans that came from them as he did so. Salty pre-come leaked from both of them, and Scott lapped it up as if it were the most important thing in his life.

Simultaneously, the two of them pulled back.

'Good boy,' grunted Gus. 'You've been a good boy and now you deserve a good fucking.' He nodded at Greg, and Scott noticed that Greg had produced condoms, seemingly from nowhere. 'Fuck him,' Gus ordered.

Greg's fingers were cold with lube now: he greased Scott's arse. Seconds later, Scott felt the pressure forcing his ring open. As he relaxed, he used the muscles of his arse to draw Greg's cock inside, further and deeper until Greg's whole length was inside him. Then he clenched his arse around Greg's cock, squeezing it rhythmically and enjoying the gasps of pleasure it elicited.

Greg started to withdraw, until his helmet was just inside Scott's ring; then he plunged back inside. It was Scott's turn to gasp, as the force of Greg's cock inside him began to bring him close to orgasm. After about five long, deep penetrations, Greg pulled out completely.

'My turn,' said Gus, and Scott hesitated: taking Greg's cock had been one thing, but Gus's was over twice as thick. Oh well, you got yourself into this, he told himself. Scott braced himself for that huge dick inside him.

As Gus's sheathed helmet touched him, Nathan relaxed as much as he could. The thick cock probed and pushed its way inside him. For long, agonising seconds, there was only scorching pain; but then his arse learnt to accommodate Gus's massive dick, and pleasure took over.

As Gus started to slowly pull and push his cock inside him, Scott was aware that Greg and Larry were standing right in front of his face, their dicks almost touching his mouth. Scott leant forward and hungrily took both of them, his tongue playing with their helmets, teasing the sensitive ridges and dick slits, lapping up their salty pre-come. Larry and Greg gasped with pleasure, and started to kiss each other, pulling on each other's tits, tearing at each other's chest hair.

More groans came from behind him: Gus was obviously very close, and the trembling in both Greg's and Larry's cocks indicated that they were, too. After holding himself back, Scott allowed himself to embrace the pleasure of Gus's thick cock inside him, and sensed the tingling feeling that was growing around his own dick.

When they came, it all happened at once. With one last thrust, Gus forced himself into Scott and yelled in ecstasy; in turn, both Larry and Greg forced their cocks into Scott's mouth and shot load after load of hot come against the back of his throat.

At the first taste of their spunk, Scott abandoned himself, reaching down to administer the last few strokes to his desperate cock. Still swallowing the double load, he shot his own over the fabric of the vaulting horse, white gouts of come against the beige.

Finally, he released the two cocks from his mouth and virtually collapsed on the horse. Gus gently pulled himself out of Scott and lay down over him, giving him a big strong hug as he did so.

'How was that?' he whispered in his American drawl as he removed the rubber from his thick cock.

Scott smiled. 'Great.'

'I was going to get some drinks,' said Greg a little breathlessly. 'Do you want one? Then we can carry on.'

For a second, Scott considered taking his leave of the three horny men and finding Leigh. But there was something so sweet, so imploring in Greg's bearded face, that he couldn't refuse.

'That would be brilliant,' he replied. Three leathermen, with him as their sex slave . . . what better way to spend a Friday night in Brighton?

'So – you're a friend of Lawrence,' said Brett, before sipping his Margarita. The Silver Lounge was comparatively quiet; there were only a couple of other people sitting at the long, marble-topped bar or at the tables. Just the sort of environment for the conversation that Nathan envisaged having with Brett McMasters.

Nathan shrugged. 'Let's just say that he and I have something in common – as do you and I, I gather.'

Narrowing his eyes, Brett hissed his response. 'Delancey.'

'Exactly. The man is pure poison,' said Nathan, mirroring Brett's obvious bitterness. Then, in explanation, 'Thanks to him,

I have no boyfriend, no job, and virtually no money.' Nathan realised that sounded selfish – me, me, me – but that was what Delancey did. He took everything of value and tainted it, brought it all down to his own mercenary level. He wouldn't know the meaning of love, of friendship. To him, nothing mattered but power and the bottom line.

Brett placed a reassuring hand on Nathan's. 'Perhaps I've been luckier: I do have a boyfriend at home, and I'm not exactly poor. But Delancey took other things away from me.' He looked up, a distant expression on his face. 'When he forced me to leave the country, I had to leave everything, including my family. When my mother died, I couldn't return to England in case I was arrested. My own mother's funeral, and I couldn't go.' He drained his Margarita and slammed the glass on the bar, causing a cascade of salt to snowfall on to the marble. 'I want him brought down, Nathan. I want him to go through what I've been through – what we've all been through.'

Nathan thought about Scott, about Marco, about his own life – all of it taken from him by one man, all because he had got in his way. His response was simple.

'How?'

Brett nodded to the barman to order another round of drinks before answering. 'Adrian Delancey has taken great pains to cover his past. Almost nobody knows anything about him, anything that they can use against him.

'But I do. I know where the bodies are buried, Nathan. I can provide proof that will put Delancey away for the rest of his life. Murder, fraud, corruption – all of it.'

'So why haven't you used it before?' asked Nathan suspiciously. If Brett hated Delancey as much as he claimed that he did, why hadn't he moved sooner?

'Because I was scared, Nathan. Even when he was just a City trader, Delancey was an evil bastard with some very nasty friends. Then he became involved with the Elective. And now . . . well, the Syndicate is simply Adrian Delancey writ large. I needed protection . . . and Lawrence has promised me that. The Hellfire

Club is the only thing capable of tackling Delancey, and the only thing capable of protecting me.'

Well, that made sense, anyway. 'So, what's the next step? How do you plan to attack Delancey?'

'Not here,' said Brett. 'Germany. All of the evidence is there, locked away in a bank vault. Also, it happens to be my home now,' he said wistfully. 'I assume that you can arrange travel?'

Nathan nodded. 'Of course.' He liked Germany – especially Munich, which was his second home. 'Where exactly?'

Brett put a finger to his lips. 'Not yet. I'll tell you when we're airborne.'

'I look forward to it,' said Nathan. Hopefully it would be somewhere where they could relax for a little while. Nathan knew that the stakes were high, but it had been a long time since he had been able to indulge himself, and he intended to take full advantage of it.

'Tomorrow, though.' Brett smiled. 'Now that I'm here, I fancy having a bit of fun,' he said, mirroring Nathan's thoughts. He leant forward across the bar. 'That Gary that you're with – is it business or pleasure?'

Nathan felt an immediate stab of jealousy. Without thinking, he said, 'Business,' even though he knew he didn't mean it. Gary might be Nathan's PA for the duration of his mission, but it was more than that. Something had happened, something deep inside him, and he just didn't know what to do.

'That's good.' For a second, Nathan was confused: was Brett after Gary? Then he understood the broad inviting grin on Brett's face: it was Nathan that he was after! Nathan wasn't quite sure how to react – his plans all seemed to revolve around Gary – but there was no denying that Brett was an attractive man. The thought of spending the night with him was one that Nathan could quite easily handle, he decided. As long as Gary didn't mind . . .

Brett squeezed Nathan's hand. 'Let's see if our luck's still good at the tables. I feel like celebrating.'

Nathan frowned. Why did life have to be so confusing?

★

Hugging Gus, Greg and Larry in turn, Scott reluctantly said his goodbyes and left them. He had no idea how many times he had come in the last couple of hours – the four of them just hadn't wanted to stop. Apparently, Larry and Greg were partners, and Gus was a frequent visitor to their relationship.

Wandering down the corridor, he sighed. It had been great – perhaps not in the same league as last night's encounter with Eddie, but still memorable – but it hadn't been real. Once again, he was in the fantasy world of the Elective, the world that he had begged Nathan to leave, the world that had driven a wedge between them. This represented everything that Scott detested – so why had he enjoyed it so much? Why did life have to be so confusing?

It was past one o'clock in the morning, but Nathan couldn't remember the last time he had enjoyed himself so much, and he just didn't want the night to end. After the last three months, to feel so alive was almost intoxicating.

He, Brett and Gary were still on the roulette table, each of them with an impressive pile of chips in front of him. It turned out that Gary had quite a flair for the game, and Nathan watched him with the sort of pride that he had last felt over Scott. When all of this was over, perhaps they could see whether there was a future for them.

'Are you sure that there's not something going on between the two of you?' asked Brett, nodding towards Gary, who was engrossed in the latest spin of the roulette wheel.

Nathan shrugged. 'Not yet,' he answered truthfully. 'But I hope so.'

Brett elbowed him playfully. 'Good for you.' Yes, there was a trace of disappointment in his words, but Nathan was pretty sure that he was taking it OK. It wasn't as if anything could have happened between him and Brett anyway – he did have a boyfriend in Germany, didn't he?

'Ten thousand on black twelve.' At that everyone at the table looked round. It was Gary!

'Are you sure about this?' Nathan hissed in his ear.

Gary grinned, and it was clear that he'd had slightly more to drink than he ought to have had. Then again, the money was irrelevant: despite the fact that he was betting enough money to keep Nathan very happy for six months, to Lawrence it was a drop in the ocean.

'I feel lucky,' said Gary. 'Trust me.'

'Twenty thousand on red twenty-one.' The counter-bet definitely silenced the table. A new player was standing there, a staggering pile of chips on the table in front of him. Nathan guessed that he was about thirty, with slicked-back red hair and a hawklike face. There was something about him that Nathan immediately disliked, something in his expression, his bearing. His instincts immediately told him that the man was trouble – but why? Although bets of that magnitude weren't unusual given the type of people playing, most of the high-rollers had already decamped to the bar.

'All bets in, gentlemen,' said the croupier, before spinning the wheel. All eyes were on the silver ball as it skipped from number to number, from red to black and then to red again. Even though the money wasn't really important, Nathan realised that he was holding his breath.

The wheel slowed, and the ball's movements did the same. Finally, the wheel came to a halt, and the ball made a couple of final leaps . . .

And landed on black twelve.

Without thinking, Nathan grabbed Gary and gave him a warm hug. 'Well done, mate!' he shouted, oblivious to the stares of the others. Winning wasn't a problem here; displays of emotion clearly were. He gently unwound his arm and gave an embarrassed smile.

'I think I'd better leave while I'm ahead,' said Gary breathlessly, as the croupier pushed pile after pile of chips towards him. Nathan took a rough guess that Gary had just won nearly sixty thousand pounds. *Nice*.

'Let's go to the bar to celebrate,' said Brett, with the slightest slur in his words. 'It's not like we can't afford it, is it?' He placed an affectionate arm around Gary, and Nathan couldn't help but feel jealous. Suddenly, another idea sprang into his mind: if the three of them fancied each other, why didn't they just go with their feelings?

What's this? The old Nathan Dexter finally resurfacing? said his inner voice. He ignored it.

Breaking into a grin, he summoned a waiter. 'I'll get them to send up some champagne to my room. How does that sound?'

The looks that passed between the three of them were answer enough. This was going to be fun.

As Gary scooped up his winnings and went over to change chips for cash, he didn't see the look of complete and utter contempt that came from the ginger-haired man.

His name was David. And he had some very unpleasant associates.

Eight

_____

Scott was beginning to get worried. Fine, so he hadn't explored every single room of Club Extreme, but, after his recent experiences, he didn't really want to: I'd be here all night, he thought wryly.

Yet there was no sign of either Leigh or Pete. After nearly half an hour, Scott finally gave up. He had no desire to spend any more time at the club – even if he picked anyone up, he didn't have the energy to do anything anyway. Oh well, he decided, Leigh's a big boy, more than capable of looking after himself. Himself and Pete, Scott reminded himself. He just hoped that neither Leigh nor Marco got hurt by this. Having a fling was one thing, but Scott had seen the looks that had passed between them.

Leaving the club through the main door, where a queue of people were still waiting to get in, he decided to have a stroll along the seafront. It was a lovely evening: cloudless, full of stars, with a huge full moon beaming down on the sea. He would wander back to the hotel, have a quick drink in the bar, and then have a good night's sleep. And tomorrow he would go back to London . . . and see Nathan.

Satisfied – both with what he had done and what he was going to do – Scott sauntered off into the mild night.

Unaware of the figure in the shadows, watching him carefully.

By the time they reached Nathan's room, the champagne had
been delivered, a magnum of Krug and three glasses sitting on
the long mahogany dresser. Nathan ushered Gary and Brett inside
before shutting and locking the door – the last thing he wanted
was for room service to turn up at a critical moment.

Gary threw off his dinner jacket and sat down on the edge of
the enormous bed. Brett did the same. Nathan picked up the
champagne and undid the wire around the cork.

'All in all, a successful evening, gentlemen,' he announced,
popping the cork and filling the three flutes.

'That remains to be seen,' said Brett.

'Sorry?' said Nathan as he handed over the glass.

'We still have to get back to Germany and get the evidence,
Nathan. Without that, Delancey could still win.'

'What exactly is this evidence?' asked Gary.

Brett frowned for a second, obviously trying to decide whether
Gary could be trusted. Nathan knew he could: the way Nathan
felt at the moment, he would have trusted Gary with his life. But
this was Brett's life they were talking about at the moment:
Nathan had no doubt that Delancey would eliminate Brett
without a second thought if he suspected he was a threat to him.

'Well, there are two main pieces of evidence,' Brett began,
having decided to trust Gary. 'There's a lot of paperwork which
proves that Delancey's guilty of various offences. However,
Delancey's a devious bastard, and there's no guarantee that he
wouldn't wriggle his way out of all of it.' He sipped his
champagne before looking up. There was an odd expression on
his face, and it took Nathan a few seconds to recognise it. It was
triumph.

'More importantly, I've got a witness.'

'Witness to what?' asked Nathan.

Brett gave an evil smile. 'What else? A witness to murder.'

★

Scott reached the steps of the Grand and bounded up them. He had decided to forgo the drink – he was so tired that he just wanted to slump into bed and sleep. He approached the reception desk and asked for his key.

The night porter checked the computer and looked up at Scott, a puzzled expression on his face. 'I'm sorry, Mr James, but our records indicate that you checked out about an hour ago.'

'What?'

'Mr Robertson settled up the bill before leaving.'

Scott's head whirled. What was Leigh playing at? 'Are you sure about that?' he asked, just in case there had been some sort of mistake.

'Absolutely sure. We do have some spare rooms available if you've changed your mind,' he offered.

Unfortunately, I don't have any spare cash, Scott realised. 'No, it's OK – I've obviously misunderstood what's going on,' he said lamely, leaving the hotel.

What the hell are you up to, Leigh? Scott thought as he stood on the steps, trying to decide his next course of action. It was already one in the morning, so there was no chance of getting a train – even if he had a ticket. Cursing himself, he remembered he had told Leigh to look after the tickets. And he didn't have enough money, either on him or in the bank, to afford a ticket anyway. So a taxi was completely out of the question.

He was stranded in Brighton, without friends, and with absolutely no idea what to do. He couldn't return to the club, he couldn't do anything. Great way of cheering me up, Leigh, he said to himself. I suppose you think I'll look back on this and laugh.

He crossed the road and went down on to the beach. The only thing he could think of doing was kipping down somewhere and phoning Marco the next morning. Perhaps he could explain what the hell was going on.

Marco was standing by the window, looking out over Lawrence's immaculate garden. Lawrence was asleep, looking more innocent than he had any right to.

Than *either* of us has a right to, come to that, Marco thought. As betrayals went, what Marco had just done ranked right up there at the top of the list. He had slept with his ex-boyfriend. He remembered Nathan once describing it – melodramatically – as a crime beyond imagining. It didn't feel that melodramatic now.

The problem was, Marco didn't want it to stop. For five years, he had dreamt about seeing Lawrence again, about being with him again. Now it had happened, he just didn't know what to do next. He didn't even know what this had meant to Lawrence. Perhaps it had meant nothing to him, just a convenient one-night stand. But Marco couldn't believe that. The passion that had flowed between them, the intensity of the emotions . . .

No, Lawrence *had* to feel the same way.

He *had* to.

Because if he didn't . . . Marco just didn't know what he would do.

Brett had declined to give them any further details after dropping that particular bombshell, and Nathan had been unwilling to push him. All he knew was, the sooner they reached Germany, the better.

The magnum of champagne was nearly empty. Nathan considered ordering another one, but decided not to. He already felt a little unsteady. Any more and he wouldn't be of use to anyone.

Brett was lying on his back, his shirt completely undone. He was solid and smooth, and Nathan suddenly felt very, very mischievous. He nodded towards Gary, indicating for him to get to work. He had discussed this with Gary earlier, while Brett had been in the bathroom, and Gary had thought it was a wonderful idea.

Leaning over, Gary ran his tongue up Brett's body, from his navel to his chest, making a small diversion to lick and then chew on each of his nipples. Brett let out a satisfied sigh, and undid his suit trousers. Kicking off his shoes, he shuffled his trousers off and let them drop to the floor.

Nathan was impressed by what he saw: Gary's actions were having an obvious effect, if the thick outline beneath the cotton of Brett's briefs was to be believed. Gary's attentions were drawn to the bulge, his tongue lingering over the outline of the helmet before gently biting the shaft.

Watching his boyf– Watching Gary pleasuring Brett was turning Nathan on. He unbuttoned his shirt and removed it, glancing at Brett to see whether he had noticed. He had.

'I've got a thing for hairy men,' he said enthusiastically.

'Then it's your lucky day,' said Gary, pulling his own shirt open to reveal the forest beneath.

Brett grinned. 'Two bears. I must have died and gone to heaven.'

As Gary continued to undress, Nathan took off the rest of his clothes, making sure that Brett got a good look at his thick cock, now hard and ready. He also ensured that he watched intently as Gary stripped off: Brett wasn't the only one who liked hairy men. He stared at Gary with undisguised lust, that hairy body, the thick cock bobbing between his legs. It was taking every ounce of Nathan's willpower not to fall to his knees and take it in his mouth.

There'll be time for that later, he told himself.

Finally, both Gary and Nathan were naked, their big hairy bodies standing side by side in front of the bed, in front of Brett. Brett sat up and removed his shirt, revealing muscular arms, with a Celtic knot tattooed around his right bicep. Brett reached out and took each of their cocks in a hand, wanking them firmly with even strokes.

'I take it you approve?' said Nathan, putting his arm around Gary and stroking the hair on his chest.

'What do you think?' Brett replied, leaning forward. 'I want both your cocks in my mouth.'

Gary and Nathan did as they were asked, moving forwards so Brett could take them both. His erection was still constrained by the fabric of his briefs, but it was already threatening to break free. It looked like he had one of the biggest cocks Nathan had ever seen, and Nathan just knew that he wanted it inside him, filling him up.

Brett's mouth toyed with both their cocks, managing to swallow both of their helmets without difficulty. As he pleasured them, Nathan continued to stroke Gary's body, touching his shoulders, his chest, his stomach, and finally his balls, cupping them in his hand and squeezing them gently.

'I want to suck your cock,' said Nathan, beginning to get desperate for a glimpse of what lay within Brett's briefs.

Brett smiled. 'Well, that's easily arranged.' He pulled down his briefs. Nathan wasn't disappointed. Brett's dick must have been about ten inches long and three inches wide – definitely one of the largest he had ever seen.

'Lie down on the bed,' Brett ordered. 'Both of you.'

Fitting two bears and a Muscle Mary on to the bed started to prove problematic, but it was a situation Nathan had been in many times.

'Let's try this,' he suggested. Choreographing Gary and Brett, he manoeuvred them around the wide bed so that his cock was brushing Gary's mouth, while Gary's own cock was against Brett's face. Of course, that meant that Nathan was exactly where he wanted to be: nuzzled up to Brett's cock, his face buried in the thick blond bush of his pubes.

'Right!' growled Brett, unable to wait any longer. He swallowed Gary's dick in his mouth, forcing it deeply down his throat. He started to suck it firmly, and Gary groaned. Brett was clearly a master at giving blow jobs, thought Nathan, with only the slightest trace of jealousy. But that didn't last very long: seconds later, he felt Gary's mouth clamp around his own cock. The feeling urged him on: he took as much of Brett as he could. Feeling a cock that big in his mouth was an unbelievable sensation. He strained his jaws to taste as much of it as possible, which wasn't that much. Brett's helmet alone seemed to fill up his mouth, and Nathan's tongue lapped at his dick slit, enjoying the salty-sweet taste of his pre-come.

Nathan felt a hand, which he assumed to be Gary's, stroking

his arse, the fingers probing and finding his anus and gently penetrating it. While trying not to pull his cock from Gary's mouth, he urged Gary on, urged him to finger him deeper and deeper.

The three of them continued like that for timeless moments; all Nathan could think about was the mouth around his dick and the dick in his own mouth, while Gary's finger went further and further up his arse, probing and reaching for his prostate gland.

Nathan suddenly moved his hand so it was gripped around the enormous width of Brett's cock and began to wank it, trying to find the rhythm that would bring Brett close. But he didn't want Brett to come: he had something else in mind for that.

Pulling away, drawing his own cock from Gary's mouth, Nathan got on to all fours. 'I want that inside me,' he said, pointing at Brett's huge tool.

Brett raised an eyebrow. 'I hope you're ready for it.' He thought for a second. 'I'll make you a deal. While I'm fucking you, I want Gary to fuck me.'

Nathan nodded. He wanted to know that Gary's cock was inside Brett while Brett was inside him.

Gary grabbed a couple of condoms and the lube bottle – was there nothing that Gary had forgotten to pack? – and handed one of the condoms to Brett. Nathan crouched there, almost unable to contain his eagerness, as the two men rolled their condoms over their stiff dicks and lubed themselves up. Finally, Nathan felt the cool touch of lube inside his arse, and started to relax himself. Taking all of that was going to be difficult, but he knew that was what he wanted.

'Ready?' said Brett.

'Yep,' Gary replied as Nathan nodded.

'Get on to your back,' said Brett. 'I want you to see your mate screwing me as I fill you up.'

Nathan did as he was told, allowing Brett to hoist his legs in the air. All three of them were ready now. Nathan braced himself for Brett's massive tool.

As Brett's helmet touched his ring, Nathan relaxed as much as he could, but even that wasn't enough. The three-inch-thick cock bullied and bruised its way inside him, and Nathan felt as if his arse were on fire. For long, agonising seconds, the pain was worse than he had ever imagined; but then his arse learnt to accommodate Brett's huge dick, and pleasure took over.

Brett's expression was wild and brutal as he rested his full length and width inside Nathan, and Nathan guessed that this was going to be one hell of a rough fuck.

Just what he wanted this evening.

The pain returned for a second as Brett withdrew slightly – then it was his turn to gasp as Gary ploughed his dick inside him, before pulling out. Brett started to drive himself into Nathan once again, and Gary copied his rhythm. Nathan lay there with his legs on Brett's shoulders, taking all of that big cock inside his arse, feeling it hurt him and fill him with burning pleasure at the same time. He watched as Gary slid his cock in and out of Brett's hole, a look of rapture on Gary's face. The three of them moved with one rhythm: Gary into Brett, Brett into Nathan, and Nathan squeezing his arse around Brett's dick.

The three of them started moving faster and faster, building up to the easy rhythm that Nathan knew would bring him off. Brett's cock wasn't just rubbing against his prostate, it was bullying it, battering it, forcing it to relinquish Nathan to his orgasm. Nathan was trying to hold off as long as he could, but it was going to be difficult to wait much longer.

Gary grunted, a loud, guttural sound, and Nathan knew that he was coming, shooting his hot load into Brett's arse. This must have been Brett's trigger: with an even louder yell, he drove his dick into Nathan's hole so hard that Nathan also cried out. He could feel Brett's thickness pumping inside him, filling him with his spunk, and that was enough for Nathan. Using his hand to administer the final strokes, Nathan came over his chest and stomach, more spunk than he could remember ever shooting.

He slumped back on the bed, waiting for Brett to withdraw; Brett did so carefully, gingerly, trying not to hurt Nathan, and Nathan had to admit that it was a relief when he felt it removed.

The three of them, all flushed and sweating, just lay there for a minute. Finally, Brett spoke.

'You two make one hell of a team.'

Nathan smiled. 'We aim to please.' Then he remembered the last time he had said that: after the threesome with John Bury. With Scott. Unable to help himself, he shivered. A sudden sense of dread overcame him. Surely nothing could go wrong now, could it?

There was a knock at the door. Nathan got to his feet and grabbed the dressing gown from the bathroom. The room was arranged in such a way that anyone at the door couldn't see into the main bedroom.

He opened the door, and was surprised to see the ginger-haired man from the roulette table standing there.

'Yes?' he asked. Before he could say anything else, a punch to the stomach knocked all the wind from him, and he collapsed to the floor. He lay there, helpless, as the man strode over him and stepped into the bedroom.

Scott sat under the ruins of the pier, staring out to sea. Thankfully, it was a warm night, and the spot he had found was quite comfortable, but that didn't exactly help much. He was totally pissed off and confused. For a second, he had considered phoning Nathan, but what could Nathan do? He didn't have a car, and his finances weren't up to getting a taxi to Brighton and back.

No, he was stuck here for the duration. As soon as it got light, he would find the main road out of Brighton back to London and hitch a lift home.

And Leigh had better have a bloody good explanation.

The man hauled Nathan to his feet and threw him on the bed with the others. While he had been lying there, unable to move, Nathan had heard the sound of a fight, and was scared of what he might see. Brett had the beginnings of a black eye, but thankfully Gary didn't seem hurt. Even so, this man was obviously quite a fighter, and was clearly in control of the situation, as neither of the others seemed willing to move against him.

'What do you want?' Nathan demanded.

'You must be Dexter,' the man surmised. 'And McMasters. Don't know who you are,' he spat towards Gary, 'and, frankly, I don't actually care.' He leant down and grabbed Brett by the throat. 'You've been causing a lot of trouble, McMasters, threatening to blow the lid on certain things that don't concern you. I'm here to make sure that you don't.'

'Delancey sent you,' Nathan hissed.

'*Mr* Delancey. But that won't do any of you any good. My instructions are to make sure you never leave Monte Carlo.'

Nathan frowned. How had Delancey known to find them here? Lawrence had been certain that he was 'undetectable', so what had gone wrong? With a growing chill, Nathan wondered whether Lawrence was quite as powerful as he thought he was. Perhaps the Syndicate now dwarfed the Hellfire Club as well.

'What are you going to do? Kill us?' asked Gary.

'Eventually. After Mr McMasters here has told me exactly where he's keeping a few bits and pieces that aren't his.'

Nathan guessed he meant the evidence. Hang on, though – there wasn't any suggestion that he knew about the 'witness'. From what Brett had said, the witness alone could put paid to Delancey.

'You're wasting your time,' said Brett. This did nothing to improve the red-haired man's temperament: he slapped Brett viciously with the back of his hand. 'I don't think so. Everybody's got their price, McMasters. All of you: get dressed. And don't try anything.' He reached into his pocket and drew out a gun.

Nathan stood up and reached for his shirt. He knew that there was nothing that he could do: the man was clearly a much better fighter than Nathan. He just hoped that they would get the chance to act before they ran out of time.

Leigh opened his eyes. The last thing he remembered was leaving the club with Pete. Scott had left – or had he? Leigh didn't remember seeing Scott after he decided to have a look around.

There was something not quite right going on – a huge gap in his memory that resisted any attempt to probe it.

So, where was he? Definitely not in his room in the Grand – it was far too cold for that. Not only that, but he was moving – or, rather, the room was moving. And there was the sound of an engine, and that of tyres against the surface of a road. He tried to get up, but immediately discovered that he couldn't: his arms were tied behind his back and to the wall, and his legs were bound together.

The thought that suddenly occurred to him brought him out in a cold sweat.

There was only one answer. He'd been kidnapped.

A year ago, something like that would never have occurred to him – why would anyone kidnap an innocent graphic designer?

That was before Adrian Delancey, before the Elective. He had been kidnapped once before, and shipped off to Germany. It was a memory that he would never forget – a month of slavery, all at the orders of that bastard Delancey. There was no reason to doubt that they – and he knew exactly who *they* were – would do it again, if it served their purposes. As far as Delancey was concerned, Leigh would make an ideal pawn against the Elective.

But how had they got away with it, under the very noses of the Elective? Pete had been there all the time . . .

'I'm an idiot,' he muttered. Of course they had been able to get away with it. Because Pete had been behind it all along.

What proof did Leigh have that Pete worked for the Elective in the first place? OK, so he had been brandishing the names of Elective officials around, but what did that prove? Before creating this Syndicate, Delancey had been the Comptroller of the UK branch of the Elective. He would know all that information as well.

Once again, Leigh knew that he had been led by his dick, against his better judgement. He had walked into a trap – and had no idea what to do about it. Resigning himself to his fate – at least until he could do something about it – Leigh lay back against the corrugated metal of the lorry and waited.

★

Dressed in their dinner suits, there was nothing to indicate that Nathan, Gary and Brett were anything other than normal guests in the hotel, although Brett's now noticeable black eye had garnered more than one quizzical stare. But nothing would have been said: for all anyone knew, he might have been into a bit of rough stuff, and, as far as the Elective was concerned, anything went.

The red-haired man was taking them along lesser-used corridors, away from the casino and the majority of people. In any other hotel, he could have counted on the lateness of the hour, but, with the Elective temporarily overrunning the Palais du Cypresse, the place was still buzzing with its heady mixture of money and sex.

Timeless minutes later, they stopped: obviously they were reaching the end of their journey. In front of them was a plain service door. It was locked, but the red-haired man didn't let that deter him: he simply shot the lock off.

Gun's got a silencer, Nathan noted. Although what earthly use that bit of information would be, he had no idea. He thought back, trying to see if there was anything in his experience that could help him: but, even though his years of journalism had taken him to some pretty dangerous places, and put him in some tight spots, he had never been at the end of an assassin's gun – if you discounted that experience with Marco in Amsterdam.

Pulling open the door, the man ushered the other three inside. A set of forbidding concrete steps led upward. 'Start climbing,' he ordered.

Nathan tried to remember what the Palais du Cypresse had looked like from above, when they had landed on the roof. He vaguely recalled some sort of roof garden, and guessed that that was where they were headed. Perhaps the open space will give us an advantage, he wondered. OK, so he had a gun, but there were three of them. If they could somehow coordinate their efforts, they might stand a chance.

Because, if they didn't, the whole situation would play into Delancey's hands. He could imagine the explanations, the newspaper headlines, grist for a hundred and one lurid rumours and salacious gossip.

MILLIONAIRE HOMOSEXUALS IN CASINO DEATH LEAP

And wouldn't that just suit Delancey? Brett and Nathan silenced – permanently, the Elective publicly exposed . . . and Gary, dead on the pavement far below. The thought of his beautiful, gorgeous bear cub, lying broken on a street in Monte Carlo, galvanised him. There had to be a way to stop Delancey's hired hand – there had to be!

Reaching the top of the stairwell, Brett pushed open the door and stepped out. Nathan and Gary followed, with the red-haired man behind.

The roof garden was empty of people. It was a flat concrete area dotted with shrubs and decorative urns, a vain attempt to turn some empty space into something useful. Not particularly successful.

A dining area lay to their left, with tables and chairs and a wonderful view of the city. It was dark and quiet, the only noise the muted revelry of the hotel below them. But the view wasn't what was interesting Nathan at the moment – at least not the view to the city. On their right, their helicopter waited patiently, proud in the silver livery of the Hellfire Club.

That had to be the key, thought Nathan. Something was nagging at him, something that could save them . . .

He remembered. He remembered what Gary had said to him, only hours ago: 'I hadn't been in a helicopter until about two years ago. And now . . . well, I even learnt how to fly one.'

If they could overpower their kidnapper, if they could reach the helicopter, then Gary could fly it.

And I always do three impossible things before breakfast! Nathan thought wryly.

'This is as far as you go,' said the man, brandishing the gun. Nathan had no doubt that he would use it; indeed, Nathan had no doubt that he was *going* to use it. Unless they acted now, it would be the end.

'I won't tell you,' Brett protested. 'My solicitor has instructions to release the information in the case of my death, so this won't do you any good.'

The man gave a cruel smile. 'Oh, come on. We'll find the solicitor before he has a chance to do anything. Haven't you realised by now? We're everywhere, we know everything.' He adopted a falsely reasonable tone. 'Just tell me and you can all go.'

Which was a lie. Nathan knew that the man – that *Delancey* – couldn't take the risk of letting them go now. They would have to die, just to cover up the Syndicate's dirty work.

Gary, lying broken on the pavement . . .

It was only later – much later when Nathan thought carefully – that he would know what had happened. Somehow, both he and Gary acted in the same way at the same moment.

In a blur of movement, without even thinking, Nathan threw himself at the red-haired man. While he was off-balance, Gary kicked the gun from his hand, sending it flying across the roof garden.

'The helicopter!' shouted Nathan, heading towards it, pulling a stunned Brett with him. Nathan checked that Gary was following, and managed to spare a glance at the red-haired man. The follow-through of Gary's kick had knocked him to the ground, his gun now yards away from him, but he was battling against the pain to reach it. Nathan just hoped that the three of them could get into the helicopter before he retrieved it.

By the time Nathan and Brett reached the silver helicopter, Gary had already opened the door. 'Inside!' he urged, although Nathan needed no urging.

A single shot rang out, shattering the Monte Carlo night.

Brett fell heavily against Nathan, a growing red stain clearly visible against the white of his dress shirt. Trying not to panic, Nathan climbed into the helicopter as quickly as he could, pulling Brett up after him. He could see the red-haired man urgently checking his gun: hopefully it had jammed, which might give them the few seconds that they needed. Now they had to get away – and get medical attention for Brett.

Nathan slammed the door of the helicopter behind him. Gary was already buckled into the pilot's seat.

'Come on!' shouted Nathan. 'We're not bulletproof in here!'

'I know, I know,' said Gary. 'Give me a chance.'

'I thought you knew how to fly this thing.'

'I learnt to fly in a simulator, Nathan!' Gary replied. As he spoke, the whirr of the blades began. 'Won't be a second . . .' Another gunshot – and the window next to Nathan cracked into a spider's web. It was still holding together, but another shot would breach the cabin – and Nathan into the bargain.

'Here we go!' Gary yelled over the noise of the blades. With a lurch, the helicopter inched away from the roof garden, banking first one way, then the other, as Gary tried to control it. Finally they were about four feet above the roof; Gary executed a sweeping curve over the hotel, and Nathan was able to see the red-headed man aiming his gun at them. But they were too far away for it to matter now. He watched as the man ran over to the stairwell.

'He's going to follow us,' Nathan pointed out. 'Radio ahead to Nice – get the Learjet ready to fly to Berlin.' Even though part of him was crying out to return to the safety of England, he knew that he would have to see this through. If Delancey wasn't stopped, no one would be safe.

He turned to Brett, and was horrified to see how pale he was. His shirt was now sodden with blood, and his chest was moving irregularly as he tried to draw breath. 'Don't worry – we'll get you medical attention when we get to Nice,' Nathan reassured.

Brett shook his head. 'Too late,' he gurgled, and Nathan remembered another time, another place, another man dying in his arms. During a brief spell as a foreign correspondent, he had been in an Israeli hotel when a terrorist bomb had exploded. One of his colleagues, a French journalist, had caught a shard of shrapnel in his back, penetrating his lung.

He had drowned in his own blood. And he had sounded exactly like Brett.

'You must get to Berlin,' Brett hissed. 'Safety deposit box . . .

Tacheles Bar in East Berlin ... Tell you where to find ... Harvey ...' He lapsed into unconsciousness. Nathan felt for a pulse on the side of his neck, and realised that he was wrong. He wasn't unconscious.

Brett was dead.

This time, the panic came very close to overwhelming him. Forcing it back, he looked behind, and saw a small bright dot coming from the direction they had just left.

'He's following!' Nathan neither knew nor cared where the other helicopter had come from. As far as Adrian Delancey and his operatives were concerned, nothing seemed beyond them.

Gary must have opened the throttle: the helicopter surged forward in the air, and Nathan realised that they were now well out over the ocean. 'How's Brett?' he asked into his headset.

Nathan decided to wait until they had landed to tell Gary the truth. The last thing he wanted was for them to drop out of the air. 'Just get us to the plane,' he said evasively.

The five-minute journey seemed like a lifetime. Gary had radioed ahead, getting the pilot to secure landing space for the helicopter and a departure window for the plane: it seemed that the Hellfire Club could wield the same privileges as Delancey and the Elective. They needed only a few minutes to get clear, but the bright dot was now clearly recognizable as a red and black helicopter – and it was gaining on them. Even though the airport was now below them, it was going to be a very close shave.

'Hang on!' warned Gary. 'I'm bringing us down. It won't be a soft landing, I'm afraid.'

Nathan was willing to suffer a bit of discomfort, and Brett ... well, Brett wouldn't notice, would he? he thought sadly.

The helicopter hit the tarmac with a jarring thud which rattled Nathan to the core. As soon as he was sure that they were down and weren't going to take off again, he opened the door and jumped out.

'What about Brett?' asked Gary as he climbed from the cockpit.

'Brett's dead,' said Nathan softly. 'He was shot in the back.' Nathan held his hands out, and was shocked to see that they were red with Brett's blood. 'There was nothing anyone could have done. He died just after we took off. Gary – we have to get to the plane.'

'What?' The colour drained from Gary's face. 'We can't just leave him here!'

Nathan didn't feel any better about leaving Brett's body behind than Gary did, but it was a matter of priorities. 'Look!' Nathan pointed to a spot a hundred yards away. The red and black helicopter was already landing, and Brett's murderer was clearly visible inside. 'We *must* reach the plane.' But Gary was rooted to the spot. 'Now!' Nathan grabbed Gary and dragged him to the waiting Learjet. He virtually propelled him up the short flight of boarding steps, well aware that their adversary had landed and was even now running towards them, trying to take aim at them.

Shoving Gary into the plane, Nathan followed, pushing the steps away and securing the door. Even as he did so, he heard the sound of gunfire, and prayed that the Learjet was hardier than the helicopter had been. He activated the intercom to the pilot.

'Go!' he yelled. 'Go now!'

The engines powered up as Nathan helped Gary into one of the seats. He was limp and pale, clearly in shock. But Nathan wasn't unmoved: his thoughts were elsewhere, in the lonely cabin of the helicopter, where a lifeless body was stiffening in the cool Monte Carlo night. Somebody who had trusted Nathan, and was dead as a result.

No, Nathan told himself. Yes, Brett was dead, but he was the latest victim of Adrian Delancey. Delancey, who destroyed everything and everyone who got in his way.

How many more people would die before that bastard was forced to pay for his actions?

As the plane accelerated along the runway, Nathan looked at the pain on Gary's face and came to a decision. A final decision.

He would stop Adrian Delancey. Whatever the cost.

Nine

The sun was shining through the shuttered window as an urgent knocking woke Marco with the worst hangover he could remember. He tried to sit up in bed, but finally conceded defeat and slumped back into his pillow.

But it *wasn't* his pillow. It wasn't even his bed. Where the fuck was he? His memory of the previous evening was foggy, but he seemed to remember . . .

Lawrence. Oh God. What have I done?

'Good morning, sir.' The greeting was cold, unfriendly, and could only have come from one person. Hadleigh. Marco looked up to see Lawrence's butler standing over him, bearing his ubiquitous tray and ubiquitous sneer. This morning the tray appeared to be bearing a cup of coffee – just what Marco needed. The sneer simply represented the way that Hadleigh felt towards anyone who dared to share his master's affections.

'The master is in his playroom, Mr Capiello. He asked if you would care to join him immediately.'

'Uh . . . yeah, give me about five minutes.'

'I'm sure that the master is more than willing to accommodate you,' said Hadleigh archly, and Marco couldn't help recalling more than one morning that had started off like this. Hadleigh's jealousy would be the death of him, Marco concluded. With that, Hadleigh deposited the coffee on the bedside table and left the room.

Marco finally managed to manoeuvre himself into a position where he could reach the coffee, and took a deep drink from it. As the caffeine hit the spot, he looked around the room. Nothing much had changed in the last five years: a different shade of wallpaper, a new carpet, but it was still definitively Lawrence.

And Marco knew that he was still in love with him.

Draining the coffee cup, he pulled himself out of bed and wandered over to the *en-suite* bathroom. Then he glanced at the bedside clock and had to double-check. It was only five in the morning – no wonder he felt so bloody awful: he'd had only a couple of hours' sleep. Hoping that Lawrence had a good reason for waking him up in the middle of the night, he continued into the bathroom and started splashing cold water over his face.

Despite his unscheduled orders for departure, the Learjet's pilot hadn't balked at being ordered to fly to Berlin. Gary and Nathan watched out of one of the windows as the plane accelerated along the short runway, while Delancey's operative stood impotently in front of his own helicopter. Nathan knew that they wouldn't have much of a head start – he could see a number of private jets dotted around the airport, and guessed that one of them was Delancey's – but, the way things were going, even half an hour counted now.

'Bastard,' was all Gary could say as he slumped back into one of the armchairs. 'I can't believe that he would have someone murdered.'

Nathan felt for Gary. Although he worked for the Hellfire Club, he probably hadn't encountered machinations as blood-thirsty and terminal as Delancey's. Nathan remembered how he had felt when John Bury had been murdered – after another threesome, came the sick recollection – and knew exactly what was going through Gary's mind.

What made it worse, if that was possible, was that Nathan's instincts had warned him that something was up. For years, he had trusted his instincts. But, ever since his involvement with the Elective, he had been ignoring them more and more – he was getting soft, complacent.

Nathan knelt down next to Gary and put a comforting arm around him as the jet continued its emergency take-off, soaring from the runway and away from Delancey's thug. For the moment.

His voice was warm but firm. Now was not the time for Gary to go into shock – he needed him, damn it! '*Now* you see what we're up against. Our only hope is to reach this Harvey in Berlin before Delancey's people get there, and get him back to Britain. Hopefully, Lawrence will be able to protect us from the Syndicate until we can finally track Delancey down and stop him once and for all.'

Gary looked up at Nathan, and Nathan was moved to see that there were tears in his eyes. 'I saw the look on that bastard's face, Nathan. When he fired that gun, he didn't care what happened. How can people become like that?' he whispered.

Nathan hugged him. 'It's Delancey, Gary. He taints everyone who comes into contact with him.' Nathan remembered the way that he had worked his way into his relationship with Scott, poisoning it, corrupting it. *Ending* it. 'That's why we're doing this, Gary. To make sure that Adrian Delancey never gets the chance to do this again.'

They sat there in silence, holding each other, as the Learjet penetrated the Mediterranean dawn.

Adrian Delancey listened to David Kirsten's report with mounting anger. How could David – one of his top operatives – have failed him like that? Not only was Brett's information still secure, its location unknown, but Nathan Dexter was still alive.

Kirsten had told him how he'd had to shoot Brett, wounding him, and how he'd subsequently found Brett's body inside the silver helicopter. The smallest part of Delancey regretted Brett's death – he and Brett had once been very close – but Brett had been on the point of betraying him. And betrayal was the worst of crimes, and demanded the worst of punishments. Death was no more than he deserved.

'Have you any idea where they're going?' he demanded into the mobile phone. Brett might be dead, but Delancey couldn't take the chance that he had perhaps lived long enough inside the fleeing helicopter to have told Nathan everything. Nathan had to be stopped – now more than ever. He had ceased to be a minor irritation – he was now a major threat to Delancey's plans.

'I've just checked their flight plan with air-traffic control,' said David. 'They're heading towards Germany.'

'Germany?' Delancey had expected Nathan to return to Britain, to come running back to his mysterious benefactor. So why was he going to Germany?

Unless . . .

A cold chill ran through him. He had always suspected that Brett was a lot more devious than he had given him credit for, and this could be Brett's legacy to Delancey. 'Whereabouts?' He knew that Brett had been living in Hamburg, but he had had him traced for the last six months: there hadn't been a single clue in that time as to where he was hiding this evidence of his, nor any sign that he had contacted anyone else.

Because it wasn't Hamburg that Delancey was worried about. It was somewhere else in Germany. Somewhere where Delancey had buried his deepest, darkest secret.

Was that where they were going?

David Kirsten's next words were like a dagger to Delancey, even though something inside him had been expecting it. Brett's revenge.

'Schönefeld Airport – Berlin.'

Delancey froze. A unfamiliar feeling started to grow inside him.

Fear.

'Are you sure about that?' Delancey barked. It couldn't be.

How could Brett have tracked Harvey down? How had Brett known about him?

'Absolutely, Adrian. We're just getting clearance to leave Nice at the moment. But Dexter's got a good half-hour head start. I don't know where to go once we reach Berlin.'

'Leave that to me. As soon as you get there, I'll tell you. Just keep me informed, David – every step of the way. And don't make any more mistakes.' With that, he put the mobile phone on the desk. Berlin. It couldn't be . . . could it?

When Adrian Delancey had been twenty-five, he had fallen in love for the first time. The *only* time. The pain he had felt when they parted had torn him apart, torn his soul apart. And that pain had been the catalyst for his own personal metamorphosis into the Adrian Delancey that he was today. Love no longer mattered. Sex could be bought. All that counted was power, the power to make sure that no one ever hurt him again.

Until now. If Delancey's suspicions were correct, that mantra, the code that had determined his life for the last decade, was about to be sorely tested. Part of him wanted to get to Berlin, to utterly destroy Nathan Dexter before he could uncover the truth. But he knew that would be pointless. By the time he reached Germany, it would be far, far too late.

All he could do now was wait. And hope that David didn't let him down again.

'I hope you can explain yourself,' growled Marco as he entered the playroom. He had grabbed one of Lawrence's sweatshirts and a pair of his boxers on his way out of the bedroom, and was still struggling with the sweatshirt.

Lawrence was sitting at his computer, but his gaze was beyond that, out into the breaking dawn of a London summer morning.

'There's been . . . an incident,' he muttered.

'An incident? What the fuck does that mean?' said Marco, pouring himself a very strong mug of coffee from the cafetière on the table.

'Brett's been killed in Monte Carlo. Shot by one of Delancey's operatives, if the description's correct. A very unpleasant hired hand called David Kirsten.'

A cold knife of fear stabbed at Marco. 'Nate?'

'From what Nathan's told me, he and his PA are OK, which is a small blessing. They're on their way to Berlin at the moment. It seems that Brett was able to pass some information to Nathan just before –'

'When do you want me to leave?' said Marco. Nathan was getting out of his depth, and Marco wanted to be there to add his support. He wanted to find this David Kirsten and rip the bastard apart.

'I don't,' said Lawrence, finally looking at him. Marco was shocked at how drained he looked, as if the news had taken all of his strength from him. The Hellfire Club might be bigger than either the Elective or the Syndicate, it might be as powerful as both of those organisations put together, but it was clear that Lawrence had never had to deal with anything like this. Breaking legs was one thing, but murder? Lawrence may have read about Delancey's machinations, have heard about them, but Marco had seen it at first hand. For God's sake, Delancey had sent him to Amsterdam to kill Nathan!

Lawrence's words finally registered. 'What? Why not? What the fuck are you talking about? Nathan needs me, Lawrence,' he pleaded.

'And so do I. I am not putting you in danger as well. If my information is correct –'

'Your information!' Marco bellowed. 'Your information has just led to someone being murdered!' As soon as the words left his lips, Marco regretted them. Lawrence hadn't pulled the trigger, and Marco could see how badly he was taking it. 'I'm sorry,' he whispered. 'I shouldn't have said that.'

Lawrence shook his head. 'No, I deserved it. All this James Bond stuff – I was treating it like some sort of a game. And someone's dead because of it. That's why I can't put you at risk as well.'

As Lawrence slumped back in his chair, Marco came to a

decision. Despite what Lawrence wanted, Marco would be there for Nathan.

Whatever the consequences.

'The Tacheles Bar,' muttered Nathan.

'What?' Gary was bearing up well, and had showered and changed. Nathan had watched him as he undressed, watched him reveal that fit, hairy body, but sex hadn't seemed right. He just hoped that there would be another time once all of this was over.

'That's where we go. Brett's last words – he wanted us to go to the Tacheles Bar. Have you heard of it?'

Shaking his head, Gary got up and went over to the computer which sat on the oak desk – the Hellfire Club had thought of everything. He spent a few seconds typing, before turning to Nathan. 'I've just done an Internet search – it's real, at least.'

'A gay place?'

Gary shook his head. 'Not quite. According to the Internet, it's a "mixed trendy bar leaning towards the gothic and techno". Doesn't sound like Brett's scene at all.'

Nathan had to agree that Brett would have seemed rather incongruous in those surroundings. 'Then there's this Harvey, his "witness". Who's he? How are we going to find him?'

Gary looked at his watch. 'We'll be in Berlin in about ten minutes. Why don't you get changed? We'll find a hotel and get a few hours' sleep. *Then* we can worry about Harvey and the Tacheles Club.'

Nathan nodded. 'There's nothing we can do until this evening, I suppose.' He got up and walked over to the shower room, shedding his clothes as he did so. Gary came over and started to massage his shoulders. 'Nathan, I . . .'

Nathan turned to face him. He knew what Gary was going to say – he just didn't want to hear it. Everyone who got close to him got hurt, and he didn't want that to happen with Gary. When anything happened – *if* anything happened – between him and Gary, it would be when they had put all of this behind them, when they were free of the Elective, the Syndicate, the Hellfire

Club . . . and Adrian Delancey, hovering over the whole affair like some obscene vampire.

Nathan placed a finger on Gary's lips. 'Not now. Please?'

Gary seemed to understand, and gave Nathan a hug. As he released him, he still looked a bit upset.

'What's the matter?'

Gary seemed to be having trouble saying the words. Finally, he managed it. 'If it became necessary, could *you* do that? Could *you* kill a man?'

Nathan froze. That had been Lawrence's hidden question when he had recruited him into his holy war against Delancey. Could Nathan do it? Could he break through the final restraint and murder a man in cold blood?

The answer he gave Gary was the most honest one he could give. 'I don't know,' he whispered. 'I just don't know.'

Scott woke with a start. He hadn't intended to sleep – he hadn't thought he would feel comfortable enough – but obviously he had slept. He looked at his watch: it was nearly six in the morning, and the sun was just beginning to rise, casting an orange glow over the sea.

He jumped to his feet and stretched, taking deep lungfuls of the morning air. It looked like it was going to be a nice day. But all Scott could think about was getting home. He would hitch a lift to London, then he would try to track Leigh down and get an explanation.

And then he would see Nathan. And try to bring some order back into both of their lives.

Scott had a quick piss against the rusting metal of the pier before making his way off the beach towards the coast road. For the best chance to get a lift, he ought to head in the direction of the main road towards London, he decided.

He didn't spot the lone figure watching him from a distant bench.

★

The Learjet touched down at Schönefeld Airport at about seven o'clock in the morning, local time. Nathan and Gary walked down the steps towards the terminal building. It was already light, and a cool breeze was blowing.

'Any ideas?' asked Gary as they walked through passport control.

'Delancey will know what's happened – and he's not going to give up now. His . . . associate will probably be here within the hour, but we'll be long gone by then,' said Nathan as they stepped out of the terminal building.

'We should get a hotel in the city. There are hundreds of hotels – he can't possibly find us.' Gary gestured towards the silver Mercedes that was waiting for them.

'No,' said Nathan. 'Not the car. Send it to another hotel. Delancey's people will be watching for it.'

As the car sped off, Nathan hailed one of the cream-coloured taxis.

'You're good at this,' said Gary. 'All this cloak-and-dagger business.'

Nathan laughed, but Gary was right. As they climbed into the taxi, he wondered – not for the first time – about what was happening to him. What had he said to Gary about Adrian Delancey? 'It's Delancey, Gary. He taints everyone who comes into contact with him.'

Nathan had had enough contact with Delancey for it to have had an effect. Was he changing? Was he becoming as ruthless and manipulative as Delancey? Or worse . . . did he need to become like that to defeat him?

The questions remained unanswered as the taxi headed towards the centre of Berlin.

Marco awoke from his nap with the smell of fresh coffee wafting towards him. He had fallen asleep on the sofa; glancing at the timer on the hi-fi system, he noted that it was nearly eight in the morning.

'Any word?' he croaked.

Lawrence nodded. 'They touched down in Berlin about ten minutes ago.'

'I want to go there, Lawrence,' Marco insisted as he sipped his coffee. His short sleep hadn't changed his mind at all.

'Out of the question,' said Lawrence. 'I'm hoping that Nathan will be back in the country tomorrow morning. Then we'll have a clearer idea of what we're doing.'

Marco got to his feet. 'I better get going,' he said. 'I need to check up on few things at home.'

A brief flash of disappointment crossed Lawrence's face, but he said nothing about it. 'OK. We'll touch base later.'

'I'd better give you my phone number.'

For the first time in hours, Lawrence actually smiled. 'Oh, don't worry about that. I know where you live,' he said with mock menace.

'Of course you do,' said Marco, as he went upstairs to get dressed.

Scott felt as if he'd been standing at the junction for hours, even though a glance at his watch showed that it had been only twenty minutes. He had expected the traffic to be heavier, even though it was a Saturday, but only a few cars and lorries had passed him, and none of them had paid him the slightest attention.

That's what comes of looking like a thug, he thought ruefully. You might like it, Nathan, but it doesn't help me to hitch a lift.

A rumble made him look up. An HGV was slowing as it approached the lay-by where Scott was waiting. With a grunt of air brakes, it stopped as it drew level with Scott.

'Where you going?' asked the driver. He was about thirty, thickset with short curly hair.

'As close to London as I can get,' Scott explained.

'No problem. Hop in.'

As Scott climbed on to the footplate and got into the cab, he was relieved that he had finally got a lift. That the lorry driver was quite a looker was an added bonus.

★

The Crowne Plaza Hotel on Nürmburge Strasse was a typical city-centre hotel, specifically catering for the business community. Checking in was quick and easy, and, only minutes after getting out of the taxi, they were putting their luggage on the big double bed of their room.

Berlin was living up to its reputation for being liberal-minded: the check-in woman hadn't batted an eyelid when Gary had asked for a double room, even though Nathan was hovering behind him.

'What time should we leave for the club?' asked Gary, throwing his heavy brown leather jacket on to one of the chairs.

'Oh, not till about nine o'clock,' said Nathan, yawning. 'I don't know about you, but I definitely need some sleep.'

Gary nodded. Within a couple of minutes, the two of them were naked: they stared at each other for long seconds, each mirroring the other's desire. Finally, Nathan pulled back the duvet and gestured for Gary to get in.

Nathan followed, pulling the duvet over them, and snuggled up to Gary, with his stomach and chest against Gary's back – 'sleeping spoons' was how Nathan's mother described the position. Gary's body, fit and furry, was warm and comforting, like having a living breathing teddy bear in bed with you. Nathan tried to remember the last time he had felt so relaxed in bed with someone, and realised it had been with Scott. But he didn't feel any pain – not any more. Perhaps the time had come to move on.

As soon as his arm encircled Gary, Nathan felt his hard-on growing as it nestled against Gary's thigh, and, as Nathan's hand brushed Gary's stomach, he briefly stroked Gary's erection. But Nathan was too tired to do anything at the moment. He just wanted to feel safe and secure for a few hours, away from gun-wielding murderers, helicopter chases and Adrian Delancey.

He was asleep within minutes.

The lorry thundered along the quiet motorway, heading towards London. The driver – Phil – had obviously been grateful for someone to chat to, because he hadn't stopped talking since Scott had jumped into his cab. He had been driving through the night, going from Devon, along the coast to Brighton to pick up something – Scott hadn't really been paying attention to the details – before heading up to London.

'So, what do you do?' Phil asked.

'I'm a student,' said Scott.

'In Brighton?'

'No, in London. I came down with a friend, but we got separated, and he's got the train tickets.'

Phil nodded. 'Bummer, eh? Spent the night in Brighton, did you?'

'Under the pier.'

Phil looked ahead. 'There's a service station about a mile away. Fancy breakfast? I know I do – I'm starving.'

Scott had to admit that the thought of a hot cup of coffee was irresistible. He was feeling both exhausted and a little hung over from the previous night. 'Sounds good to me,' he replied.

The lorry turned off the motorway and parked up in the HGV area of the car park. Scott and Phil got out, and Scott had to admit that Phil was actually quite horny. He was wearing a red hooded sweatshirt and jeans, but even under the baggy sweatshirt Scott could see that he was stocky. But it wasn't just his physical appearance: as he came round the lorry, he gave Scott a broad grin – the sort of grin that made Scott want to fall to his knees and suck on Phil's cock.

'What's it to be? Full English?'

Scott knew what he wanted, but he'd settle for a plate of bacon and eggs – and quite a few coffees.

Lawrence sat in the Summer Room, nursing a glass of Louis XIII and his own, troubled, thoughts. He needed to concentrate on Hellfire business, but all he could think about was Marco. After five years, five long years during which he had convinced himself that it was all over, Marco had walked back into his life and into his heart. Lawrence knew that he loved him, loved with the same intensity as he had always loved him.

But the timing couldn't have been worse. The Elective was moving in for the kill, threatening to destroy everything for which Lawrence's family had striven for the last two hundred years. Nathan and Gary were in danger, risking their lives for him – and all he could think about was Marco's big hairy Australian body, holding him, taking him.

He drained the glass and touched a button to summon Hadleigh. He wanted another couple of brandies before he made his next move.

Scott sat back in the plastic seat and gave a contented sigh. He hadn't realised how hungry he had been, and had wolfed down the fry-up as if there were no tomorrows.

'Looks like you needed that,' said Phil, nodding towards Scott's empty plate.

Scott agreed, his mouth still full. 'Thanks,' he said in a muffled voice.

'No problem,' said Phil, getting to his feet. 'Ready?'

Scott followed Phil out of the service station, across the mostly empty car park. Most of the traffic was heading the other way, towards Brighton, and the whole place was quiet.

Phil pulled his door shut and looked round at Scott. 'I don't know about you, but I can do with an hour's kip before I set off. Or were you in a hurry?' he said, his tone indicating that he sincerely hoped not.

Scott shrugged. 'I'm not rushing off,' he replied. To be honest, he wasn't actually looking forward to getting back to London: there was something odd going on. Last night, it just seemed that there had been some sort of misunderstanding, but now, after some sleep, Scott had to admit that he didn't believe that Leigh would have just left like that – it wasn't like him. And, after that, Nathan . . .

Phil was closing a curtain around the interior of the cab, and

Scott remembered the other lorries nearby, the interiors of the cabs curtained off to stop people disturbing them.

Then he leant over to Scott and put a strong hand on his knee. 'You're a good-looking kid,' he whispered.

Scott didn't know what to say. He returned the gesture, rubbing his hand up Phil's knee, getting as far as the groin before going back in the other direction. Encouraged, Phil kissed Scott on the neck, then on the cheek, and finally on the lips. He was gentle at first, his tongue lightly pressing at Scott's lips. But soon Scott's tongue was responding, forcing its way into Phil's mouth – and Phil went wild. His tongue battled with Scott's, pushing past it and entering his mouth. Scott turned in his seat, his hands pulling at Phil's sweatshirt, while Phil started to tug Scott's shirt from his jeans. Somehow they managed to remove each other's top without having to stop kissing for more than a few seconds, and Scott took a moment to appreciate his new friend's body.

Although he wasn't as muscular as Eddie, Phil obviously worked out fairly regularly, with a well-defined chest and arms. Hair covered his chest, before trailing off in a line that joined up with the hair on his stomach. His left nipple was pierced with a silver bar, and there was a tattoo of a cross gripped by a dragon on his right shoulder.

'Nice,' said Phil, pulling back from the kiss to admire Scott. He placed a hand on Scott's chest, and then gently tweaked each of his nipples. Scott could see the bulge in Phil's jeans, and desperately wanted to get inside, to hold that cock, to suck that cock, to take that cock inside him. Scott's own dick was painfully constrained in his jeans, and he wanted to get it out, to show it to Phil, to let Phil do whatever he wanted with it.

Phil must have read his mind – or his expression. He leant over and undid the belt and then the flies, pulling Scott's cock out and squeezing it in his hand. Scott returned the favour, unzipping Phil's jeans, allowing his cock to spring free. And what a cock!

Scott had thought that Gus's cock in the club had been thick, but compared with Phil's . . . It must have been about four inches thick, a dark, veined shaft that climbed about eight inches before ending in a wet red helmet. Scott didn't hesitate: he leant over and took as much of it into his mouth as he could. Phil shuddered as Scott's tongue touched his helmet, grabbing Scott's head and forcing him to take more and more of it. Scott could just about take that big helmet in his mouth, his tongue still playing with it, licking at the dick slit and running round the ridge.

Phil was holding on to Scott's thick hard cock, gently wanking it with his firm grip. But Scott wanted Phil's mouth round his cock – preferably at the same time. Scott tried to figure out whether there was some way to recline the seats.

Phil must have guessed what Scott was looking for. He pulled a lever at the side of his seat and pushed the backs: they reclined, giving them the area of a reasonable bed to work with.

Or play with, thought Scott. He reached down to Phil's trainers and pulled them off, allowing him to slip his jeans down his hairy legs. As he did so, he allowed his hands to stroke Phil's thighs. As soon as Phil was naked, he gently pushed Scott back on the reclined seats and did the same. Phil climbed over and lay on top of Scott, and began to grind his thick cock against Scott's.

Scott could feel his helmet rubbing against Phil's, two helmets lubricated by pre-come. Phil started to kiss Scott once more, frantically, violently, his hands pulling and tearing at Scott's chest, tugging on his nipples. One hand moved downward, finding Scott's cock and grabbing it. Scott realised that Phil was wanking them both off at the same time, and the feeling was almost more than he could handle.

After a few moments, Phil moved his hand even lower, reaching between Scott's legs and finding his arse. A brutal finger invaded him, pushing his ring open and entering. Scott yelled with the pain, but Phil didn't stop – if anything, it urged him to force his finger deeper into him.

Scott's hand sought out their two cocks, still rubbing together: he continued from where Phil had left off, seizing their dicks and wanking them together, his hand now wet with pre-come.

Phil's finger was now in as far as he could go, his fingertip stroking the hot nut of Scott's prostate. Pain turned into pleasure as Phil rubbed with a building rhythm: Scott synchronised his wanking so he was pulling them both off in time to Phil's stimulation of his arse. Phil continued to kiss Scott, even more brutally, even more forcefully, and Scott guessed that he too was close.

Scott felt a familiar sensation growing in the pit of his stomach, and sensed his balls tightening with the imminence of his release. He could feel Phil's cock grow even stiffer, that huge tool pressing into his own dick. Finally, he couldn't stop himself. With Phil's finger still inside his arse, Scott pushed Phil away slightly so he could see their cocks being wanked as one: the sight was enough to finish him off. A stream of come shot from him, spraying both of them. As the white drops fell on to Phil's dick, he came as well, a torrent of warm come that flowed over Scott's hand, his own cock, mingling with his own come. The two of them bellowed with the intensity of their orgasms, as come continued to flow from both of them for long moments.

Eventually, Scott slumped backwards on to the seat and sighed.

Phil gave him one of his wicked grins. 'You weren't in a hurry to get back to London, were you?'

Scott smiled. After that, he could have stayed in the cab all day. And, looking at the smile on Phil's face, he very probably would.

Marco looked at his watch. It was just past five in the afternoon. Where had the day gone? He had sat on his sofa, hoping to get a couple of hours' sleep, but all he had done was try to figure out what was happening. Only twenty-four hours ago, he had been sitting with Scott, discussing Nathan, thinking about the Elective.

Now, he could think only about Lawrence.

They hadn't discussed what had happened. Partly because events in Monaco had overshadowed everything else, but mainly because Marco was worried what would happen if they did. At the moment, it was like some sort of a dream, a fantasy – the moment either of them started to analyse it, to dig deeply into the whys and wherefores, they could lose the lot. And that was something that Marco simply couldn't face.

He checked his watch yet again, and came to a decision. He was going to go out. If Leigh could have fun in Brighton, Marco was bloody well going to have fun in London. He smiled: he still had time to catch the Bear Sauna in Soho.

Determined, he looked around for his boots.

Sion cursed himself as he hurried through Soho. He had fully intended to deal with this matter last night, but he was mother to his charges, and one of his 'daughters' – Brendan – had needed his advice. Sion had spent the entire evening in the Crossed Swords trying to sort out the poor boy's tangled love life; by the time Brendan had felt happy enough to face the rest of the night, the Brave Trader had already closed.

And today, even though it was a Saturday, Sion had been tied up with business until the early evening. Damn Lawrence – why did he always choose Saturdays to impart whatever vital snippets of importance he saw fit? But Sion couldn't be too angry with Lawrence: he had been Sion's first 'daughter', and that demanded a certain degree of both loyalty and indulgence.

Passing through Old Compton Street, he was pleased to see how busy it was: the pavement cafés were buzzing with clientele, and a steady stream of people were packing into both the cosy confines of the Europa Arms and the two-storey Club Nebula. Normally, he would have had time to stop for a coffee, a pint or a quick quad vod, but he owed it to Nathan to talk to the Royal Enclosure of the Brave Trader as soon as possible.

Brushing past the dawdling tourists on Wardour Street, Sion tried to work out what he was going to say. He knew that he couldn't persuade the Elective to drop its pursuit of Nathan: he didn't have the authority, and nor did the Royal Enclosure. But he was sure that, between him and the Enclosure, at least *somebody* could be made to see reason. All he would ask for was that Nathan could take up his old position in the Royal Enclosure, a place of safety, where he could relax without living in constant fear of the revenge of the Elective.

Because, although the Elective knew nothing of the Hellfire Club, Sion knew that the members of the Royal Enclosure were quite aware that he had some friends in very high places indeed.

Almost out of breath, he finally reached Poland Street. Saturdays tended to be a little on the quiet side, which suited Sion perfectly. A chance to talk, a chance to reflect.

Just what Sion needed.

Scott picked up the receiver, still not sure whether he was doing the right thing. But he couldn't really see any other option. There was no sign of Nathan anywhere: he wasn't at home, he wasn't in the Crossed Swords . . . Coupled with his annoyance towards Leigh, Scott just wasn't in a very good mood at all now.

Scott hadn't spoken to Marco for months – not since Scott had split up with Nathan. But Scott liked the guy, and hoped that he still had time for him. If he had spoken to Nathan over the last couple of days, there was a chance that he knew where Nathan was. And he really ought to make contact with Leigh and find out what had happened.

Punching in Marco's mobile number – Nathan had taught him to always use mobiles wherever possible, since they were more difficult to tap into – Scott waited. Part of him hoped that it would go straight to Marco's voice mail: he was still a bit nervous about talking to him. What if he asked about what Leigh had been up to in Brighton? Before he could even consider that one, he heard the familiar Australian accent saying hello on the other end of the line.

'Marco . . . it's Scott.'

'Scott! How are you? How's Brighton?'

How's Brighton? Why did he think he was still in Brighton? Hadn't Leigh spoken to him?

For a second, Scott considered playing along, allowing Marco to believe that he was still in Brighton. Just in case Leigh was up to something, and wanted Scott to cover for him. Bollocks to that, Scott suddenly decided. If he didn't have the decency to explain to Scott what he was up to, why should Scott lie for him?

'I'm not in Brighton, Marco – I'm in London. On Oxford Street, actually.'

'Oh. Is Leigh with you?'

There had been too many lies, Scott decided. The time had come for openness, but what actually came out was confused, muddled. 'We got separated. I'm not entirely sure where he is, actually. I thought he was with you.'

Marco was silent for a second before replying. 'I see.'

I see? He didn't exactly sound very worried. Oh well, a mystery for another time. 'I'm trying to find Nathan. I need to talk to him.'

'Nathan's not here. He's . . . gone abroad for a couple of days.'

'Abroad?' From what Scott knew, Nathan had no job, no money. How could he afford to go abroad? What the hell was Nathan up to now?

'Look, Scott – we need to talk. How close are you to the Brave Trader?'

'About two minutes' walk. That's where I was headed.'

'I'm round the corner in the Crossed Swords. I'll meet you in the Brave Trader in about ten minutes, and then I'll explain everything. OK?'

Well, actually, it wasn't OK, but, if Marco knew something about Nathan, then Scott needed to know as well. 'OK. I'll see you in there.' With that, he put the phone down. Nathan abroad, Leigh missing, Marco being mysterious . . . Something was going on, and Scott had to get to the bottom of it. Frustrated and confused, he headed towards Poland Street and the Brave Trader. After all that, he needed a drink.

Lawrence looked at the phone for the umpteenth time. Should he ring Marco? He knew that Marco still wanted to fly to Berlin, but there wasn't much chance of that: Lawrence had ensured that the forces of the Hellfire Club were watching every port and airport.

What if he did phone Marco. What would he say? Thanks a lot for last night, must do it again in five years? It had meant much, much more to Lawrence than a simple shag – he could get that with a snap of his fingers. No, it was almost as if Marco's reappearance had been some kind of an omen, a sign that Delancey would soon be wiped out, bringing to an end a five-year cycle of revenge. Lawrence didn't know how Marco felt, but he just hoped it was reciprocated.

He looked up as the phone rang. He wheeled himself over to the phone and picked it up – and his face froze as he heard the words coming down the line.

He clicked the hook and quickly dialled for Hadleigh. He answered within seconds, but even that was too long.

'Hadleigh, Get the car round. Now!'

'Sion?' Scott's tone was accusatory, harsh, but why not? Sion was supposed to be the one person whom Nathan trusted, the one person who hadn't turned his back on him when the whole of London had disowned him. So what the hell was he doing, standing in the Royal Enclosure of the Brave Trader, chatting away to known members of the Elective as if they were old friends?

Anger overriding everything else, Scott pushed past the busy Saturday night crowd of bears and clones and entered the Royal Enclosure. The whole royal court was there: Suspenders Alex, Little John, JT, Morgy . . . and, at its centre, Sion.

'Sion? Can I have a word, please?' said Scott in a monotone, trying not to show any outward signs of his emotions. How could Sion have betrayed Nathan like this? *Betrayed? Like you did, Scott, when you walked out on him, when you left him to face the wolves alone?* But he ignored the voice. He just wanted to know what was going on.

Sion turned round and regarded Scott with a mixture of shock and surprise. 'Scott. I –'

'We need to talk, Sion.'

'Not now, Scott.'

Scott didn't notice Willie coming out of the toilet, looking rather flustered, talking to his partner Ron in a low, urgent voice.

Scott finally lost it. 'What the fuck do you think you're doing?'

Sion tried to place a reassuring hand on Scott's shoulder, but Scott threw it off, ignoring the stares of the other members of the Enclosure. He knew what they thought of him, and he didn't care. All he cared about was Nathan.

'I want to know, Sion. I want to know what you're playing at.'

Before anyone could answer, Willie's Scottish brogue cut through the conversation.

'Everyone get out. Now!'

'What?' someone shouted. Scott didn't know who'd said it. All he heard was Willie's reply.

'There's something in the lockup. I think it's a bomb!'

Mike Bury sauntered down Poland Street, a smile on his face. Yesterday, with Nathan, had been great. It had been a while since they had spent any time together, and yesterday had proved to Mike that he had missed Nathan. Perhaps it was time to make it a bit more . . . regular.

However, he had to confess to a little nervousness. There was a pretty good chance that Scott was in the Brave Trader, and he wasn't sure whether seeing him would be such a good idea. He was fairly sure that Scott knew about Mike's . . . arrangement with Nathan, and he didn't know how he would react to seeing him.

Mike was standing virtually opposite the Brave Trader when it happened. The sound stopped him in his tracks, a concussive boom that echoed up and down Poland Street. Simultaneously, the front of the Brave Trader exploded outward, its glass-panelled frontage shattering into countless shards, the wooden frame and door splintering across Poland Street. He fell to the pavement as an entire pane of bevelled glass shot past him, and watched from there as a gout of flame rolled out from the ruined façade. Putting his hand over his face to protect himself from the heat, he clambered to his feet and tried to get closer, to see if he could help. Only now, as the rumbling of the explosion and the crashing of masonry and glass subsided, could he hear it.

The screaming.

Mike went to run inside, when a heavy hand planted itself on his shoulder. He turned to see Marco standing there, his expression one of pure horror, his voice a growl.

'Scott's in there.'

Ten

_____

'What?' Mike yelled, pulling away from Marco's restraint. 'We have to help him!'

'It's too dangerous,' Marco shouted back. He wasn't going to stand by and watch Mike put himself at risk. 'You stay here.' With that, he headed towards the broken wreck of the Brave Trader, even as the sirens from the fire engines started, homing in from the station on Shaftsbury Avenue.

Stepping over the broken frontage, Marco was terrified of what he might find. He had told Scott to wait for him in the Brave Trader – how could he handle it if anything had happened to him?

The interior of the pub was chaos. A cursory glance suggested that the centre of the blast had been towards the rear of the bar, possibly the toilet. But the whys and wherefores were irrelevant: the only thing that mattered at the moment was to get as many people out as possible. Because, unless Marco was very much mistaken, that was gas that he could smell.

It looked like the majority of people at the front of the bar weren't too badly hurt: stunned by the blast, suffering cuts and bruises, but able to move. He saw Peter and Sean lying by the fruit machine, unhurt but dazed. Marco gently pulled them to their feet and urged them towards the street, before turning to address the pub.

'There's a gas leak: get out of here as quickly as you can. If you can walk, help the people who can't!' he bellowed above the groans. As he climbed over the shattered stools and tables, taking care not to hurt himself on the broken glass, he desperately looked for Scott, helping people to their feet as he went. Nobody looked too badly hurt in this part of the Brave Trader, although Marco couldn't help noticing the cut down Postman George's face.

The worst of the damage was centred around the Royal Enclosure. The explosion appeared to have come from the toilet: the toilet door was broken like matchwood and scattered over the gap between the bar and the kitchen, and the pillar between the toilet door and the stairwell had cracked.

As Marco got closer, he could see that the kitchen door was off its hinges, but that wasn't a bad thing: he could see people behind it, and it might just have offered some protection to them.

It turned out to be Morgy and Little John, slumped in the doorway. Marco couldn't help smiling when he saw that they were still clasping their drinks. But they weren't moving. Kneeling over them, Marco was relieved to see that they were still breathing. But there was no sign of Scott.

'Are they . . .?' asked Ron, climbing to his feet behind the bar. Kevin and Trevor, the other two barmen, also seemed OK: the bar had obviously protected them from the blast.

'They're alive. Get them out of here,' Marco ordered. 'Get everyone out of here.' A creak came from behind him – the stairs to the upstairs bar. And that pillar looked a lot less supportive than it had a couple of moments ago. 'Is anyone still up there?'

'A few people,' said Trevor. 'Do you want me to look?'

'No – you make sure everyone gets out. I'll check upstairs.' He paused. 'Is anyone in the flat?' Willie and Ron's flat was on the top floor of the pub.

'No,' Kevin called out as Marco clambered out of the wreckage of the Royal Enclosure.

At the foot of the stairs, the smell of gas was far stronger: Marco remembered that there was a gas pipe in the lockup. If that had ruptured, a single naked flame or electrical spark would ignite the lot. Taking care not to lose his footing on the broken stairs, Marco clambered over the wreckage and made his way upstairs, knowing that he might have only minutes.

The worst damage was at the top of the stairs. The explosion had been directly below the ladies' toilet, and that had been blown apart. Marco just hoped that no one had been inside at the time. The stairs to the flat had also been torn apart – Marco was glad that no one was up there.

There was a lot of smoke and dust around, which made it difficult to see what was going on. He peered into the gloom – unsurprisingly, the electricity had gone off – and tried to see who was up there. By some strange quirk, the upstairs bar was rarely busy on a Saturday, and Marco could make out only about five people, three sitting and two on the floor. All seemed relatively OK, thankfully.

'We've got to get downstairs,' he shouted, and was pleased to see the five of them get to their feet. He let them out first as he gave a last double check that no one else was up there, before following them downstairs.

By the time he reached the lower bar, most people had left. Through the ruined façade of the pub, he could see a crowd of dazed and bloodied people standing on Poland Street. He made a gesture for them to move further away – the gas smell was almost overpowering now.

'Someone's trapped under there,' said Kevin, who was helping the last few people to their feet. He pointed towards the bar. A section of ceiling had fallen during the explosion, and Marco could see that there was someone underneath.

'Someone give me a hand,' he shouted. Kevin continued helping the others, while Willie and Marco took a corner each and pulled. After agonising moments, the masonry moved – seconds later, they had enough room and enough leverage to pull it off.

Marco saw who it was and felt his heart skip a beat: Scott was on top, but his body was shielding someone beneath him.

Marco knelt down. 'Scott – are you OK?'

Scott turned his head and looked at Marco blearily. There was a cut on his forehead, blood trickling down. 'I've been better,' he said with a dazed smile. 'Help me with Sion.'

As Scott moved and rolled the other person over, Marco was shocked. It was Sion. *Sion?* What the hell was the head of the Round Table doing in the Royal Enclosure? It didn't matter, he decided. That could be figured out later, when they weren't in danger of being blown sky high.

Sion was unconscious: Marco gently lifted him to his feet, and he and Kevin carried him out of the Brave Trader, with Willie and Scott just behind.

'Is that everyone?' Marco called out.

'I think so,' said Willie as they walked over the debris. 'If there was anyone else, I didn't see them.'

They had just reached the other side of Poland Street when the inevitable finally happened. Whether it was a stray spark, or the gas meeting a smouldering cigarette butt in an ashtray, no one would ever know.

Everyone dropped to the pavement and put their arms over their heads as the huge gas explosion tore apart what was left of the Brave Trader – a bright orange mushroom cloud of flame which lifted the roof off the pub before allowing it to fall back and shatter into thousands of tiles that bombarded Poland Street like shrapnel. At the same time, the mirrored windows of Marks and Spencer's side exit shattered, raining silver on to pavement and person alike.

As soon as there was no danger of being stabbed by a piece of shrapnel, Marco tried to get himself and the others as far away from the Brave Trader as he could – he was sure that he could hear another explosion, not too far away. As his heartbeat returned to normal and he finally calmed down, a host of questions suddenly presented themselves to him. Why had the Brave Trader been bombed, and by whom? Had it been bombed, or had it been some sort of accident? Marco just hoped that it wasn't the obvious answer. But he knew, deep down, that it was.

As they reached the junction of Poland Street, Marco turned to Scott. 'How's Sion?' he asked. He still wanted to know what Sion had been doing in the Royal Enclosure in the first place, but that could wait. Sion didn't look like he was going to be talking to anyone in the next few hours.

'I think he needs to be looked at – he's out cold,' Scott replied. 'Has anyone called an ambulance?'

Marco nodded, remembering hearing someone doing it from their mobile. 'You should get yourself checked out as well,' said Marco. He pointed to the cut on Nathan's forehead. 'That looks serious, mate.'

'It's nothing,' said Scott. 'What happened? The last thing I remember is Willie shouting something –'

'I saw a package in the lockup,' explained Willie, next to them. Despite his covering of plaster and dust, he seemed to be unhurt. 'The next thing, it blew up.' He looked at what was left of the Brave Trader – nothing more than a heap of burning rubble – and Marco saw a tear in his eye. 'Gone,' he muttered. 'All gone.'

Marco felt for him, but now was the time for practicalities. From Willie's description, it was clear that it had been a bomb. 'Is everyone OK?' he called out to the crowd around him. Although he wasn't a regular in the Brave Trader, his role in the Elective meant that all of the Royal Enclosure recognised him, and that gave him a certain gravitas.

'No one died, if that's what you mean,' said Little David. 'Nobody's been too badly hurt, and I don't think that there was anyone left in there.' He looked at the rubble. 'What the fuck happened?'

Before Marco could reply, a shout came from behind him. A youngish bloke – early twenties, with bleached blond hair and wearing a crop-top – was running towards them, trying to make himself heard. Only when he was about five yards away from him could Marco make out what he was saying.

'The Europa Arms,' he was yelling. 'There's been an explosion!'

An explosion? That couldn't be coincidence. Pubs just didn't blow up for no reason. Before Marco could even begin to consider what was going on, a bleep from his belt attracted his attention. Taking his mobile phone from its pouch, he pressed the receive button.

The conversation was short, and mostly one-sided, but, when Marco ended the call, he felt as if all the blood had drained from his body. This just couldn't be happening.

'What is it?' asked Scott, spotting his reaction.

Marco's voice was quiet when he replied, quiet and incredulous. 'That was a colleague of mine. They got the Harness as well.' He thought of his club, burning in the night sky. He just hoped that no one had been killed.

'The Harness?' said Scott, his voice betraying the fact that he knew the significance of the Harness. In many circles, it was nothing more than a popular S&M club in Vauxhall. But it held a very special position in Marco's life, because it was also home to the London headquarters of the Elective.

Just as the Europa Arms and the Brave Trader had been important Elective outposts, he realised. Any last doubts that he harboured had vanished. There was only one man who could have had both the motive and the ability to stage a terrorist attack against the Elective.

Adrian Delancey.

Marco was so preoccupied that he didn't notice the large silver BMW pull up alongside him.

'Well, are you going to stand there all day?' Marco turned to look at who was speaking, and was extremely surprised to see Lawrence in the passenger seat.

'What are you doing here?'

Lawrence nodded towards the broken, burning Brave Trader. 'I came as soon as I heard about it. I presume you know about –'

'The Europa Arms and the Harness, yes. I think we can take a good stab at who's behind this, can't we?'

'Get in,' said Lawrence. 'Bring Scott, Sion and Mike as well. Things are beginning to get out of hand.'

Gary and Nathan had spent the whole of the afternoon making love, taking advantage of the huge double bed that their room afforded them. After their frantic lovemaking on the Learjet, they had taken it slowly, savouring each other's body, acquainting themselves with each other, until Nathan felt that he had known Gary all of his life.

'I suppose we'd better make a move,' said Nathan. 'The club will be opening soon.'

'I love you, Nathan,' was Gary's reply.

Nathan closed his eyes. He had known that Gary felt that way, knew that Gary had almost said it on the flight from Nice.

But that didn't make it any easier. He couldn't allow someone else into his life, he couldn't take the risk that they would be hurt like everybody else. As much as he cared for Gary, as much as he wanted Gary, he couldn't do it. He had no choice.

'I love you,' he said. As the words came out, he knew that all of his previous arguments, all of his reasons why it was a bad idea, meant nothing. All that mattered was that he did love Gary.

Leaning over the bed, Nathan kissed him, long and deep. Finally, he pulled away. 'I love you,' he repeated.

Oh well, said an inner voice. *Here we go again.*

The journey to Russell Square took minutes, but Marco used them to explain as much as he could to the others. The others being Mike and Scott – Sion knew exactly what was going on. The four of them were sitting in the back of the car – which had as much room as a London cab inside – with Lawrence and the driver in front.

'There you have it,' Marco concluded. 'The final battle between the Elective and the Syndicate, and we have ringside seats.'

'Where's Delancey?' asked Mike quietly. Marco knew that he was thinking about his twin brother, John, dead at Delancey's hand. Finding Delancey had been the whole reason that Mike had got involved – and got involved with Nathan. He just hoped that the presence of Scott and Mike together wasn't going to be explosive. After this evening, that was all they needed.

'We don't know,' Marco replied. 'That's what Nathan's trying to find out.'

'Hang on, hang on,' said Scott. 'There's one thing that I'm not entirely clear about. Who is Nathan working for? The Elective hate him, and he's hardly going to work for Delancey, is he?'

Marco knew that this was coming, but there was nothing he could do. He looked at Lawrence, who turned to face them.

'He's working for me, Scott. I'm Lawrence Dashwood – Marco's boyfr– *ex*-boyfriend.' *That* didn't go unnoticed. 'I believe that Marco has mentioned me?'

They reached the town house in Russell Square at that point.

'I think you all deserve an explanation,' said Lawrence. 'And I need a drink.'

Nathan was dressed casually in black jeans, blue Levi shirt and Caterpillar boots. He pulled on his black leather biker's jacket to complete the ensemble. Gary was wearing jeans and a white T-shirt, but he could have been wearing an old sack as far as Nathan was concerned. His feelings for Gary were stronger than ever – something that Nathan hadn't thought possible.

'How far is this Tacheles Bar?' he asked as they waited for the lift to the hotel reception.

'A good taxi ride away – it's in East Berlin,' he said as the lift arrived.

'Who's Harvey?' Nathan muttered, more to himself than anything. 'Brett seemed to think that he was the key to everything, and I can only assume that he's this mysterious witness.'

'More important, Nathan – how are we going to find him? And the safety deposit box, come to that?' He stepped out of the lift and into the foyer.

Nathan had to admit that he didn't have a clue.

★

Lawrence had brought them into his playroom, while Hadleigh handed round drinks. Marco drained his vodka in one go and asked Hadleigh for another, eliciting another sneer. Marco didn't care: events were spiralling out of control, and he needed to calm his nerves.

Lawrence had just finished giving them a potted history of the Hellfire Club and its relationship with both the Elective and the Syndicate. Considering the secrecy that Lawrence had shrouded himself and the Club in, Marco found it disconcerting that he was letting so many people in on it: he could only assume that matters were now so far out of hand that he needed all the help he could get.

'Delancey is panicking,' said Lawrence. 'Blowing up three Elective strongholds was nothing more than a knee-jerk reaction – and I can only assume that it's a reaction to Nathan.'

'Where is Nathan?' asked Scott. The concern was clear in his voice.

'Berlin. And Delancey's on his trail. I've had word that his paid assassin arrived in the city about two hours after Nathan and his PA.'

Marco couldn't help noticing a flash of jealousy cross Scott's face. Marco knew what he was thinking: PA? It should have been *me* over there with him.

'Thankfully,' Lawrence continued, 'we've been able to cover Nathan's tracks – Kirsten, who is Delancey's man, has no idea where Nathan is. But that could all change. Nathan told me where he was going. If it's as important to Delancey as I think it is, Kirsten is going to be waiting for him.'

'A trap?' asked Mike. 'Does Nathan know?'

Lawrence sighed. 'I'm hoping that Nathan is as resourceful as I've given him credit for. I daren't take the risk of trying to contact Nathan. Remember, the Syndicate has a worldwide monitoring network every bit as powerful as the Elective. And there's evidence to suggest that Delancey still has his claws into the Elective's communications network. If I contact Nathan, there's the possibility that we'll alert Delancey. It's going to be hard enough for Nathan, without them finding him before he makes his move.'

Scott stood up. His whole body language suggested restrained anger. 'But you don't mind him walking into a trap?' He strode over to Lawrence and stood over him; Marco had to force himself not to intervene.

This is all getting too personal, he realised. Scott and Nathan, him and Lawrence . . .

'What the fuck is so important to you that you'd put Nathan's life in danger, eh?' Scott demanded.

Lawrence looked up at him, his expression unreadable. 'The final end of Adrian Delancey. For everything that he's done, for everything that he would do if left unchecked. I'd make a deal with the devil to stop him, Scott.'

Scott's eyes narrowed. 'It looks like you already have,' he hissed, before sitting down. But he seemed a little less angry: as with all of them in the room, the poison touch of Adrian Delancey had polluted his life. He understood what that bastard was capable of.

Lawrence's words mirrored that. 'That's why I'm glad all of you are here: all of you. In fact, there's only one person missing – Leigh.' He turned to Marco. 'I'm afraid I have some bad news.'

Marco froze. Leigh was in Brighton, wasn't he? Then he remembered how evasive Scott had been when they had spoken on the phone earlier that evening. In the chaos of the explosion, he had completely forgotten about it.

'Has something happened to him?' he asked.

Lawrence nodded. 'I had Hellfire members watching all the ports and airports to ensure that you didn't try to follow Nathan and make matters worse,' he said in a matter-of-fact tone. Marco was taken aback – he knew that Lawrence wielded unimaginable power through the Hellfire Club, but he hadn't suspected that he would use it to keep tabs on Marco's movements. But he said nothing. What had this to do with Leigh?

'About twelve hours ago, a known Syndicate agent took the Eurostar to Paris. He wasn't alone. According to *my* agent, he was accompanying an unconscious man in a wheelchair. The description matched that of Leigh.'

Marco laughed. 'For God's sake, Lawrence, that's circumstantial at best.' But a worrying, nagging doubt was beginning to grow.

'There's more,' said Lawrence.

'Hang on,' said Scott, before Lawrence could continue. As he explained the events of the previous night, Marco's doubts became all-out panic. There was no way that Leigh would have acted in that way.

At the end, Lawrence steepled his fingers and rested his chin on them. 'This "Pete" is actually Colin Chambers, one of Delancey's inner retinue of agents. But you're right, Marco – this is circumstantial. In fact, I didn't even check until I heard this.' He clicked his mouse. Immediately, familiar words came from the speakers.

It was the message on Marco's answering machine. If he hadn't been so concerned about Leigh, he would have said something: the idea that Lawrence was monitoring his every move . . . Before he could react, the voice changed.

Marco felt his stomach knot in apprehension.

'Marco – it's been a long time.'

The voice was unmistakable: Adrian Delancey.

'I thought you'd like to know that a graphic designer of your acquaintance has decided to take advantage of my hospitality. If you want to make sure that he has a pleasant holiday, I expect two things. One: you order the Elective to allow my takeover bid of all their holdings. And don't plead ignorance, Marco: I know that you and your friends have been watching me, just as I have been watching you.

'Two: you call off Nathan, order him back to Britain. Unless you comply with these . . . suggestions by the end of today, I'm afraid dear Leigh won't be saying "wish you were here".'

A click terminated the message.

'When did you receive this?' Marco demanded. 'When?' He didn't care that Lawrence had been watching, eavesdropping, whatever. All he cared about was making sure that Leigh was safe. Fair enough, things were going to be difficult between them: there was no way that Marco could walk away from Lawrence, not now. But Marco couldn't stand by and let that bastard Delancey hurt Leigh.

'About an hour ago.'

'What are we going to do about it?' said Sion, the colour returning to his cheeks after a quad vod. 'I can't see the Elective surrendering – because that's what this is, Lawrence: a demand for unconditional surrender.'

Lawrence nodded. 'It's not just the Elective. If we agree, the Syndicate gains control of the Hellfire Club's assets by default. Knowing Delancey, it won't be long before he realises that he's bought more than he bargained for.'

'Fuck the Hellfire Club!' Marco bellowed, jumping to his feet. 'Leigh's in danger! We all know what that bastard is capable of doing. He doesn't make empty threats.'

'Marco's right,' said Scott.

Lawrence leant back in his chair and looked at his watch. 'If Nathan is going to succeed, we'll know about it in a couple of hours. I suggest we wait – however difficult that's going to be.'

As Marco poured another vodka from the bottle of Smirnoff Black that Hadleigh had left next to him – the butler had given up serving him – he knew that the next two hours were going to be the longest of his life.

The taxi drove through the darkening streets of Berlin, and Nathan had to admit that he was impressed. Munich was one thing, but Berlin seemed bigger, more alive. He and Gary stared out of the BMW's windows, as they headed through the Brandenberg Gate, and back in time.

Nathan had half expected East Berlin to resemble a building site, but it was nothing of the sort. If anything, most of the building was happening in what had been West Berlin, as the city prepared to become the seat of government. But East Berlin . . .

There was a sense of history that was lacking in the West. The

191

buildings all seemed older, but not neglected. He remembered his friend Neil telling him about it. Neil had spent a couple of years in Berlin, on either side of the Wall coming down; he had explained to Nathan that the West had felt a need to tear the old buildings down and start all over again, filling the west of the city with buildings indistinguishable from those in the city centres of other 'modern' countries. But in East Berlin a combination of economic factors and tradition had ensured that the old buildings weren't demolished but cared for, renovated and lived in. Seeing East Berlin was like travelling back in time to an earlier age.

But that wasn't to say that East Berlin was caught in a time warp – far from it. History sat side by side with the most modern of buildings: as the taxi drove them down Friedrichstrasse, Nathan was impressed by the exclusive clothes stores, the restaurants, nestling next to tall thin residential blocks painted in pastel colours. The road itself was busy with BMWs and Mercedes – not a Traband in sight! It was hard to believe that he was in a city that had been on the point of economic ruin only a decade before.

That was not to say that prosperity was everywhere. Down side streets, dark and dingy buildings were just visible; the ubiquitous curse of the late twentieth century – beggars – sat on corners, the only difference between them and their London cousins being the language.

But none of that mattered tonight. In an ideal world, Nathan would have had time to sightsee, to experience Berlin's excellent gay scene. But not tonight. Tonight he had a job to do.

As the taxi came to a stop, Nathan wondered whether this would ever end. Would they ever be free of the Elective, or the Syndicate, or the Hellfire Club? Would there ever be a time when he and Gary would be able to get on with their lives?

Putting such thoughts behind him, Nathan paid the cab driver and gave him a hefty tip. As the BMW roared away, Nathan looked up and down the street. This was a side turning from Friedrichstrasse, but it had obviously been neglected over the years. The buildings were old and hadn't been looked after: their façades were dirty, the pastel shades decayed into dull browns and greys.

'There,' said Gary, pointing to a building a couple of doors along from them. A large open doorway didn't exactly invite them in, but the spray-painted words above it confirmed that they had reached their destination: TACHELES BAR was written there in lurid, angular letters.

As they entered, Nathan looked around, checking for familiar faces. Or, rather, one familiar face: the man who had murdered Brett. He was almost certainly in Berlin by now – the Hellfire Club was powerful, but even it didn't have the power to hide a flight plan. Their only chance was that this wasn't somewhere of special significance, somewhere that meant something to Delancey. If it was – and if Delancey had directed the red-haired man there – they might as well give up. The game would definitely be over.

'This is . . . interesting,' muttered Gary as they stood by the bar. The Tacheles Bar had clearly once been an apartment block; but all of the interior walls and floors had been removed, leaving a large open area with brick and concrete walls. They were their natural colours, but their browns and beiges had been brightened up by the addition of various pieces of 'art': gaudy statues made of plastic and glass, indecipherable objects constructed from wrought iron and draped in fabric. The furniture was as utilitarian as the walls: table and chair legs were made from more wrought iron, while the seats and tabletops were unvarnished wood.

A bar was set against the left side of the room: it was roughly square, but each side of it was a different height, an effect that made Nathan slightly giddy. A single metal pillar rose from one corner of the bar, reaching up to the ceiling: Nathan guessed that it was one of the original support beams. A stylised dragon's head made from welded metal plates was affixed to the pillar about twelve feet up.

Even as Nathan was looking at it, he jumped: a ball of orange flame erupted from the jaws before dissipating.

'Cool,' said Gary. 'Fun place.'

'Drink?' Nathan went over to the bar and ordered a couple of beers, but he constantly looked around, from the bar to the door and back again.

Handing Gary his beer, Nathan considered the clientele. Although it wasn't strictly gay, there were enough people around who clearly *were* gay for the bar to warrant being called mixed. A couple of lesbians sat in the corner, their arms around each other, while a group of leathermen were standing by the window. Two men − boys really − were holding a loud discussion at the bar: they sported short cropped hair and thick goatee beards, and Nathan couldn't help a brief spot of fantasising, imagining them both naked, their fit bodies next to his. He thought about the darker-haired one on all fours as Nathan fucked him, while the blond one forced his cock into his friend's mouth. There was a good chance that they were straight: short hair and goatee beard was a grunge uniform in Germany − but that made the fantasy all the better. Straight friends, being forced to have sex with each other, being forced to suck each other's cock, each forced to take the other's dick into his arse, fucking till they both came, while Nathan took full advantage of them both.

Aware that he was developing a hard-on, Nathan turned away from them.

'I wish I knew where to start,' said Gary, sipping his beer. 'Harvey, safety deposit box . . . it's not exactly a lot to go on, is it?'

Nathan shrugged. 'As clues go, it's a lot more than some cases I've worked on.' He thought for a second. 'When in doubt, ask the barman.' That advice held true in London, anyway: like Mike Bury in the Brave Trader, Nathan had once gone undercover and worked as a barman. 'When people drink in a pub, they ignore the bar staff, forget that they're there. Bar staff become privy to everything that's going on. If you want to know the truth, get friendly with a barman.' That was what Marcus Moore had told Nathan, and it had stood him in very good stead over the years.

In fluent German, Nathan asked one of the bar staff whether he knew someone called Harvey. Although the response was negative, it wasn't the right kind of 'no'. Not 'no, I don't know,' but 'no, mind your own business'.

Oh well, Marcus, it was worth a try.

Nathan returned to Gary. 'No joy,' he whispered.

'You were asking about Harvey?' Nathan turned to see a man about his height and age standing there. He had short dark hair and a thick clone moustache, and was wearing jeans and a checked shirt. Clichéd, but practical, thought Nathan.

'Yes – we're from Britain. A . . . friend asked us to look him up. Send his regards. Someone called Brett.'

The man nodded thoughtfully for a second before replying. 'I'm Harvey,' he said quietly. 'You must be Nathan Dexter. Welcome to my bar.'

Nathan shook his hand. 'Is there somewhere we can talk?'

'Why not here? This is my bar, after all.'

Nathan had to agree that he had a point. It wasn't as if they would be overheard over the throbbing techno that blared out from the speakers above them.

'How is Brett?' asked Harvey.

Nathan hesitated. Should he tell him? But he knew that time was short – he really had little alternative.

'Brett's dead,' he whispered.

Harvey cast his gaze to the floor. 'I warned him,' he muttered. 'I warned him that Delancey would get him the moment he broke cover.'

'I take it you know Delancey,' said Nathan quietly.

Harvey looked up at him, his eyes full of immeasurable sadness. 'I should do. He's my boyfriend.'

Eleven

'His boyfriend?' Nathan couldn't believe what he had just heard. 'Delancey?' The idea that a creature like Delancey could have a boyfriend, could be in love . . . Nathan would have sworn that love of anything save power and money was a completely alien emotion to Delancey.

'*Was* my boyfriend, I suppose I should say. It was a long time ago, Nathan. I presume you know him?'

'Better than you could possibly imagine,' Nathan hissed. 'He's systematically destroyed everything that ever meant anything to me.' He stole a glance at Gary, hoping that he wouldn't take offence at that. But why should he? Gary represented the future – a better future, a future without Adrian Delancey.

'Adrian's calling card,' said Harvey. 'We split up nearly ten years ago, but he's never let go. He constantly reminds me that I can't hide from him. Whenever I move, he finds me. When I bought this place, he managed to virtually ruin me financially, before stepping in and buying half of it. His way of telling me that he's still in control.'

'You're the witness,' said Gary.

Harvey nodded. 'I suppose I'm luckier than most: everyone else who has ever posed a threat to him has either been framed

196

or murdered. There's nothing to connect it to Adrian, though – he's far too devious for that, far too clever.'

'His cleverness is coming to an end,' said Nathan. 'I don't know how much Brett told you before . . .'

'About Lawrence? About bringing Adrian to justice?' Harvey gave a sad smile. 'Everything, Nathan.'

'So where's the safety deposit box?'

Harvey raised an eyebrow. 'He told you about that? It's here, don't worry. Everything that you need is in there. Dates, signed confessions, the lot. Coupled with my evidence, Adrian won't stand a chance.'

'Why now?' asked Gary. 'You've as much as admitted that you know what's been going on. Why wait until now to act?' (Why wait for so many people to die? was his unspoken codicil.)

'Because I vainly hoped that he would change. I hoped that he might realise why what he was doing was wrong. And because I love him – even after all of this, I still love him.'

Nathan couldn't begin to understand how anyone could love someone like Delancey, but it was clear that Harvey did. 'It's a fair bet that Delancey's people are on to us, Harvey. We've got a plane waiting at the airport, ready to leave at a moment's notice.'

And how much had *that* cost? The Hellfire Club was paying a king's ransom to keep a take-off slot on permanent standby for the Learjet.

'Let me get the box and I'll be with you. I'll tell the bar staff I'm taking a holiday.' He gave a wan smile. 'They'll probably be glad to see the back of me.'

As Harvey vanished behind the bar, Nathan frowned.

'What's the matter?' asked Gary. 'Isn't this exactly what we wanted to happen?'

'Exactly. It's too smooth, too easy. Every instinct is telling me to get out of here – and this time I'm going to make sure I pay attention to them.'

Because, the last time he hadn't, Brett had died as a result.

Harvey reappeared. He had thrown on a leather biker's jacket, not dissimilar to Nathan's. 'Ready when you are,' he called out.

'Glad to hear it.' The voice was familiar, and Nathan momentarily froze as he heard it. He turned to face the door: the redhaired man was standing in the doorway, his right hand in the pocket of his brown leather jacket. Nathan didn't doubt that his gun was in there. He stepped closer.

'I want the three of you outside,' he said quietly. 'Make it look like we're old friends.' Then he turned to Gary. 'And don't think I haven't forgotten what you did to me, you little bastard.'

That was enough for Nathan. Without thinking, he spun round and punched the man in the face, feeling the satisfying sound of bone being ground into gristle. As the man fell, Nathan shouted out for them to run.

'Where are we going?' shouted Harvey.

'We need to get a cab to Schönefeld,' Nathan replied. 'We've got to get away from here.'

The sauna's proper name was forgotten – everyone who went there simply called it the Bear Sauna, hiding behind a respectable façade off Soho Square. Marco had first heard of it years ago, but hadn't got round to going to it until Nathan had persuaded him – just a few months ago. Marco shook his head to dispel the memories: he was here to enjoy himself. Because that had been the first time, but it certainly hadn't been the last.

The reception area belied what actually went on: it was spacious and old-fashioned, like an Edwardian drawing room, with the receptionist sitting behind a huge mahogany desk taking the money. Not that Marco had to pay, of course.

'Afternoon, Bill,' said Marco.

'Afternoon, good sir – after a bit of R and R?' Bill was in his mid-thirties, with short, jet-black hair, a bushy black moustache, and swarthy, Mediterranean looks. He also had a solid, muscular body with a gorgeous hairy chest, as Marco had discovered one wonderful, rainy afternoon, a few months ago. It had been quite a pleasant surprise to find that he worked at the sauna, and his occasional visits into the steam room or the Jacuzzi were always welcome.

'Why not?' said Marco. 'Will you be joining us this evening?'

Bill cocked his head. 'I wasn't, but knowing that you're in there . . . might see you in a little while.' With that, he pressed a concealed button, and a click issued from the door that led to the sauna proper.

Once he was through the door, the Edwardian atmosphere changed, swept away by the wall of hot air that hit them, sweeping out of the sauna and through the changing rooms. Moving over to the lockers, Marco started to undress, under the watchful eye of Auntie: Auntie was the owner of the sauna, a large bear with a full beard and twinkling, wicked eyes. In his late forties, Auntie was owner, father-confessor and all-round good guy, and treated his regulars like members of his family. As he was currently demonstrating.

'Marco!' he called out, coming to greet him in person and grasping him warmly by the hand. 'Lovely tan, I must say. Been somewhere nice?'

Marco caught sight of his reflection as he pulled off his rugby shirt and had to admit that it was impressive, his whole body a nice golden brown. And what a body, he had to admit: built like a brick shithouse and covered in thick black body hair over his stomach, chest and shoulders.

Despite his attempts to bury the memory, he couldn't help thinking about the last time he had been in the sauna – with Nathan.

Marco had to admit that he still found Nathan attractive: their fling together had been brief but enjoyable, but they had soon both realised that their future together was as friends, not lovers. But what did that mean? Five months ago, they had been sitting in Nathan's house on Christmas Day, Scott and Nathan, Marco and Leigh . . . And now? Leigh had gone off to 'find himself', and Nathan was trying to recover his reputation by risking his life for an organisation that was at least as sinister as the Elective and the Syndicate.

What had happened to them?

'Well?' Auntie urged. 'Where have you been?'

'Las Vegas,' Marco answered. 'But that was months ago.'

Auntie raised an eyebrow. 'You obviously know how to keep your tan, Marco. Anyway, it's going to be a good afternoon – I can feel it. A few regulars have brought some friends in to sample my humble establishment, and I'm sure they'll appreciate your company.'

Marco couldn't help smiling as he wrapped the white towel around his waist. Coming to Auntie's Bear Sauna was always an experience, and this afternoon promised to be exactly that.

He stepped through into the main part of the sauna.

In front of him, the large room contained an enormous Jacuzzi, and even this late at night it was extremely busy. About five bears were taking it in turns to suck off a sweet-looking bear cub who was sitting on the edge of the Jacuzzi, his short but thick cock jutting out. Marco watched as an older bear, his body covered in thick grey hair, took the cub's cock in his mouth and slid his lips up and down the shaft. Marco felt his cock stiffening under his towel as the bearded face buried itself in the cub's groin, and was sorely tempted to get into the Jacuzzi and join in. But the Jacuzzi wasn't what he had had in mind when coming here: Marco preferred the steam room.

Waving at Nick, a blond bear cub whom he'd had sex with a few times, Marco padded over the marble flooring and stopped at a wooden door. He pulled it open, and a blast of hot air hit him in the face. Ignoring it, he walked into the steam room.

The steam room was about the size of an average living room, with wooden benches against three of the four walls. The steam was provided by a heater in the centre of the room: as Marco watched, a thin, hairy man poured some more water on to it; a cloud of steam billowed upward.

The steam room was fairly quiet, but Marco didn't mind too much: fair enough, he wouldn't have said no to a bit of anonymous sex, but his main aim was to relax, to get away from everything else that was happening. He looked around the room to see who else was there.

Apart from the thin man, there were two bears sitting to the left of the room: they were gently playing with each other's cock. A larger, older bear was wanking his huge cock with measured strokes across the room, but Marco's attention was grabbed by the young bloke sitting on his own. Marco guessed that he was about twenty, with thinning blond hair and a very hairy chest. He looked up at Marco and his bearded face broke into a smile.

Needing no further encouragement, Marco sat down next to him, allowing his towel to fall to the marble floor.

'Hi, I'm Marco,' he whispered. Marco always found it more of a turn-on if he knew the other person's name.

'Matt,' said the bear cub, placing his hand on Marco's hairy thigh. Marco grinned, and did the same, before moving his hand further up and cupping Matt's big balls in his hand. Matt responded by laying his hand on Marco's cock, grinning as it grew larger under the attention.

Marco took Matt's cock and began to wank it slowly, feeling it stiffen in his hand. Matt's cock was about seven inches long, and quite thick; Marco pulled the foreskin back to expose the red helmet.

Pulling back, Matt fell to his knees in front of Marco and took Marco's own cock in his mouth. Marco shivered as he felt Matt's tongue exploring his shaft and his helmet, flicking in and out of his dick slit with teasing darts of his tongue.

Greedily, Matt pushed his face even further into Marco's groin, swallowing all of Marco's erection while his fingers toyed with Matt's balls and the skin behind. Growing more daring, Matt's fingers began to explore Marco's arse and ring.

Matt's lips brushed against Marco's pubes as he managed to take all of him. Then they slid back until only Marco's helmet was in his mouth. Marco placed his hands on Matt's shoulders, pulling him closer, urging him to swallow all of him again. Matt looked up at him, his eyes gleaming.

Marco knew that he wanted Matt's cock and balls; pulling away from him, Marco stood up and gestured for Matt to sit down.

As soon as he did, Marco wasted no time in falling to his knees and licking Matt's large balls, taking each one of the hairy sacs into his mouth in turn. Matt gasped with pleasure, so Marco intensified his efforts, sucking and nibbling even more furiously. His hand moved up Matt's thigh until it found his arse, but, rather than Matt's gentle exploration, he forced his forefinger into the young guy's arse, pushing into his ring and making him groan with pain. Further and further he went, opening Matt up so that he would take all of Marco's cock when the time came.

While his fingers continued to fuck Matt, Marco moved on from Matt's balls to his dick, running his tongue along the thick shaft until he reached the helmet, which was wet with glistening pre-come. Marco hungrily drank it, licking it off until the only moisture was Marco's spit. Then he took the shaft in his mouth and ran his lips up and down, up and down, in time with the pressure of his finger up Matt's arse.

Finally he knew that Matt was ready. He manoeuvred Matt so that he was lying on his back on the wooden bench, and then lifted his legs into the air to reveal his hole, which was noticeably larger than it had been: large enough for Marco to slide his cock into. Marco reached down and pulled a packet of condoms and lube from one of the many containers underneath the benches. Pulling the condom from its wrapper, he rolled it on to his stiff, sensitive cock before applying lubricant to both the condom and Matt's waiting arse.

Placing both hands on Matt's shoulders, Marco manoeuvred himself so that his cock was level with his ring. Then he touched his helmet to Matt's hole and exerted the slightest amount of pressure, and was glad to see that the first inch of his cock slid in effortlessly. Slowly, he fed more and more of his meat into Matt's willing arse, until all of his length was inside him: then he pushed with all of his weight, and Matt groaned. Marco pulled out, slowly, deliberately, until he was half withdrawn; then he drove himself back in. He increased the speed, pulling out, then forcing his way back in, until he reached the rhythm that he enjoyed. One of his hands moved down Matt's chest until he found his nipple: taking it between his fingers, he squeezed it, tighter and tighter and harder and harder, then released it. Matt's cries of pleasure increased, so Marco squeezed it once again, delighting in the sounds being forced from the bear cub. He moved his other hand down, past the solid stomach, down towards the navel and then following the thin trail of light-brown hair till he found Matt's cock. Grasping it, he started to wank it in time to his fucking, while his other hand continued to grip the cub's nipple.

All the time, his cock forced its way in and out of Matt's arse, in and out, in and out. Marco knew that he was close, and Matt's heavy breathing suggested that he was too. Marco increased his speed, fucking him faster and faster, more and more desperately, until he could feel his climax growing inside him.

Just as it began to explode, Marco pulled his cock from Matt's hole and, taking his hand from Matt's nipple, aimed his dick at the young man's chest. With a groan of release, Marco came, shooting one, two, three gouts of warm load over Matt's chest and face. At the same time, he continued to wank Matt, and was pleased when, with a groan to rival his own, Matt shot – thick droplets that mingled with the damp hair and the pools of Marco's own come.

Marco slumped on to the bench in exhaustion, his arm around Matt's shoulders. Matt looked up at him and smiled.

'Have you got to go now?' he asked innocently.

Marco grinned. 'Not quite yet, no.'

They were lucky: a cab was idling outside the Tacheles Bar. Jumping in, Nathan ordered the driver to get to the airport as quickly as possible. The offer of a thousand marks if he did it – Nathan thrust the notes into his hand before he could question it – had cemented the deal. The cab sped off, even as the red-haired man staggered out of the bar, his nose streaming blood.

'We won't have much of a head start,' said Harvey. 'There are always cabs waiting outside the bar.'

Thank you, Mr Cheerful, thought Nathan. They didn't need long – only a couple of minutes.

'I'll phone the pilot,' said Gary. 'Where are we going?'

There was only one place they could go. 'London. We need to get Harvey and his evidence back to Lawrence.'

As Gary instructed the pilot on his mobile, Nathan turned to Harvey. 'Do you know where Delancey is?' he asked.

'Not exactly. Although . . .' He reached into the steel box on his lap and pulled out a postcard. 'This arrived last week. I think it was Adrian's attempt at a party invitation.' He handed it over.

Party invitations? Nathan shuddered: he didn't even want to begin to think about the sort of party that Delancey would host. He examined the card with increasing puzzlement. The front of the postcard was plain, apart from the address of the Tacheles Bar; the postmark was indecipherable. On the other side, there was a signature, which could just about be interpreted as saying 'Adrian Delancey', but that was all. Apart from a series of raised dots. Braille? No, it didn't look like Braille. Nor did it look like a familiar code. Just four sets of raised dots –

Nathan's attention was diverted from the card as the cab served violently. Looking out of the window, Nathan could see a white Mercedes trying to force them out of the way. No – force them off the road. He could see who was behind the wheel: it was the red-haired man.

'Oh shit,' he muttered. Leaning forward, he spoke to the driver. 'Another ten thousand marks if you can get away from him.'

'What do you think I'm trying to do?' he shouted back in German. But he still complied: as he pushed down on the accelerator, they began to widen the gap between the two cars. The only hope that they now had was that their driver was more experienced than their pursuer.

Lawrence sat in the darkness of his playroom, the only illumination coming from the monitor of his PC. He knew where Marco was, but it didn't bother him – much. Indeed, he knew where everyone was. And, with a click of his mouse, he could summon them all back for the final scene of this drama.

But when then? What if they did defeat Delancey? What if the

Syndicate was destroyed? Did they really want to return to the old status quo? All of them had been changed by this, all of them. Nothing could be the same any more.

With that thought preoccupying his mind, he sat back in his wheelchair and waited for some sign from Nathan.

'We might still do it!' Gary cried out.

The other car was far behind them now, after their driver had gone like a bat out of hell towards the airport. That had scared the shit out of Nathan, but it was a damn sight better than what would happen if the red-haired man caught up with them. After Monte Carlo, Nathan knew that he would kill them all, just to satisfy his paymaster.

Nathan told the driver where to head for. For a second, the driver looked as if he was about to refuse: driving on to the tarmac wasn't exactly legal. But the thousands of marks that he had earned so far would pay for any fines. On balance, the driver realised where his best interests lay and carried on into the airport.

'We should be able to lift off in a few minutes,' said Gary. 'The plane's warming up at the moment.' Even as he said it, they passed a couple of angry-looking security guards as they approached the silver Learjet.

'Here.' Nathan thrust the rest of his money into the driver's hands. 'See if you can't slow that other car down,' he added in German. With that, the three of them leapt from the cab and headed towards the boarding steps of the Learjet.

'There he is!' cried Gary, pointing into the distance. But he didn't seem to be making any move towards them ... With mounting horror, Nathan realised that he was heading towards the black and red Learjet. There was no way that he could follow them in the plane – planes just didn't work like that. So what was he planning?

Kirsten closed the door and picked up the hotline to Delancey. 'They're already in the jet, Adrian.'

'Then stop it, David,' said Delancey calmly.

'How?' The moment they were in the air it was over.

'Use your own jet to stop them from taking off.'

'What?' Kirsten repeated.

'Ram them, you fool!' Delancey shouted down the phone.

Ram them? 'Don't be an idiot, Adrian. That'll kill us all!'

'What a pity,' said Delancey quietly. ' "It is a far, far better thing that I do . . ." ' he muttered.

The bastard. 'No, I won't do it!' Kirsten worked for Delancey for many reasons. Suicide as an end result wasn't one of them.

'Erik?' Kirsten realised that Delancey was talking directly to the pilot. 'Stop them at all costs. Ram them!'

'Delancey!' screamed Kirsten.

'Ram them, damn you! Ram them!'

Kirsten ran over to the door and tried to open it, but it was locked.

'You failed me, David. And you know the price of failure.' Delancey's voice echoed through the cabin. 'Goodbye, David.'

Kirsten could feel the plane accelerating around him.

'Oh my God!' Nathan yelled. 'Get on to the plane! Now!'

As they ran up the stairs, Nathan realised how high the stakes were. If Delancey had been willing to kill Nathan before, what about now? Now that Nathan had the evidence, now that he had Harvey?

'We've got to take off!' he bellowed as he secured the door behind him. Even as the engines started, he looked out of one of the windows and saw the other jet starting to turn on the tarmac.

'What is it?' Gary asked.

'He's going to ram the plane!' Nathan shouted. 'He's suicidal! Gary – tell the pilot we need to be airborne in two minutes or we're all dead.'

'We're not going to make it, are we?' said Harvey quietly. Their plane was already thundering down the runway towards an emergency take-off, but the other jet would still be able to intercept them unless they got airborne in the next few moments.

Before Nathan could reply, it suddenly struck him. The Braille dots on the card – it was obvious! 'Gary, get me Lawrence. Now!' he ordered. Gary handed over the mobile phone. It was already ringing.

'Lawrence, it's Nathan.' Before Lawrence could reply, Nathan shouted down the phone at him. 'We haven't got much time. He's at this map reference, Lawrence –' Nathan started to call out a series of numbers. Even as he did so, he felt the jet lifting off the runway. Perhaps they still had a chance.

That was before he heard Gary shout out. And before all hell broke loose.

From the terminal building, spectators had a ringside view of the disaster. By the time air-traffic control realised what was happening, it was far, far too late. Their frantic calls to both pilots were met with nothing but static. They could only watch in horror as the events unfolded before them.

The silver Learjet's nose just lifted from the tarmac – it was only a few feet in the air – when the red and black jet smashed into it at over fifty miles an hour. Although it struck only a glancing blow, the Hellfire jet itself was travelling at nearly one hundred miles an hour.

The impact sent the Hellfire jet skating across the ground, before it tipped to port and overbalanced. Its port wing crumpled as it was rammed into the tarmac by the weight of the plane, releasing its fuel.

The other jet wasn't quite so lucky. After hitting the Hellfire jet its momentum made it continue in the same direction: a direction that terminated with an aircraft hangar. And, since the pilot had died in the initial impact, there was no one to stop it. Seconds later it hit the brick and metal of the hangar wall and exploded, a huge fireball rising up into the Berlin night.

Even as he heard the explosion, Nathan pulled himself up from the floor and tried to stand, despite the fact that everything was at an angle. Although it was pitch-black, he could see that the mobile phone was in pieces on the floor – had the message got through to Lawrence? Then other concerns took over: through the window, he could see the ruined wing, and see the fuel flooding the tarmac. They had seconds before it would ignite, sending the Hellfire jet to kingdom come.

'Gary! Harvey!' he screamed, trying to find them in the dark. Feeling his way, he found something warm nearby; looking closely, he could see it was Harvey. His right arm was clearly broken, but he was still breathing. Nathan slapped him around the face, more violently than he had wanted. But they had to get out of there!

'Harvey, get out!' He helped the man to his feet, and pointed him towards the door. As Harvey limped towards it, Nathan continued to look for Gary. The smell of jet fuel was becoming overpowering, but there was another smell reaching the cabin – something was burning. They had seconds.

He found Gary next to the oak desk. He wasn't breathing.

Fighting back panic, Nathan realised that it would be suicide to attempt cardiopulmonary resuscitation inside what was effectively a great big bomb. He hoisted him over his shoulder and reached the door. Harvey had managed to open it; Nathan looked at the six-foot drop, and decided that he had to take the risk. Sitting on the edge, he jumped, and just about managed to hit the tarmac without dropping Gary.

Harvey was well out of danger now – it was Nathan's turn. Slowed by Gary, he just about managed to get far enough away before the fuel ignited.

The force of the explosion hit him in the back and threw him to the floor; he twisted to protect Gary. As the light of the flames illuminated everything in shades of red and orange, he started to pump on Gary's chest, willing him to breathe, willing him to open his eyes, to look up and tell him that everything was going to be all right. He gave mouth-to-mouth, filling his lungs with air, then more CPR . . .

Harvey laid a hand on his shoulder. 'It's no use, Nathan. His neck's broken.'

For the first time, Nathan saw how Gary's head was lolling,

angled in a way that just wasn't right. He stood up, tears brimming in his eyes. The pain he felt was indescribable, as if his soul had been burnt in the funeral pyre of the Learjet.

'My God, Gary . . . I thought we had more time,' he breathed. All his hopes, all his dreams and aspirations, gone, wiped out. Nathan wished that he had died as well: anything was better than the agony that tore into every part of him.

'I'm afraid your time is up,' said another voice. Nathan had to force himself to look up. A huge black man – as wide as he was tall – was standing behind them, a gun in his hand. Another red and black Learjet stood in the distance.

'I have a message for you,' he growled. 'I was told to tell you, "We play the game again, Mr Dexter."'

Nathan looked from the jet to Gary and back again. *A game?* Everything he had ever cared about, everyone he had ever loved, destroyed by Adrian Delancey. He had invaded Nathan's relationship with Scott, alienated his friends, cost him his career . . . But Nathan would gladly have sacrificed them all over again to have Gary back. He was glad that he had been caught. Glad that he was finally going to face Delancey.

Because Nathan would make that bastard pay a thousand times for the hurt he had caused. Before Nathan Dexter was finished, Adrian Delancey was going to burn in hell.

Twelve

The Learjet went only as far as Paris, but Nathan hardly noticed, and cared even less. As far as he was concerned, all of this was dead time, wasted time. Without Gary, his life consisted of a single point, in the future: the confrontation between him and Delancey.

Arriving at Paris airport, Nathan and Harvey were ushered on to a larger plane. Nathan knew roughly where they were going – he had worked it out from the map reference – but it was irrelevant. There was no place on Earth that Delancey was safe. What was it that Lawrence had called him? His avatar? But this had nothing to with Lawrence any more. This was personal.

And final.

Marco sat with the others in the playroom. The atmosphere was funereal.

'I just wish the news had been better,' said Lawrence.

'So,' sneered Scott, 'he has Nathan, he has Leigh, and he has all of the evidence that Nathan was searching for. What a result, eh, Lawrence?' Scott's bitterness was palpable. And understandable.

'Not the result I would have liked –'

'This isn't some fucking experiment!' Scott screamed. 'Nathan trusted you!'

'And I intend to repay that trust.'

'How?' asked Mike Bury, considerably calmer than Scott.

Lawrence smiled. 'By doing what I always do for an encore.'

'And what might that be?' spat Scott.

'I win.'

Twenty-four hours after leaving Berlin, Nathan and Harvey stepped off yet another plane – Nathan hadn't been counting the number of transfers they had made – and down the steps. The atmosphere was humid and almost unbearably hot, but that was only to be expected. The sign welcoming them to the airport confirmed what Nathan had suspected: LIMA AIRPORT.

They were in Peru.

A car was waiting for them on the cracked tarmac. No BMWs or limos this time: it was a dull-green jeep. Nathan climbed into the back, Harvey next to him, and waited as the jeep drove out of the airport. Under other circumstances, Nathan would have been fascinated by his surroundings – the sound of exotic birds, strange fragrances, the South American jungle – but not now. Nothing mattered any more: Nathan had lost his curiosity along with all of his other emotions.

All expect one.

Hatred. The most potent fuel for revenge.

They drove for about two hours, stopping once for Nathan and Harvey to relieve themselves against a tree. Finally, the jeep reached a walled compound, fairly deeply hidden in the jungle. Stopping at a set of impenetrable gates, the driver pressed a button on the dashboard and waited as the gates slowly opened. As soon as there was enough room to pass, the jeep carried on.

The complex was huge: vast, sculpted gardens, statuary, various outhouses and storage rooms. But none of these mattered: all of Nathan's attention was focused on the villa that they were approaching.

It was single-storey, the walls a brilliant white beneath the terracotta of the tiled roof. In another time, Nathan would have considered it stylish, beautiful even. But now . . . now, all he could think about was the evil that it housed.

The jeep stopped in front of the main entrance, a covered walkway. The driver gestured for them to get out.

'We meet again, Mr Dexter.' Nathan looked up at the sound of the oh-so-familiar voice. Adrian Delancey was standing in front of them, dressed in a plain white shirt and cotton trousers. 'I'm afraid I can't say that it's been a pleasure.'

'*You bastard!*' Instinct, anger, hatred, revenge, all igniting together in a blazing fire as concentrated as the heart of the sun.

Nathan threw himself at Delancey, his hands outstretched, desperate to grab his throat and choke the life out of him, the way he had choked the life out of John Bury, out of Brett, out of Gary . . . the thought of Gary, his wonderful, irreplaceable Gary, was just too much. He knocked Delancey to the floor and started to strangle him, paying no attention to Delancey's body-guards as they tried to pull him off. Nothing else mattered. They could hit him, pull at him, but he wasn't giving up until Adrian Delancey was dead.

That was his last thought as something hit him on the back of the head and unconsciousness overcame him.

When Nathan finally woke up, his head was splitting. Harvey was watching over him. 'Are you OK?' he asked.

'I've been better. A lot better.' He looked around. 'Where's Delancey?'

'He's waiting for us in the courtyard.'

Nathan sighed, and gingerly touched the back of his head. He winced at the pain. 'Well, we don't want to disappoint him, do we?' The anger that he had felt earlier was fading, but the desire for revenge hadn't. If anything, it had been hardened, quickened. What was that old proverb: 'Revenge is a dish best served cold'? As cold and as dead as Nathan's heart.

Escorted by one of Delancey's big black guards – were they

for security, or was Delancey living out another of his fantasies in his super-villain HQ? – they walked through an ornate archway into the courtyard. Nathan had to admit that he was impressed: it had been laid out as an enormous chessboard, with life-size statues acting as the pieces. Their heads were hooded, and their sculpted bodies were crisscrossed with harnesses.

Delancey was sitting at a table to the right of the huge board: Nathan noticed that he was wearing a cravat around his neck, presumably to hide the bruises. Nathan was led to the table, where the guard forced him to sit down. At this range, he could see the gun holster at his side.

'I do hope you haven't recovered,' said Delancey pleasantly. 'Welcome to my little *pied-à-terre*, Nathan.'

Nathan said nothing. There was something about the chess pieces, something not quite right . . . He looked down at the table between himself and Delancey, and realised that there was another, normal-sized, chessboard there.

They weren't statues. With mounting horror, Nathan realised that the masked and harnessed chess pieces were people. In another situation, Nathan wouldn't have raised an eyebrow – he had seen such living chess games before. But with Delancey in control . . . there had to be a sinister purpose to all of this.

'Admit it: you prefer it this way, Nathan. Man to man,' said Delancey.

Nathan shook his head. 'I just want this to finish, Delancey. I want to put an end to all of the games.'

Delancey replied with a chastising finger. 'Not all of the games, Nathan. There will always be people who only exist to manipulate others – bigger games, better games. Defeat me, and another will take my place. In fact, *you* could take my place. What about it Nathan? You and I are not that dissimilar.'

'You stand for everything I oppose, Delancey. Love, affection, respect . . . You corrupt everything you can corrupt, and destroy everything you can't. I will never be like you.'

'We'll see.' Delancey looked down at the board. 'The rules are very simple, Nathan. A game of chess, a tournament between us.

If you win . . . I will let the Elective survive. I will release you and your friends. I will stay out of your life for ever.' *Friends?* What was he talking about?

'And if I lose?'

'You die, Mr Dexter – it's as simple as that.'

Simple – and melodramatic. The problem was, Nathan knew he meant it.

'You can make the opening move, Nathan.'

Nathan studied the board. He hadn't played chess for a long time, and he was rusty. But, if Delancey wanted to play games, they would play games. They would play this game long enough for Nathan to determine Delancey's weakness. And then he would strike.

There – that would do it. With a confident hand, he moved his knight and took Delancey's rook.

'A good move,' said Delancey, looking over at the black and white marble of the human chessboard. 'Phillipe – take Antonio.'

As the rook was removed from the board, the action was mirrored on the life-size chessboard beyond them. Nathan felt his excitement building as he watched his human knight, wearing nothing but a leather thong and harness over his smooth, muscular body, force the defeated rook to the marble floor. As he knelt on the marble, the knight pulled the leather mask off the rook, revealing a handsome boyish face, twisted into a look of fear and submission. Unable to act, unable to protest, he did nothing as the knight pulled his body round so that he was on all fours, his arse towards the knight. It was time to surrender himself to his new master.

Delancey looked over at Nathan as the two men began to have sex – no, as Phillipe forced himself on Antonio.

'Every time you take a piece, its human counterpart will be taken as well. I have chosen these people because of the emotional ties between them. Phillipe's boyfriend Robert is one of your pawns. Imagine how he feels, knowing that you are forcing his boyfriend to have sex with someone else in front of him. And Antonio: his boyfriend is one of my pawns, watching as Phillipe has him, in front of everyone.' Delancey's eyes narrowed. 'And I don't approve of precautions,' he added.

'You bastard,' hissed Nathan. 'Is there no level to which you won't sink?' But Nathan couldn't take his eyes off the two men.

Delancey shot him a snakelike smile. 'Actually, no. Take a careful look at the pieces, Nathan. Despite the hoods, I'm sure that you won't have any difficulty recognising your erstwhile boyfriend, Leigh.'

Nathan froze. Even though he knew that Delancey was the king of deceptions and lies, Nathan was familiar enough with Leigh Robertson's body to immediately spot him – the dragon tattoo was the final proof.

He was Delancey's queen. If Nathan was to win the game, he knew he would have to take the powerful pieces off the board first of all. And the queen was the most powerful of all. How could Nathan win the game, knowing that he could do it only by ordering someone to rape Leigh? Because that was what it was – rape, pure and simple.

But Nathan couldn't give up now. That wasn't an option: given enough time, he knew that something would present itself. All he had to do was stall for time, and trust to his instincts.

Meanwhile, Phillipe had forced Antonio on to all fours. Nathan could see a couple of hooded figures watching intently, and guessed that these were the respective partners, helpless observers to the violation that Delancey had ordered.

Delancey ordered it, but you made the move, said Nathan's inner voice. *So who's really to blame?*

Nathan watched as Phillipe pushed Antonio face down on to the marble so that his arse was exposed and available.

'Beg for it, Antonio,' said Delancey languidly.

In response, Nathan heard Antonio's accented voice call out, 'Fuck me! I want to feel you in me, filling me!' Nathan tried to imagine how Antonio felt, and was shocked and disgusted with himself when he realised the idea was turning him on. The thought of being a slave to Phillipe, who was pulling off his thong to reveal a thick, meaty cock, already glistening with pre-come. Nathan shuddered, but continued to fantasise . . .

Antonio screwed his eyes shut, ready to feel Phillipe's cock enter him and fill him up with its thickness. 'You've got a tight arse,' said Phillipe. 'A cock this size is going to rip you apart. You need loosening up, boy.' Phillipe knelt down so that his face was opposite Antonio's hole, still guarded by the leather of his thong. Phillipe roughly tore the straps away and threw them to the floor. Antonio groaned as Phillipe's fingers probed the narrow crack of his arse, widening his hole. But it was what he did next that drove Antonio to new levels of pleasure and excitement.

Phillipe licked the rim of Antonio's arsehole with his tongue, probing the ring of muscle, and then sucked on it. Antonio gasped. As Phillipe's tongue went in deeper, Antonio pushed back on to him, feeling the slinky wetness move inside him.

Phillipe's tongue started to flick in and out of Antonio's arsehole, hot darting flicks that made Antonio gasp with the sensation. Phillipe's hands pulled his arse cheeks even further apart. Phillipe was becoming greedy now, burying his face in Antonio's arse, his tongue sucking him and fucking him at the same time. Antonio felt Phillipe grab for Antonio's cock, pulling it down, jerking it in time to his tongue as it probed Antonio's tight hole, the two actions in perfect rhythm, in and out, up and down. His arse was now wet with Phillipe's spit, while his cock was soaked with pre-come.

Phillipe removed his tongue from his hole and started tenderly kissing his bare and hairless buttocks. 'Keep it inside me,' Antonio begged 'Keep fucking me with your tongue.' He didn't want that feeling to stop; he wanted to feel Phillipe's tongue, then Phillipe's fingers, then finally Phillipe's dick, penetrating him, taking him . . .

Phillipe started to bite Antonio's arse cheeks, gently at first, and then, as his own excitement mounted, more and more roughly. Biting deep into the soft tender flesh that was thrusting itself into his face. Pulling hard on Antonio's rock-hard stiffness. Bringing him to the heights of ecstasy. Pleasuring him. Hurting him. Driving him mad with desire. Making him fucking beg for it!

'Please, Phillipe, now. I need it. Now. I need it in me now!' Phillipe inserted a finger into Antonio's waiting arsehole, slowly widening the

resisting ring of muscle with sure circular motions. Antonio wriggled his arse, pushing himself backwards on to Phillipe's probing finger, relaxing himself to take as much of it as he could.

'Now, Phillipe. Please. In me. Now. Please . . .'

With one hand Phillipe held Antonio's arse steady, while, with the other, he gently guided his thick cock towards the waiting moistness of Antonio's ring. The head of his cock pushed gently at the opening, forcing its way into Antonio.

Antonio yelped with the initial pain, and Phillipe started to withdraw: whether this was out of consideration or to pleasure himself, Antonio didn't know, and cared even less. Antonio grabbed Phillipe from behind, and pulled him on to him, ignoring his virgin's pain as Phillipe's cock entered him. He was in a frenzy of passion now, all he wanted was Phillipe's cock up his arse, pounding away at him, thrusting deep and long inside him.

Antonio pushed backwards, impaling himself further on to Phillipe's thick cock. The thrusts became stronger as Antonio forced the muscles of his ring to relax even more, to allow Phillipe free entry into Antonio's arsehole.

The feeling was indescribable: a deep pain that was so overpowering, so overwhelming that it touched Antonio like nothing else had ever done before.

'That's it,' Antonio said through gritted teeth. 'Shove it all in me. Make me take it all. Fuck me!'

Antonio screamed with pleasure, as Phillipe's cock buried itself deep inside him.

Phillipe threw back his head, and his thrusts became slower and more direct; Antonio could tell that Phillipe's climax was only moments away. At that point, Antonio felt a sharp pain as Phillipe pulled his cock from his arse.

'I'm coming!' Phillipe yelled. Antonio looked over his shoulder and saw Phillipe pumping furiously on his dick. He continued to roar with ecstasy, as he finally found release: the shower of thick white come spurted out of his cock, covering Antonio's back with its creamy warmth.

He hung his head, beads of sweat dripping from his brow, and *squeezed the last drops of come from his still swollen cock. 'I just couldn't wait . . . That was so good. Fuck, that was so good.'*

Nathan broke out of the daydream, aware that he himself was close to coming. He looked across at Delancey and realised that he was well aware of what had been going through his mind.

'You bastard,' Nathan hissed, watching as Antonio limped off the chessboard.

'Admit it, Nathan – you enjoyed that. Join with me, and that sort of power will be yours as well.'

'Never,' said Nathan. But the nagging doubts remained. Could he be like Delancey? And, more worryingly, would he become like Delancey?

Trying to dispel such ideas, he returned his attention to the chessboard and watched as Delancey made his move.

Finally, after what seemed like hours, they were approaching the endgame. Nathan was pleased with himself: he had managed to get this far without endangering Leigh. Unfortunately, even as he congratulated himself, Delancey made an audacious move with his rook. As the rook on the real-life board grabbed Nathan's pawn and forced his cock in his mouth, Delancey gave Nathan a grin of triumph.

'As far as I can see, Nathan, you have to take my queen.' He pursed his lips. 'In my opinion, you simply have no alternative.'

Nathan studied the board with rising panic, realising that he had been outmanoeuvred. Unless he took the queen with his knight, unless he ordered his man to rape Leigh, he would put himself in check.

And he knew what would happen then. Understanding dawned on him: Delancey didn't care about winning or losing – Nathan was dead already. All he wanted was to put Nathan in the position where he would have to order Leigh's submission. His fingers were poised over the board – what could he do? End the game now and die, without a chance for revenge? Or let Leigh be raped, just to buy some more time? *You could take my place:* was that Delancey's plan? To see if he could corrupt Nathan?

Nathan jumped to his feet, knocking the board to the floor. Delancey stood up as well, but Nathan had already picked up the table. He swung it round, catching Delancey a glancing blow to the head – more than enough to topple him. Nathan moved over to him before his guards could react and pulled the gun from its holster. He touched the barrel to Delancey's temple.

'Go on, Nathan – do it. Strike me down. Do this, and you will become like me – you will be me,' Delancey hissed.

'You've taken everything from me,' Nathan shouted. 'Everything.'

'All I have done is to remove those weaknesses that were holding you back, Nathan. Emotional ties, dependencies ... You're free of them Nathan, free to fulfil your destiny!'

'Never.' But the gun was wavering. Nathan tried to think about Gary, to use that anger, that pain, but it was useless. He wasn't a murderer. He couldn't do it. The gun clattered to the tiled floor.

'You disappoint me, Nathan. The gun was empty – I just wondered whether you would have the strength of character to use it.' Delancey sighed. 'But I see that you're a little man, just like all the others. Our revels now are ended, Nathan –'

The single shot echoed across the courtyard. Delancey's mouth opened, but nothing came out. He looked down in surprise at the spreading stain that was colouring the white of his shirt.

Nathan was rooted to the spot. What had happened? Then he looked over Delancey's shoulder and understood.

He finally understood.

Delancey touched the blood stain and pulled his hand away. He reached out for Nathan, his fingers clawing at the air, before he finally crumpled, hitting the black and white floor with a dull thud.

Nathan looked at Delancey's lifeless body for long moments, unable to believe what he was seeing. Finally, he looked up. Lawrence was standing there, the barrel of his gun still smoking.

'That was your intention all along, wasn't it? You wanted me to find him, to smoke him out. You never wanted me to kill him, did you?'

Lawrence shook his head. 'Nathan – I knew you couldn't do it. If I'd thought you could, I would never have approached you. I knew that you had reason to, but that acted as the motivation to find him.

'Indeed, I would never have forgiven you if you had cheated me out of this.' He gave the body a slight kick. 'The final end,' he muttered.

Nathan looked around the courtyard. Paramilitary-style troops were swarming around the complex, seizing all of Delancey's guards: Nathan assumed that these were more of Lawrence's agents. But it was the group of people standing behind Nathan that demanded his attention: Marco, supporting a visibly shaken Leigh; Mike Bury, there to see his brother's death finally avenged.

And Scott.

Nathan didn't know how he felt at the moment: what he had experienced with Gary had been real. But, after everything, he needed someone just to be there for him. Someone to chase the monsters away and tell him that it was all going to be all right.

He needed Scott.

Almost running, he grabbed the young man in his arms and hugged him, squeezed him, the tears rolling down his face. Nathan had no idea how all of this was going to play out, and at the moment he didn't care. Standing there, surrounded by his old friends, by people who cared about him, people who loved him . . .

Because in the end, it hadn't been about revenge. It hadn't been about destroying Delancey. It hadn't been about the King of Swords. It had been about getting back what was rightfully his.

His soul.

Epilogue

Lawrence had decided that they all needed a holiday. Not just to rest, but to keep out of sight until everything died down. He was certain that the influence of the Hellfire Club would be sufficient to clear everything up, but even that organisation needed time to work its miracles.

That was how they had all ended up on a private Caribbean island, guests at an exclusive resort that was only one step removed from paradise. Leigh, Marco, Lawrence, Sion, Mike, Scott and Nathan – but for each of them the holiday was coloured by memories of recent events.

The Lawrence–Marco–Leigh scenario was still to be played out: Nathan and Scott had decided to keep well out of that until their friends made up their own minds about what they were going to do. Nathan couldn't even begin to guess the final result, but he was there for them if they needed him.

Mike Bury finally seemed to be at peace with himself: he could mourn his brother at last, and had started taking long, solitary walks around their Caribbean paradise.

Sion, on the other hand, never seemed to leave his apartment. Lawrence had charged him with overseeing the dismantling of the Syndicate, a delicate task given that the hand of the Hellfire Club was not to be detected. But Sion was in his element.

That just left Scott and Nathan.

Nathan had told Scott everything – or, rather, almost everything – a flood of near honesty that went a long way to healing many old wounds. It reminded Nathan of their heart-to-heart soon after they had first met, but the emotional intensity was a thousand times greater. In turn, Scott had tried to explain why he had done what he did. But all the time Nathan kept one thing back.

Then Nathan told him about Gary. How could he explain that he had fallen in love with someone else? Even Scott was taken aback by the intensity of Nathan's feelings for Gary – it was clear that Nathan had been hurt more badly than he had ever known.

It was late by the time they finished talking: the sun was on the horizon, turning the calm sea a warm red. A soft breeze flowed across the beach. Nathan and Scott were sitting in silence on their patio, a half-empty jug of beer between them. A half-empty jug and a lot of hurt.

Finally, Scott turned to Nathan. 'Come inside.'

'What?' After all that Nathan had told him, Nathan was convinced that he and Scott were history.

Scott shrugged. 'I don't know what's going to happen, but I do know that you and me need one another at the moment. Probably more than we ever have done.' He stood up and took Nathan's hand, urging him inside.

They sat on the low, wide bed, looking at each other as if this were their first time together. Because, in many respects, it was. They were different people now – different people who needed to get to know each other all over again.

Scott pulled off Nathan's T-shirt with a gentleness that belied the months since they had last been together. After all they had been through, they could afford to wait, to take their time in reacquainting each other.

Nathan removed Scott's shirt and let it fall to the floor, before leaning down and seeking out Scott's nipple with his teeth, finding it in the thick chest hair and teasingly biting it with sharp yet playful nibbles. He had forgotten how Scott smelt, that musky smell that went straight to his cock, hardening it inside his shorts.

Scott stroked Nathan's firm back, urging him to carry on biting, harder and harder. As the pleasure almost became too much to bear, Scott pushed him away and pulled him into a standing position.

'You're one hell of a guy,' he said. 'I've missed you.'

'I've missed you, Scott. More than you could realise.' Nathan embraced him, entering Scott's mouth with his tongue and finding Scott's tongue waiting to do the same. It felt right – very right. Nathan knew that he would never forget Gary: there would always be a part of him that cherished the memory of their too short a time together. But Scott – Scott was part of Nathan's soul.

As they kissed, Scott's hands moved from Nathan's back to his shorts, pulling at the waistband, his hands gently touching the hard-on that waited inside. Nathan shivered at the touch, and began to remove Scott's own shorts.

Finally they were naked, their cocks stiff and expectant. Moving as one, Nathan and Scott seized each other's dick, squeezing them gently at first, before growing braver, more desperate, wanking each other with firm, constant strokes.

Nathan looked at Scott's solid body, his furry chest and stiff erection exciting him even more than he thought possible. Dropping to his knees, he continued to wank Scott, but took his balls his mouth, sucking on one, then the other, through the soft skin of his sac. Scott gasped as Nathan did this, urging Nathan on: still wanking, he took Scott's cock in his mouth, relishing the hot warmth and salty taste of his helmet.

Scott groaned, and put his hand on the back of Nathan's head to urge him on, to take even more of his dick in his mouth. Nathan took his hand away and slid his lips over the shaft, remembering the rhythm that had always excited Scott.

Nathan continued, swallowing as much of Scott's cock in his

mouth as he could, until Scott, already trembling slightly with the closeness of his orgasm, pushed him away.

Scott guided Nathan on to the soft quilt of the bed and urged him to lie down. Getting on to the bed, Scott knelt over Nathan and kissed him full on the mouth, allowing their bodies to rub against each other. Nathan could feel the hardness of Scott's cock sliding alongside his own, its motion lubricated by their juices flowing together, and the sensation, the thought of it, abruptly brought him to the point of coming.

He tried to pull back, to make it last longer, but Scott had other ideas. Clearly sensing how close Nathan was, Scott stopped kissing him, and drew his tongue down Nathan's hairy chest and stomach until he reached his dick, burying his face in Nathan's furry groin as he did so, nibbling at his thighs and bringing him so very, very close. Scott finally took Nathan's cock in his mouth and sucked it, hard, relentless sucks that made Nathan groan with pleasure. Scott's tongue teased Nathan's helmet, playing with his dick slit.

As he did so, Scott started squeezing Nathan's right nipple; his other hand reached between Nathan's legs and found his arse. Gentle fingers began to play with the hole, teasing strokes that were too much for Nathan to bear. Nathan tried to hold off, but the moment that Scott's fingers reached inside his arse it was too late. Within seconds of Scott's passionate assault on his body, Nathan's body exploded in orgasm, and he thrust his cock even further into Scott's mouth.

Scott didn't resist: his mouth continued to play with Nathan's cock as each drop of come shot from Nathan's hard, thick cock. Nathan continued to shoot for endless seconds, urged on by Scott's teasing licks and sucks, before the sensations finally faded into an all-consuming warmth.

Nathan sighed: the last time he had come like that had been months ago – with Scott.

His whole body was shivering and tingling with the experi-ence, and he grinned as Scott looked up at him, a dribble of come on his chin. Scott smiled at him and indicated the pool of white on the bed.

'Sorry,' said Scott playfully. 'I just couldn't wait.'

Nathan pulled him closer and hugged him. But his voice was serious when he spoke.

'I do love you very much, you know.' And he did. He wanted Scott beside him, now and for ever.

Scott nodded. 'I know. But what are we going to do, Nathan? What's going to happen to us? All of us?' he added, gesturing outside of their apartment.

Nathan shrugged. 'Who knows? Only time will tell.' He broke into a huge grin. With the fall of Delancey, they were free: a whole world of opportunities and experiences was theirs to savour. And Nathan fully intended to take advantage of that.

For a moment, Nathan thought of all those people who hadn't made it this far: John Bury, Brett, Gary . . . People whom Nathan would always honour. They all owed them a debt of gratitude that could never be repaid.

'Only time will tell,' he repeated. 'It always does.'

IDOL NEW BOOKS

Also published:

THE KING'S MEN
Christian Fall

Ned Medcombe, spoilt son of an Oxfordshire landowner, has always remembered his first love: the beautiful, golden-haired Lewis. But seventeenth-century England forbids such a love and Ned is content to indulge his domineering passions with the willing members of the local community, including the submissive parish cleric. Until the Civil War changes his world, and he is forced to pursue his desires as a soldier in Cromwell's army – while his long-lost lover fights as one of the King's men.

ISBN 0 352 33207 7

THE VELVET WEB
Christopher Summerisle

The year is 1889. Daniel McGaw arrives at Calverdale, a centre of academic excellence buried deep in the English countryside. But this is like no other college. As Daniel explores, he discovers secret passages in the grounds and forbidden texts in the library. The young male students, isolated from the outside world, share a darkly bizarre brotherhood based on the most extreme forms of erotic expression. It isn't long before Daniel is initiated into the rites that bind together the youths of Calverdale in a web of desire.

ISBN 0 352 33208 5

CHAINS OF DECEIT
Paul C. Alexander

Journalist Nathan Dexter's life is turned around when he meets a young student called Scott – someone who offers him the relationship for which he's been searching. Then Nathan's best friend goes missing, and Nathan uncovers evidence that he has become the victim of a slavery ring which is rumoured to be operating out of London's leather scene. To rescue their friend and expose the perverted slave trade, Nathan and Scott must go undercover, risking detection and betrayal at every turn.

ISBN 0 352 33206 9

DARK RIDER
Jack Gordon

While the rulers of a remote Scottish island play bizarre games of sexual dominance with the Argentinian Angelo, his friend Robert – consumed with jealous longing for his coffee-skinned companion – assuages his desires with the willing locals.

ISBN 0 352 33243 3

CONQUISTADOR
Jeff Hunter

It is the dying days of the Aztec empire. Axaten and Quetzel are members of the Stable, servants of the Sun Prince chosen for their bravery and beauty. But it is not just an honour and a duty to join this society, it is also the ultimate sexual achievement. Until the arrival of Juan, a young Spanish conquistador, sets the men of the Stable on an adventure of bondage, lust and deception.

ISBN 0 352 33244 1

TO SERVE TWO MASTERS
Gordon Neale

In the isolated land of Ilyria men are bought and sold as slaves. Rock, brought up to expect to be treated as mere 'livestock', yearns to be sold to the beautiful youth Dorian. But Dorian's brother is as cruel as he is handsome, and if Rock is bought by one brother he will be owned by both.

ISBN 0 352 33245 X

CUSTOMS OF THE COUNTRY
Rupert Thomas

James Cardell has left school and is looking forward to going to Oxford. That summer of 1924, however, he will spend with his cousins in a tiny village in rural Kent. There he finds he can pursue his love of painting – and begin to explore his obsession with the male physique.

ISBN 0 352 33246 8

DOCTOR REYNARD'S EXPERIMENT
Robert Black

A dark world of secret brothels, dungeons and sexual cabarets exists behind the respectable facade of Victorian London. The degenerate Lord Spearman introduces Dr Richard Reynard, dashing bachelor, to this hidden world. And Walter Starling, the doctor's new footman, finds himself torn between affection for his master and the attractions of London's underworld.

ISBN 0 352 33252 2

CODE OF SUBMISSION
Paul C. Alexander

Having uncovered and defeated a slave ring operating in London's leather scene, journalist Nathan Dexter had hoped to enjoy a peaceful life with his boyfriend Scott. But when it becomes clear that the perverted slave trade has started again, Nathan has no choice but to travel across Europe and America in his bid to stop it.

ISBN 0 352 33272 7

SLAVES OF TARNE
Gordon Neale

Pascal willingly follows the mysterious and alluring Casper to Tarne, a community of men enslaved to men. Tarne is everything that Pascal has ever fantasised about, but he begins to sense a sinister aspect to Casper's magnetism. Pascal has to choose between the pleasures of submission and acting to save the people he loves.

ISBN 0 352 33273 5

ROUGH WITH THE SMOOTH
Dominic Arrow

Amid the crime, violence and unemployment of North London, the young men who attend Jonathan Carey's drop-in centre have few choices. One of the young men, Stewart, finds himself torn between the increasingly intimate horseplay of his fellows and the perverse allure of the criminal underworld. Can Jonathan save Stewart from the bullies on the streets and behind bars?

ISBN 0 352 33292 1

CONVICT CHAINS
Philip Markham

Peter Warren, printer's apprentice in the London of the 1830s, discovers his sexuality and taste for submission at the hands of Richard Barkworth. Thus begins a downward spiral of degradation, of which transportation to the Australian colonies is only the beginning.

ISBN 0 352 33300 6

SHAME
Raydon Pelham

On holiday in West Hollywood, Briton Martyn Townsend meets and falls in love with the daredevil Scott. When Scott is murdered, Martyn's hunt for the truth and for the mysterious Peter, Scott's ex-lover, leads him to the clubs of London and Ibiza.

ISBN 0 352 33302 2

HMS SUBMISSION
Jack Gordon

Under the command of Josiah Rock, a man of cruel passions, HMS *Impregnable* sails to the colonies. Christopher, Viscount Fitzgibbons is a reluctant officer; Mick Savage part of the wretched cargo. They are on a voyage to a shared destiny.

ISBN 0 352 33301 4

WE NEED YOUR HELP . . .

to plan the future of Idol books –

Yours are the only opinions that matter. Idol is a new and exciting venture: the first British series of books devoted to homoerotic fiction for men.

We're going to do our best to provide the sexiest, best-written books you can buy. And we'd like you to help in these early stages. Tell us what you want to read. There's a freepost address for your filled-in questionnaires, so you won't even need to buy a stamp.

THE IDOL QUESTIONNAIRE

SECTION ONE: ABOUT YOU

1.1 Sex (*we presume you are male, but just in case*)
     Are you?
     Male ☐
     Female ☐

1.2 Age
     under 21 ☐   21–30 ☐
     31–40 ☐   41–50 ☐
     51–60 ☐   over 60 ☐

1.3 At what age did you leave full-time education?
     still in education ☐   16 or younger ☐
     17–19 ☐   20 or older ☐

1.4 Occupation _____

1.5 Annual household income _____

1.6 We are perfectly happy for you to remain anonymous; but if you would like us to send you a free booklist of Idol books, please insert your name and address

_____

_____

_____

_____

SECTION TWO: ABOUT BUYING IDOL BOOKS

2.1 Where did you get this copy of *The Final Restraint*?
  Bought at chain book shop ☐
  Bought at independent book shop ☐
  Bought at supermarket ☐
  Bought at book exchange or used book shop ☐
  I borrowed it/found it ☐
  My partner bought it ☐

2.2 How did you find out about Idol books?
  I saw them in a shop ☐
  I saw them advertised in a magazine ☐
  I read about them in _____
  Other _____

2.3 Please tick the following statements you agree with:
  I would be less embarrassed about buying Idol books if the cover pictures were less explicit ☐
  I think that in general the pictures on Idol books are about right ☐
  I think Idol cover pictures should be as explicit as possible ☐

2.4 Would you read an Idol book in a public place – on a train for instance?
  Yes ☐   No ☐

SECTION THREE: ABOUT THIS IDOL BOOK

3.1 Do you think the sex content in this book is:
  Too much ☐   About right ☐
  Not enough ☐

3.2 Do you think the writing style in this book is:

Too unreal/escapist ☐   About right ☐

Too down to earth ☐

3.3 Do you think the story in this book is:

Too complicated ☐   About right ☐

Too boring/simple ☐

3.4 Do you think the cover of this book is:

Too explicit ☐   About right ☐

Not explicit enough ☐

Here's a space for any other comments:

SECTION FOUR: ABOUT OTHER IDOL BOOKS

4.1 How many Idol books have you read?

4.2 If more than one, which one did you prefer?

_____

4.3 Why?

SECTION FIVE: ABOUT YOUR IDEAL EROTIC NOVEL

We want to publish the books you want to read – so this is your chance to tell us exactly what your ideal erotic novel would be like.

5.1 Using a scale of 1 to 5 (1 = no interest at all, 5 = your ideal), please rate the following possible settings for an erotic novel:

Roman / Ancient World ☐

Medieval / barbarian / sword 'n' sorcery ☐

Renaissance / Elizabethan / Restoration ☐

Victorian / Edwardian ☐

1920s & 1930s ☐

Present day ☐

Future / Science Fiction ☐

5.2 Using the same scale of 1 to 5, please rate the following themes you may find in an erotic novel:

Bondage / fetishism ☐
Romantic love ☐
SM / corporal punishment ☐
Bisexuality ☐
Group sex ☐
Watersports ☐
Rent / sex for money ☐

5.3 Using the same scale of 1 to 5, please rate the following styles in which an erotic novel could be written:

Gritty realism, down to earth ☐
Set in real life but ignoring its more unpleasant aspects ☐
Escapist fantasy, but just about believable ☐
Complete escapism, totally unrealistic ☐

5.4 In a book that features power differentials or sexual initiation, would you prefer the writing to be from the viewpoint of the dominant / experienced or submissive / inexperienced characters:

Dominant / Experienced ☐
Submissive / Inexperienced ☐
Both ☐

5.5 We'd like to include characters close to your ideal lover. What characteristics would your ideal lover have? Tick as many as you want:

Dominant	☐	Caring	☐
Slim	☐	Rugged	☐
Extroverted	☐	Romantic	☐
Bisexual	☐	Old	☐
Working Class	☐	Intellectual	☐
Introverted	☐	Professional	☐
Submissive	☐	Pervy	☐
Cruel	☐	Ordinary	☐
Young	☐	Muscular	☐
Naïve	☐		

Anything else? _____

5.6 Is there one particular setting or subject matter that your ideal erotic novel would contain:

_____

5.7 As you'll have seen, we include safe-sex guidelines in every book. However, while our policy is always to show safe sex in stories with contemporary settings, we don't insist on safe-sex practices in stories with historical settings because it would be anachronistic. What, if anything, would you change about this policy?

_____

_____

SECTION SIX: LAST WORDS

6.1 What do you like best about Idol books?

_____

6.2 What do you most dislike about Idol books?

_____

6.3 In what way, if any, would you like to change Idol covers?

_____

6.4 Here's a space for any other comments:

_____

_____

_____

_____

Thanks for completing this questionnaire. Now either tear it out, or photocopy it, then put it in an envelope and send it to:

Idol
FREEPOST
London
W10 5BR

You don't need a stamp if you're in the UK, but you'll need one if you're posting from overseas.